Memoirs

of a

Bow Street Runner

by

Henry Goddard

Memoirs of a Bow Street Runner

written by henry Goddard

Detecting crime in the Regency and early Victorian eras

with an introduction by
Charles Rozel
© Charles Rozel 2020
All rights reserved
email: charles@quaystonebooks.com

This paperback edition:
September 2024

isbn: 978-1-9196257-5-1
Imprint: Quaystone books
website: quaystonebooks.com

The Bow Street Runners

Bow Street Runners roamed the mean streets of London detecting crime in late-Georgian and Regency times. In fiction the Runner is usually an ex-soldier, perhaps wounded, physically or emotionally, from fighting the French, or possibly the upstart United States of America. A handsome, square-jawed enigma, he is as romanticised as Wyatt Earp in Deadwood. A sharpshooter with a brace of flintlocks, skilled with a blade, and his knuckles; he moves as easily beneath the glittering candle-chandeliers of Mayfair as in the flickering tallow-shadows of the Seven Dials. Apart from his horse, his romantic interest is usually an aristocratic beauty (possibly a spy for Napoleon or the Americans) and the buxom wench who serves his ale in the pub he calls home, within a gallows-eye view of Newgate.

In 1811 the madness of King George III required his son, also called George, to become the Regent (the *de facto* king). Thus, the Regency period started in 1811 and ended in 1820 when George III died and the Regent became George IV. However, some historians, and aficionados of the period, extend the Regency to include the years from 1820 to 1830 when George IV reigned. He died in 1830.

The Bow Street Runners were founded, in late 1748 or early 1749 by Henry Fielding, a lawyer and sometime-novelist (he wrote Tom Jones: which was filmed in 1963 winning 4 Oscars). In setting up the Runners, Henry Fielding was assisted by his brother John, who was was blind. The Fielding Brothers lived and worked from number 4 Bow Street in the West End of London. This address was also their magistrates court from where they dispensed 'justice'. Prior to the appointment of

Henry Fielding, magistrates were not paid officially, but paid themselves from the fines they imposed in their courts. They were referred to as 'trading magistrates' and reputed to be corrupt. Henry Fielding himself said as much, when referring to Thomas De Veil, his predecessor as Bow Street magistrate.

Henry Fielding died in 1754 and his brother, John, known as 'the blind beak'—he could recognise hundreds of criminal by their voices—carried on alone until he died in 1780. Thereafter, a succession of magistrates continued the work of the Fielding brothers until the Runners were disbanded in 1839, ten years after the establishment of the Metropolitan Police in 1829.

Most novelists refer to these detectives as 'Bow Street Runners' but this is a misnomer. They should be called Principal Officers. A runner was a messenger, or the person responsible for escorting a prisoner to and from a court. The common name for these Officers—Bow Street Runners—was inappropriate, and they considered it demeaning, but the name 'stuck' and I will use 'Runner' when referring to Principal Officers.

Funded, reluctantly and miserly, by the Home Department (now the Home Office), the Runners are considered to be Britain's first organised police force, albeit without uniforms and small in number. Throughout their existence of ninety years, there were never more than eleven Runners at Bow Street at any one time.

However, the Runners were augmented by Patrols. An eight-man Horse Patrol was inaugurated in about 1763, but discontinued within a few years because it was too expensive for the Home Department. It was not until 1805 that a Horse Patrol was re-established, this time in a uniform of scarlet waistcoats and blue trousers. This Horse Patrol is regarded by some historians as the first uniformed police force in England; it was absorbed into the Metropolitan Police in 1836.

Occasional Foot Patrols started in about 1765 and were discontinued within a few years. A regular Night Patrol on foot was inaugurated in 1790 and continued until it too was absorbed into the Metropolitan Police. From 1821 a Patrol, whose official name was the Dismounted Horse Patrol as its members were 'on foot', operated during the day, until also absorbed into the Metropolitan Police.

Runners were often chosen and appointed from a Patrol, and were sometimes assisted in their investigations by members of Patrols: for example, Patrol Constables helped the Runners deactivate the Cato Street Conspiracy, an attempt to murder the prime minister and his Cabinet in 1820.

The premises in Bow Street, from which the Runners had operated since the Fielding Brothers, was know as a Public Office. In 1792, the government set up seven more Public Offices in London to be run along the same lines as Bow Street. One of these new Public Offices was at Great Marlborough Street in the West End of London.

Henry Goddard

Henry Goddard, was born in Southwark, on the south bank of the river Thames in London, in 1800.

He joined the Bow Street Foot Patrol on the 7th April 1824, and, the next year, was promoted and transferred to the Police Office in Great Marlborough Street, West London, as a plain-clothes Principal Officer. Clearly, he was good at his job because it normally took ten or so years to be promoted like this. He remained at Marlborough Street until he transferred to Bow Street as a Runner in 1834. He remained a Runner at Bow Street until the Runners were disbanded in 1839.

He was then appointed Chief Constable of the newly formed police force in the English county of Northamptonshire.

In addition to his official duties, he did some work as a private detective.

Henry Goddard died in 1883.

This edition of his memoirs retains the grammar and spelling of the original handwritten draft.

CHARLES ROZEL

NORFOLK, ENGLAND

December 2020

Mr Spring's Watch	1
Chunee, the Elephant	4
Robbery at the Travellers Club	6
Burglary	13
Robbery	25
Kleptomania	28
The Duel	33
Madame Vestris	36
Dick Poacher	40
A lost Diamond Ring	55
The Murder of Mr Richardson	58
The Great Fire	78
Joseph Randall	88
Randall Montague Lewis	96
The Duke of Brunswick	104
Incendiary at Frant	126
The Gold Robbery	132
Looking at one self in the glass	136
Joseph Reiteroffer	139
Deer Stealers etc.	142
The Cold Shoulder	148
The Murder of Elizabeth Longfoot	151
Joseph Reitcroffer again	155
The Revd. R Stephens	162
Fitzherbert Batty Esq.	171
Concerning the Emperor of Russia	174
The Eglington Tournament	178
Delicate Enquiries	184
Gold Robbery	197
Sir Francis Mackenzie	204
Mr John Todd	217

The Great Robbery ... 239
Julius Tode ... 256
Edward James Farrer Esq. ... 260

Mr Spring's Watch

I received my appointment as an Officer at the Public, Office, Bow Street in April 1824. My duties at first consisted in serving Summonses, and in the execution of Assault and Peace Warrants, and occasionally, where required, in assisting the Principals in the very important enquiries, both Public and Private, which their duties called them to perform.

In the month of October of this year, Mr Elliston, the Manager of Drury Lane Theatre, applied to Sir Richard Birnie, the Chief Magistrate, for the assistance of another Officer in place of one deceased, and I was fortunate enough to obtain the appointment.

About a fortnight afterwards, while on duty at the Theatre at 11 o'clock at night, a dashingly dressed lady came running, almost out of breath, to the Box-lobby and enquired for me, saying that Mr Spring had sent her, and that he wanted me immediately, as he had been robbed of his gold watch. She stated that he was waiting at the corner of James Street, Covent Garden. I ran to him as fast as I could, and he, in a state of excitement, informed me that while he was standing there talking to some ladies, three ruffians dressed in flannel jackets ran up to him, one giving him a blow under his chin, the others at the same moment robbing him of his watch and chain, and that then they decamped, crossing the Market towards Henrietta Street. Mr Spring called "Stop Thief" as loud as he could, but without result.

I considered it useless to follow as so much time had been lost, and on retiring to the Theatre it was arranged for me to call upon him the next morning, while in the meantime he was to write a description of the Watch for Glindon the Printer in Rupert Street to print 600 bills, for distribution among Pawnbrokers and others; after which we separated.

A short time before the Theatre was over, it occurred to me that as Mr Spring had called out so loudly "Stop Thieves" the thieves may have imagined they were being closely pursued, and fearing apprehension with the stolen property in their possession as evidence to convict them, they might throw it away. Acting on this idea I called one of the linkmen, whose nickname was Jack Strawboots, to follow me with his lantern. I took the direction indicated by Mr Spring, and in less than half a minute. by the light of the lantern, on a heap of cabbage leaves, I saw the watch and chain. Jack Strawboots picked them up and gave them to me.

We returned to the Theatre and I passed through the Rotunda, up the steps towards the dress circle. Old Nettleton the Officer was standing by the side of Mr Banks the check taker, when he almost insulted me for daring to absent myself from the Theatre at such a time, as the performance would in another five minutes be over. In a sarcastic tone he asked, "Had I got the Thief?" and "What a stupid you must be!"

I replied, "No! I haven't the thief, but here's the Watch"

(shewing it).

He looked amazed, but as the performance was now over we had to attend to our several duties, and thus, for that night, matters ended.

The next morning I saw Mr Spring, who was the Box-Book and House-Keeper to the Theatre, gave him his Watch and told him how it was discovered. He expressed himself much satisfied, and that was all that Jack Strawboots and I received for our trouble in this matter.

The above particulars relating to the finding of the Watch appeared in the Globe newspaper of the following day, stating that after overhauling all the scattered cabbage leaves in Covent Garden Market I at length found the hidden treasure.

Chunee, the Elephant

In the month of March 1826 the following incident occurred while William Craig, a fellow officer, was passing along the Strand through Exeter Change, the lower part of which was very spacious and was tenanted by a Mr Clark, an extensive dealer in hardware, ladies' workboxes, and other fancy articles. This place had the appearance of a large Bazaar, and was a place of great traffic, in fact the main thoroughfare on the north side of the Strand for foot passengers. Over this was a large Menagerie kept by a Mr Cross, and at the entrance, to cause attraction, stood a gigantic powerful-looking man called a Beefeater dressed in the costume of Henry the Eighth's Yeomen of the Guard, who handed descriptive bills to the people as they passed and who shouted out as loudly as he could, "Look here! look here! the most extraordinary animals in the world to be seen alive for the small charge of one shilling; the wonderful great Elephant Chunee, and Nero the largest Lion ever seen in the whole world, the Boa-constrictor and the laughing Hyena, Ourang Otang, Birds of Paradise, Ostriches and every living animal from the Jungles in the far East."

While he was thus vociferating there was suddenly a great tumult heard upstairs, and numbers of people, the visitors, rushing downstairs in great terror and apparently for their lives. It appears that the Elephant had got enraged, and with his enormous Tusks was breaking the bars of his Den, causing the greatest alarm to all concerned as well as to the whole neighbourhood, and it was feared in his great strength he would become uncontrollable and would be the means of the Lion, Tigers, Hyena, Boa-Constrictor and the whole menagerie to be let loose.

The proprietor and his attendants, seeing the danger that appeared imminent, despatched a messenger to run for his life to Somerset House and ask the Sergeant of the guard for two soldiers to come without delay and shoot the Elephant, or the loss of life would be dreadful; the combined roaring of the Lion, Elephant, Tigers and other enraged animals was dreadful. The soldiers were quickly on the spot and discharged several bullets before they took effect. I was present with Craig, and we had great difficulty in preventing the mob from entering this part of the premises.

At last the animal was prostrated, his head resting on his tusks, and to finish the business Mr Harvey fixed a sabre on an iron crow bar and pierced it in to the animal's heart. All danger from the escape of the other animals being got over, the mob separated, the thoroughfare was cleared for traffic and matters passed off quietly.

Robbery at the Travellers Club

Towards the latter end of the year 1827, about the hour of eight o'clock in the morning, when the breakfast-tables were being got in readiness for the reception of the members of the club, the butler proceeded to the plate closet for the usual supply of silver, but to his astonishment discovered the lock of the strong double doors had been forced and seven massive silver candlesticks missing, that he had deposited there and locked up at eleven o'clock on the previous night. He immediately informed the housekeeper and the whole of the establishment, who were all soon up in arms and expressing their wonder to each other how the robbery could have been done, and by whom.

During the midst of this excitement and tumult about 10 o'clock the Secretary put in an appearance, followed by His Grace the Duke of Wellington who, having been made acquainted with the circumstances, inspected the plate closet, and after hearing all sides of the question resolved at once to proceed to Marlboro' Street police office and see the sitting Magistrate, to explain to him what had occurred. When His

Grace and the Secretary had stated the case to the Magistrate, he directed Sam Plank, the chief officer, to dispatch without delay two officers, the most fitting for such an enquiry, and I at that time felt myself much flattered to think that our chief selected me to accompany my senior, Tom Clements, to the scene of action.

On our arrival our first point was to go to the plate closet and hear what the butler had to say, then to examine all back and side doors, the area and windows, as well as the roof, skylights and gutters; after inspecting and scrutinising all these places, we could see nothing to indicate to our minds that any entry or breaking in had been effected at any of these points, and under these circumstances we agreed and came to the conclusion that whoever the thieves were they must have found their way in from the street through the front hall, and went out the same way they had come in. Coming to this conclusion caused us to fix our attention upon the hall-porter, who in answer to our questions said that no one could either come in or go out after the Club was closed at half past 10 o'clock last night till their being missed this morning, without his knowledge, because he not only bolted and barred the door, but locked it and put the key into his own pocket.

After hearing this statement we began to think that the candlesticks were concealed by some one on the premises, particularly as the butler still held to his first statement, and to which he was most positive.

On this, Clements, the Secretary and myself held a consultation and decided that, if we could rely on what the porter and butler had stated, it would be advisable for a strict search to be made in all the out of the way holes and corners of the establishment, not forgetting the servants' boxes, cisterns, chimneys, copper, copper-flues, etc. Before commencing this search we deemed it expedient to have the assistance of another officer to be on the qui-vive and keep guard with the porter at the hall door to see what came in and what went out. A messenger was therefore dispatched without delay, and while waiting his return, and to beguile the time, we asked the porter if he still maintained his former statement, and asked him to again well consider before he answered our questions whether he was quite certain that no one came in or went out during the whole of last night. He replied again that he was quite sure and that he knew for certain there was nobody else but the sweeps.

"Only the sweeps," I said. "Why have you never mentioned that before? What do you mean then? At what time did they come?"

"At five o'clock," he replied.

"How did they get in?" asked Clements.

"Why, they awoke me by giving one loud knock at the door and bawling out "Sweep! Sweep!"

"And what did you do then?" said I.

"Why, I took the key from my pocket, unbolted and unlocked the door and let them in."

"Let them in? Why, how many?" asked Tom Clements.

"Two," the porter replied.

"What did they say?" asked Clements.

"They said they had come to sweep the pantry chimney."

"What did they do then?"

"They asked for a candle, and to be shewn the way, and I shewed them the way."

"Do you know who the sweeps are and where they come from?"

"Why, certainly I do, they come from Cooks in Argyll Street."

"Who told them to come?"

"I don't know."

"How do you know they came from Cooks?"

"Because they said so."

"When?"

"When I first let them in-they told me Mr Cook had sent them, and that is all I know about it."

"How long were they in the pantry sweeping the chimney?"

"Nearly an hour."

"What time did you let them out?"

"A little before six, and as they were going out they wished me good morning and said they had had a very dry job as the chimney was very foul."

"Did they have much soot?"

"About half a sack full."

"What did you do with yourself after they left?"

"Locked the door, sat in the hall-chair and slept till seven o'clock."

Just at this point Schofield, a brother officer, arrived, who we left upon the premises while I and Clements lost no time in going to the master sweep Mr Cook. On seeing him and relating the whole business we were engaged upon in, he replied that he had not sent any of his men to the Travellers Club though he swept their chimneys. No application had been made to him at all, and he was certain it was none of his people, for they were all engaged that morning in an entirely different direction. Mr Cook began to get warm upon the matter and accompanied us to the Club, and after surveying the place volunteered to give up all his time and render what assistance he could to aid us in the discovery of the thieves, that is to say the supposed sweeps.

While St. Giles, Seven Dials, Westminster, Whitechapel and

Bethnal Green were being hunted over, George Avis, a very indefatigable officer who had spent much of his time in obtaining a personal knowledge of thieves of every description, as well as of notorious receivers of stolen property, had by some means received such information as caused him to apprehend a man named Solomon who kept a "fence" in White Lion Street, Seven Dials, in whose possession he found two of the candlesticks. This led to an enquiry at Syrells Silver Refiners in Barbican, who, it was found, had sold two others of the candlesticks to one of the Colleges at Oxford. Solomon was remanded, the case standing over in order to give us time to find out the thieves. From enquiries made, a woman of disreputable character, living in the Almonry, Westminster, informed us that she knew one of the thieves, a notorious "Cracksman" named Sam White who was living with Nance, a late friend of hers, in the neighbourhood of Bethnal Green.

Avis, hearing this woman announce the name of Nance, said, "What, Nance Castle do you mean?"

"Yes," she replied, "that's her name, and only let me see her," she said, "I'd skin her alive for taking Sam away from me."

Acting upon this information, Clements, Schofield, Avis and myself, together with a volunteer named Clement Mastry, who stood six feet three or four inches high, and who filled the post of private footman to the Dowager Duchess of Richmond, all proceeded to Bethnal Green and, knowing the desperate ruffian we were going to deal with, armed ourselves with a cutlass strapped round the waist and under our great coats, some carrying handcuffs.

When we arrived we saw the weavers in large gangs parading the streets with a band of music and carrying Banners representing the following mottoes: "Starvation", "The

Workhouse", "We are in want of bread", a Death's head, etc. This procession, with the cadaverous appearance of the people, looked sad and alarming. In the midst of this, George Avis suddenly saw a rough bull necked strong built man, drest in a short jacket, talking to Nance Castle, and calling our attention to this fact we made towards him; but he, seeing our movement, made a dash and run away as fast as his heels could carry him into the middle of the Procession, calling out "Murder, murder, they are going to kill me".

We followed him up. Being determined to capture him. I, being the swiftest runner, caught hold of him with one hand by the collar and by the other his wrist, he trying at the same time to throw me; Clements at this moment laid hold of him on the other side in the same manner and George Avis behind, while Schofield and the amateur police officer, Mastry, flourished their cutlasses to keep the mob off. In the skuffle I was thrown with Sam White on the top of me and Clements upon him, while George Avis was struggling to put on the handcuffs so that I had to bear the weight of all three. It was sometime before Avis succeeded in fastening one handcuff on to his wrist while Clements held on to the other, which enabled me, after considerable kicking on the part of the prisoner and struggling, to clasp the other. This resistance lasted, at a rough guess, full twenty minutes, the mob all the time yelling, hooting and crying out "Rescue, rescue," Nance Castle moreover throwing up her arms and screaming at the top of her voice, "They are taking my Sam, don't let them!"

At this moment Mr Gardner, the chief officer from Worship Street office, with four or five others, came to our rescue, otherwise I do believe the crowd of weavers would have rescued him from us, they believing at the time we were interfering with them and taking into custody a fellow weaver from their ranks. At length we got him into a Hackney coach and reached Marlboro' Street Office about half-past three o'clock in the afternoon, just after the Magistrates had left. We took him into the private room, Sam Plank came out from another room, and when he saw us Clements said, "Sam White!"

Our prisoner was locked up and brought before the Magistrate, at the evening sitting of seven o'clock, who remanded him for further examination to the House of Correction, Coldbath fields; a few days afterwards all the needful evidence was brought against him, he was committed to Newgate for trial and as the result he was sentenced to transportation for life. Solomon got out of it by turning King's evidence, and the remaining three candlesticks had, before it was time to recover them, found their way into the crucible.

Burglary

In the middle of June 1827, about 4 o'clock in the afternoon, I was walking down Tottenham Court Road when my attention was drawn to the window of a Jeweller's shop in which there was an attractive display of goods, when I saw a well-dressed handsome young man carrying something heavy in a blue bag, looking about him, first to the right and then to the left, and behind, as if to assure himself he was not followed. He then suddenly darted into the shop.

These movements attracted my attention, and caused me to look through the window. I could see all over the shop and, after what appeared to be a conversation with the person behind the counter, he opened the bag and emptied its contents, which looked to me, so far as I could distinguish, mutilated silver of King's Pattern; it was then taken to the scales and weighed. Afterwards some gold watches were shewn to him, which he attentively examined as with a view to exchange for his silver. While so engaged, I left the window to avoid observation, retiring to a safe position to watch his coming out. In the course of ten minutes I saw him leave with the empty bag under his arm.

Suspecting that all was not exactly right, I followed him, he walking very fast, and continually looking back and stopping, which further increased my suspicion. He took a roundabout way across Seven Dials up Short's Gardens into Drury Lane, turned down Great Queen Street, stopping at the corner and looking back. I by this time arrived at the corner of Long Acre and saw him enter a public-house, the sign of "The Sugar Loaf", Mr Bishop proprietor.

I kept the house under observation twenty minutes, and as he did not come out I entered, and looked in the tap-room; seeing no one there, I went to the parlor and sat among a number of men who were smoking and drinking. Being very hot weather the door was kept open, and from my position I could see who went in and out. He was not among the company, but I stayed with my pint of ale for nearly an hour and then left, concluding in my own mind that he lodged there.

I went to Marlboro' Street Office and mentioned this circumstance to Clements, a brother officer, who said it would be as well to search back in the Hue and Cry to see if there had been any plate robbery of late. I did so, but found nothing of any service to me.

Two days after, at two o'clock in the afternoon, Mr Sam Plank, our chief officer, asked me if I had any business on hand, and telling him that I had not, he directed me to be at Mr Styles the Silversmith of No. 28 Tottenham Court Road, at 3 o'clock, and to tell him who I was and who sent me. I accordingly went and saw Mr Styles, who related a long circumstance about a young man who had called twice lately, making purchases of two gold watches, one for himself and another for a lady, in exchange for a quantity of broken up silver which he told the shopkeeper had been left to him and his brother by their uncle, who died in Yorkshire lately, and that they had had a dispute about dividing it, and had agreed to break it up and sell it for what it would fetch.

I asked, "How much have you had of him?"

"About two hundred ounces," said Mr Styles, "and he is going to bring some more at half-past three this afternoon to agree upon what I am to allow him for it. But when he comes I shall tell him that when he brings all he has I shall be better able to judge what I can afford. He will be here soon, and if you watch outside you will see him come in carrying a blue bag, and when he goes out, after you have followed him to where he goes, come back to me and I can tell you what arrangements we have made."

I waited some little distance on the opposite side of the road, and very soon I saw pass in the same man I had followed three days previously, and in about a quarter of an hour afterwards he came out.

Following on the opposite side of the way, I held him in view across the Seven Dials, down St. Martin's Lane, along the Strand to an oyster shop, up Southampton Street, round Covent Garden Market into Russell Street, up Drury Lane, turning down Great Queen Street into the Sugar Loaf, where I had previously followed him. I took the same precautions I had done before and felt further satisfied that he lodged there.

I returned to Mr Styles and told him what I had done, and Mr Styles told me he had arranged for him to come with the rest of the silver at 2 o'clock on the following day, and if he could not give a more satisfactory account of the possession of the silver I was to be there to take him into custody. I then informed Mr Styles what I have mentioned in the outset of this relation as to my keeping him under observation in the first instance. He would scarcely believe it, and I think would have discredited it had I not produced Clements to bear out my statement; and when this fact became known to Mr Plank and to Mr Dyer the magistrate, and Mr Fitzpatrick the chief clerk, they marvelled.

The next day, as it had been arranged, I kept my appointment with Mr Styles. I seated myself in the parlor commanding a full view of the shop, and at the appointed time, two o'clock, a hackney coach drove up to the shop and Mr Styles assisted the young man in with two heavy blue bags; the coach afterwards drove off. The contents of the bags were emptied, and an immense pile of silver it was. When I saw what had been done I walked from the parlor, and handled some of the bent up Dish-covers, Coffee and Tea-pots, Soup-ladles, Gravy, Table and Desert spoons, and sundry other articles, all of which had been mutilated, weighing more than four hundred ounces.

I remarked when taking up a silver dish, bent in half, "Look here, what a pity to destroy such beautiful articles and to sell them for old silver when they are quite new. How did they come into your possession?" said I.

He told me the same tale as he had previously done to Mr Styles. I remarked, "It is King's pattern, and the crest and initials are all erased" (and it looked far beyond the explanation he had given). I then said, "What is your name?"

"George Wilson," he replied.

"Where do you reside?"

"No 1, Ebery Street, Pimlico," he said.

"How long have you lived there?"

"Over two months," he answered.

I then told him that I was a Police Officer, and "under the

circumstances you must consider yourself in custody."

I searched him and took from him some gold and silver, a gold watch, a bunch of keys and a room-door key. I then sent for a Hackney coach, the bags and silver were put in and I ordered the coachman to drive to Marlboro' Street Police Office, where we arrived just in time to take him for hearing before Mr Dyer the Magistrate, who remanded him for a week to the House of Detention, Coldbath fields.

On the same evening I went to the address at Pimlico he had given me and found his name was not known there. Afterwards I went to the Sugar Loaf, saw Mr Bishop the Landlord and enquired if he knew this key, shewing it.

"Yes," he replied, "it belongs to a gentleman from the country who occupies the first floor back room. He has been staying here about a week."

I told him who I was and that his lodger was in custody at Cold-Bath fields prison. I unlocked the door of the room and found there four large Trunks, and fitted them with keys from the bunch I had with me. One trunk was empty, two contained his wardrobe, and the other, some very heavy lumps of molten silver, which appeared to have been melted in a large iron ladle, a lady's gold watch and a letter directed to Mr Robert Webster, signed E. Wilson, Montagu Street, Russell Square. These articles I brought away and locked them up in my cupboard at the Office.

On the following morning I called upon Miss Wilson, who, after receiving my message that I wished to see her, came downstairs into the hall appearing to be very nervous and asked my business. I addressed her and asked if she knew a young man named Mr Robert Webster.

"Very well indeed," she replied. "I hope there is nothing the matter. Has anything happened to him? I have not seen him the last two days. Pray tell me the object of your visit."

I begg'd she would not distress herself; my business was important and she must be explicit. I said, "Have you received lately any presents from him? For he is in custody on a charge of stealing a large quantity of plate, gold watches, etc."

On hearing this she nearly fainted, and two female servants came and asked me what I had been doing to her and what I meant by it, but when I told them my business and who I was, they became more pacified, and then I was informed that Miss Wilson was the Lady's Maid.

By this time Miss W. had recovered and fetched a gold watch and wedding ring, giving them to me and saying they were about to be married and that he was going into the business of a Miller in Yorkshire.

In answer to my question, "You know where he comes from?"—,"Oh, yes," she replied, "he comes from Wiltshire and is on a holiday, and his master, the Rev. Mr Jones of Elmn Green, is going to advance him five hundred pounds to set him up."

'Which Elmn Green do you mean?" I asked.

"Elmn Green near Cirencester," she replied.

I asked what occupation he held.

"He is the Parson's butler," she answered.

I asked no further questions but said, "If you wish to see Webster I will call again and let you know."

I bade her good morning and returned to Marlboro' Street office and reported to Mr Dyer what I had done, and afterwards wrote to the Rev. Mr Jones the full particulars, and by the return mail received a letter stating that he would be at Marlboro' Street on the following day by 12 o'clock. Having shewn this letter to Mr Dyer, he gave me his authority to the Governor of the House of Correction to give the prisoner into my custody, who was then placed in a cell at the back of the Office.

At 12 o'clock punctually Mr Jones arrived, and on the production of the plate Mr Jones exclaimed, "Why, that is the silver I was robbed of last January: the thief committed a burglary and took the whole of it away, consisting of dinner, tea and coffee services. What an extraordinary affair! What kind of man is he you have in custody?"

I described him.

"Why, he answers the description of Webster, my butler; but surely it cannot be he, for I remember he was in bed on that night; I had to ring his bell and call him down stairs, but I will tell you the particulars," addressing himself to Mr Dyer and myself, "Early in the month of last January, after returning from hunting, I gave a large dinner party. The company left at 10 o'clock. Major Haines, who was staying with me, and myself retired to bed about eleven o'clock, and at 1 o'clock in the morning the Major was awoke by a terrible noise like the smashing and breaking of glass, which so alarmed him that he got up and partly dressed and came with a brace of loaded pistols to my door, waking me out of my sleep; and after getting a light we made our way downstairs, and as we proceeded, felt the wind blowing most furiously along the passages, and found the large Hall door wide open. I rang the butler's bell, called up the coachman and all the servants, who lost no time in coming to our assistance, the butler being the first to be there in his night dress and night cap, carrying a lighted lantern and making his way in a seeming courageous manner along the passage out of the Hall door shouting and hollowing as he went along, 'Look here! look here! they have gone this way, here is a spoon,' and on going further said, 'Here is a table cloth,' I and Major Haines and the household following, Webster leading the way, who observed a sauce ladle and, on stooping to pick it up, exclaimed, 'I wonder we were not all murdered!'

"After proceeding for some distance further and not finding anything more, we gave up the search, returned to the house and discovered that an entrance had been made into the butler's Pantry by raising the window sash from the outside, cutting out a panel from the shutter under the inside fastenings, and forcing the lock of the plate closet.

After Mr Jones had stated these particulars I was directed to bring the prisoner forward, and on taking him into the room, he was so surprised at the sudden introduction into the presence of his master, whom he never dreamt of seeing, that he almost fainted, and it was a scene that cannot easily be forgotten.

When he recovered he was asked by Mr Jones how he accounted for the possession of the silver. He made no reply and was dumb for a time, but after a while said, in a nervous and equivocating manner, that he could clear himself, but at present was not inclined to answer any questions. He was then again remanded back to the House of Correction, Cold Bath Fields, and to remain there till the time arrived for me to take him to be tried at the summer Assizes held at Salisbury.

After he was removed the Revd. Mr Jones made the following statement to Mr Dyer, "that the prisoner was the last person he should ever have suspected; so much so, that he held so high an opinion of him that he was going to advance him a large sum of money to put him in the business of a Miller, and it was only a fortnight since he gave him leave of absence for a month to see London and make his arrangements to get married, and settle about his flour-mill in Yorkshire."

The conversation ended and thus matters stood over till the July Salisbury Assizes. On the 27th of July, having arrived and as the Assizes commencing on the 20th, I obtained possession of the prisoner and took him in a hackney-coach to Hatchetts, having booked my fare. three days previously. He was handcuffed, and we mounted on the Salisbury Coach, sitting on the roof behind the coachman, and on our way going across Bagshot Heath my prisoner said to me, "I can clear myself, and prove my innocence, I'll tell you all about it."

I remarked "I hope you will but I must tell you whatever you say to me about the matter may be used in evidence against you."

Notwithstanding the caution, he said he could very easily get out of it and continued on, saying that it was his custom every morning to ride on the Pony four miles to the Post Office at Cirencester for his master's letters, and about a month after the burglary, among the letters, one of them was directed in a very odd sort of handwriting, at he peeped into it and he could see it said something about plate. On arriving home, after delivering the other letters to Mr Jones, he took the peculiar one into the pantry and held the wafer close to the spout of the boiling kettle till the steam moistened it, and it was then easily opened and "I read the following, viz: 'Sir, In consequence of the pursuit being so hot on the night we broke into your house and heard the alarm, and having so much to carry, we were afraid of being overtaken, and it was as much as we could do to have time to make our escape and conceal ourselves with the plate in the drain under the Orchard while the third man made his escape across the lawn. Since that night we were afraid of being watched and were frightened to go and fetch it away, therefore if you go there you will find it nearly all right." I thought this was all a hoax, but however, I went and looked in the drain and after trampling down a large quantity of stinging nettles, to my astonishment I saw two sacks and when I opened them, there was the plate as stated in the letter. The bags of plate I left there till I could conveniently move them away."

I asked if he had got the letter, but he had burnt it, he said. I said that was a pity; but "how is it that all the plate is broken up, and so much of melted?"

"Well," he replied, "these thieves broke open my desk and stole fourteen sovereigns, my property, and I mentioned this to Mr Jones but he never offered to make it good; therefore I brought away a small quantity of it at a time, and placed it in a large drawer in my pantry till I had got it all together, and when I had the opportunity I pulled the dresser drawer out a little way, to prevent anyone looking in at the door, which only opened about three inches, and it was in this way I broke it up and melted a great deal of it in an iron ladle over the fire."

After this statement his mind, he said, was much relieved, and he should like to have something to eat, and a glass of ale; so when the coach stopped at Hungerford for refreshment, I gave him a thick beef sandwich and some ale which he seem'd to enjoy.

On leaving the coach, at Salisbury I had to walk him for a mile before we got to the Jail at Fisherton. It was on a Sunday evening when the people were going to church, and they, seeing such a well dressed respectable looking young man hand-cuffed, surrounded us in crowds, all wanting to be informed what I had got him in custody for. At last I arrived at the Jail and having safely deposited my prisoner, The Governor gave me a receipt for his body. When the jail door was opened to let me out some forty to fifty persons were waiting outside to know what it all meant. I went on without saying a word to the White Hart Hotel, truly glad to get rid of my charge.

The next day he was taken before the Magistrates and after Mr Jones, Mr Styles and myself had given in our statements, the coachman to Mr Jones was called and gave the following evidence on oath, "that on the night of the burglary after the alarm was given and when he was down in the Hall during the confusion he saw under the prisoner's night-shirt that he had on his Black silk stockings, knee breeches buckled below the knee just as he wore them that same evening at the dinner party." After this evidence the court came to the conclusion that he had never been to bed at all, he was committed for trial on the capital charge. Two days afterwards the grand jury returned a true bill, and he was put upon his trial and pleaded not guilty.

The trial proceeded in all due form, and after the judge (Judge Best) had taken down the depositions of the witnesses, a detailed account of which had been already given, he was asked what he had to say in his defence, and he stated what in substance was the same as he had related to me on the coach crossing Bagshot Heath. The summing up of the Judge was then gone through, and after recapitulating the evidence the Jury were required to consider their verdict, who after retiring about ten minutes returned into court pronouncing their verdict "guilty". The Judge immediately put on the black cap and the usual proclamation having been read, the prisoner was asked what he had to say why he should not die according to the law.

He exclaimed, "Mercy, mercy, my Lord!"

"Mercy," said his Lordship, "to you, Webster, would be cruelty to others."

On the commencement of passing the sentence Webster fainted and fell into the arms of the Jailer. The court was crowded with county ladies, many of whom passed their scent bottles to the prisoner, who was then carried out of Court. The surgeon of the Jail was quickly in attendance, and in a quarter of an hour he rallied, and was in a sufficient state of consciousness to be carried back into court to hear the dreadful and solemn sentence of death passed upon him. At this moment there was great sympathy shewn by all the ladies towards the prisoner, who was only twenty-four years of age and a fine handsome man.

Some few hours before his execution, on the 14th August, he made a full confession, stating that the silver was locked up in one of the drawers and had never been taken out of the pantry at all, but to make believe the house had been burglariously entered, to give the appearance of an external entry. The noise was caused by the breaking of glass which was effected by the lowering of a cord from outside his bedroom window to the Pantry below, which he tied to the handle of the Tray and which was filled with tumblers, decanters and wine-glasses, and by pulling this Cord from his bedroom window, caused it to upset and falling on the stones underneath breaking the glasses, the noise of which gave the alarm and waking the inmates.

Robbery

On the morning of Monday, February 4, 1828, Mr Basil Wood Wine merchant of Bond Street, came to Marlboro' Street office and informed the sitting Magistrate, Mr Dyer, that during the interval between the closing of his counting-house last Saturday afternoon and that morning someone had obtained access thereto and stolen from one of the clerks' desks £75. He stated he should be glad to have the assistance of two officers, upon which Mr Plank, our chief, despatched Clements and myself.

On arriving at the counting-house, Mr Wood introduced us to Mr. Alexander Anderson, the chief and confidential clerk, who would furnish us with all the particulars, and he informed us that about 4 o'clock on the previous Saturday afternoon Lord Braybrook's butler paid £75 in Bank notes to the Clerk who sat next to him, and that it was very extraordinary how such a robbery could take place, as no one was present except the porter, who at the time of the transaction was cleaning the windows, and he was the only person who could have seen what then occurred; leading us to infer that this man was the thief.

Clements and I saw there were no indications of a breaking

in or out, and therefore came to the conclusion that this robbery must have been accomplished by or with the connivance of someone attached to the premises, more particularly as the desk from which the notes been abstracted was found locked by the clerk who used it on his arrival at the office that morning.

Acting by impulse, I motioned for Clements to come on one side and in a low tone I said, "Between you and I, I don't like the appearance nor the manner of this chief clerk." Clements said, "Well, we must do something," and he took the Porter away for a short distance to search him while I went to a small private room in which was the Chief Clerk.

I said to him, "Sir, you can see very plainly that this robbery rests with some person on the establishment."

He replied, "O yes, you are quite right, for who else could have done it?"

I then remarked that as there were several clerks, besides the porter, to be examined and searched, it would not look well to single out any one of them, in particular, and "as a mere matter of form, to prevent any complaining, by your setting the example in allowing me to commence the searching with you, they cannot afterwards complain; not that I suspect you."

"O no," he said, "you can begin with me to set the example, for I am quite as anxious as you are that the robbery should be found out."

I was suspecting him all the while. I then requested him to take off his coat, then his necktie and waistcoat, and to pull off his trousers, which appear'd to put him out of temper. Observing this, I said "By your submitting to this, if I am asked the question I can say that I searched you most strictly."

He unbuttoned his trousers and put his hand down from the

waist inside to the ankle, saying he could not get them over his boot—he wore bluchers. I said, "Pull the boot off" which he did, and in his temper kicked it to the further part of the Clerk's room, and in trying to slip off the other, he said it was tight, and at last with great vengeance kicked it to follow the other that was under a table, thinking it would attract my notice to go after it. He then drew his hand up from his heel inside his trousers, which I saw was clenched, and placed it behind him. As this movement of his did not escape my notice, I laid hold of his wrist and said, "Open your hand"; he resisted, and after rather a severe struggle I forced his wrist down and took the notes from out of his hand, which were folded in the same state as his fellow clerk had received them.

This discovery caused a great furore, and when his master heard of it he exclaimed, if he had known him to have been the thief he would sooner have lost the money than have to prosecute him, for he was the last man on earth he should have suspected, his family standing so high and his father holding a high position at Edinborough under the Crown.

We took him to Marlboro' Street Police Office before Mr Dyer, who remanded him to give time for further enquiry. We searched his lodging in Craven Buildings, Drury Lane, and found sundry bottles of choicest wines and many pawnbrokers' duplicates relating to jewellery and wearing apparel besides about twenty large boxes packed full of Theatrical dresses, which was accounted for he being an amateur actor. In due course he was committed to Newgate for trial, and when arraign'd at the bar his case being so clear, and trying to fix the robbery on the Porter which would have aggravated his case, his Counsel recommended him to plead guilty, when he was sentenced to seven years' transportation.

Kleptomania

In the latter part of the month of April 1828 about four o'clock in the afternoon, I was called from my duty at the Office to go with a young man to his employer Mr Simpson, a Silkmercer and Haberdasher of Regent Street near the Oxford Circus. I asked him on our way what it was for, and he told me that a young "Carriage lady" had been detected stealing ribands, and before entering the shop I saw an elegant carriage with a pair of high spirited horses, attended by two gorgeously dressed servants in livery, who were standing outside the shop door.

On my entering, I saw a young lady deeply veiled holding her pocket handkerchief to her eyes, and who appeared in great distress.

She was attended by two others, one elderly, the other about the age of twenty.

The proprietor pointed to the one that was crying, and said, "I charge this lady with theft. She has been observed stealing and putting into her reticule some rolls of valuable ribands from a drawer that was placed upon the counter, during the temporary absence of the shopwoman."

I searched her reticule and found inside three large rolls of ribands.

Her mother and sister were not aware of the theft and expressed great surprise and implored me not to take her, and made powerful appeals to the proprietor; but he was inexorable. The accused was deeply veiled and reluctantly came with me, the two livery servants looking at us hard in the face wondering where I was going to take her. At this moment the carriage door was opened by them for her mother and sister, and they drove away at a rapid speed. I walked side by side, my prisoner crying and sobbing most bitterly all the way to Marlboro Street Office.

At the period I am referring to, the Magistrates held their sittings daily from 11 o'clock in the morning till three o'clock in the afternoon, and again from seven to eight o'clock in the evening. This circumstance occurred about four o'clock in the afternoon, the Magistrates, Clerks, and Officers were therefore all away, except myself, who was what was termed the officer of the day, the office never being left, the officers taking in turn to perform this duty, and being eight in number the turn came every eighth day.

There was a bright fire in the clerks' office, and not wishing to add more trouble to this young lady, I allowed her to sit in a chair before it to make her under these unfortunate circumstances as comfortable as I could. She, however, kept on crying, and I pitied her very much, thinking what a serious business it was for a lady of her evidently high position to be placed in so degraded a situation.

It was about six o'clock when I heard the sound of swift trotting horses, and the noise of carriage wheels approaching fast, suddenly ceasing in front of the Office door. The letting down of carriage steps was followed up by a tremendous and violent knocking at the door. I hastened to open it, when a stout fine handsome looking elderly gentleman walked from the Carriage and enquired if a young lady was here, who had been brought from Simpson's in Regent street about four this afternoon. I answer'd him in the affirmative.

He said, "I am a Peer and a Magistrate, and not for twenty thousand pounds must this case be made known."

He enquired the name of the Magistrate sitting that evening and where he lived and how he could get to see him all of which was spoken in one breath.

I replied, "My Lord, the Magistrate's name is Conant and he lives next door."

Then he said, "No time must be lost, for I must see him immediately, and pray shew me the way."

I said, "Oh, yes, by all means, My Lord, if you follow me and if he is at home, I will speak to his servant and deliver your Lordship's message.

He gave me his card and ultimately he was introduced. I left them together and returned to the Clerk's Office to look after my charge, and in about half an hour the Magistrate's servant brought his Lordship to me with a message that I was to allow him to see the young lady. I did so and retired out of hearing of their conversation.

When the hour of seven was near at hand Mr Fitzpatrick, the chief clerk, came in, look'd about him, and quietly asked me what the gentleman and lady wanted. I took him into the next room and while I was telling him, Mr Conant came in, and called Mr Fitzpatrick to follow him into the private room. By this time our Chief, Mr Plank, let himself in with his key into the presence of the Magistrate and Chief Clerk, and in a short time afterwards his Lordship was admitted, and then the

Prisoner. I was ordered to remain outside till wanted.

His Lordship soon came out in great haste, went away and turned to the right in the direction of Regent Street, returning again in about ten minutes. After a pause of about five minutes I was asked by the Chief Clerk if Mr Simpson was in attendance, who gave the prisoner into custody. I replied he was not. I was then asked whether Mr Simpson understood me that after he had given the lady into custody he was to be there at 7 o'clock.

I replied, "Most certainly he did, for I distinctly told him."

"Then," said the Chief Clerk, "go to the door and call out for him two or three times."

I did so and had no reply.

He then said, "As no one appears, the prisoner must be discharged." She was then led by Mr Fitzpatrick down the passage, followed by his Lordship and Mr Plank into the hall of the Magistrate's house. The door was immediately closed after them, and the four were observed walking down the private garden at the back of the Magistrate's house into a long passage leading out to Marlboro' Mews, where there was a carriage in readiness to receive the young lady and her friend, the Peer, which drove away at a rapid pace with them. The carriage was followed to a mansion not a great way from Hanover Square, where, in the hall, were her Mother and several ladies and gentlemen, all evidently waiting in great anxiety to receive and cheer up the spirits of this young lady, who had been guilty of such folly.

After the evening sitting was over I was informed by Mr Conant that the matter I had had in hand that evening was to be considered as of a private nature, and the names in connection with it were not to be divulged, as a general knowledge of the affair would distress the Countess and be her daughter's ruin. I replied that as far as I was concerned, it should never escape my lips, and from that time to the present, it never has.

The Duel

The last occurrence was followed on the same night by my having, with my brother officers, to attend at a masquerade held at the Argyll rooms, till five o' clock the following morning.

In the middle of the following night I was woke up from my slumbers by hearing a loud single knock at the street door, and a ringing of the bell. Before I could get up to answer it there was another knock which rather alarmed me and it took me some time before I could find the door to let myself out. In the middle of my fright at length having found it, I made my way along the passage and opened the street door, when to my astonishment there stood like a statue Tom Clements, one of my brother officers, who said it was now past two o'clock in the morning, that Sam Plank our chief had just called him up and we had to meet him at Tyburn Gate without delay, as he had only just received information that there was going to be a duel between two gentlemen at Wormwood Scrubbs. (I was residing at this time at No. 12 Robert Street, Hampstead Road.)

My wife in the mean time struck a light, and I got myself dressed in less than five minutes, telling her at the same time the business I was going upon, which rather alarmed her, but there being no time for parley I bade her good morning and away I went with Tom Clements running and walking till we reached Tyburn Gate, where we found Sam Plank, who had just arrived in a Post-Chaise belonging to Robert Newman of Regent Street. We got in and the post-boy was instructed to proceed down the Uxbridge Road and turn down the Lane leading to Wormwood Scrubbs.

On arriving at the Lane we went down it for some distance, turned round a bend in an out of the way place and concealed ourselves behind a very high hedge. (It was about four in the morning.)

We had not been there more than half an hour before we heard in the distance the sound of Carriage wheels and heavy trotting of Horses which became louder and louder, and as they advanced, we distinctly heard voices till the noise of the carriage ceased. I, being the youngest of the party, climbed upon a high bank and then on to a tree commanding a distant view. I then saw the tops of three carriages, and climbing higher I counted eight Gentlemen, which I reported to my brother officers.

We then lost no time in approaching the spot, walking in a stooping position to prevent observation, advancing nearer by degrees. But seeing their hasty preparation, we sallied out upon them to their very great astonishment, so suddenly that they were completely taken off their guard. Mr Plank our chief informed them who we were and said that from all appearances at this early time in the morning and at this retired spot it was evident there was about to be committed a breach of the Peace and therefore, they must all consider themselves in custody. While he was thus engaged Clements and I took possession of three pistol-cases containing two duelling pistols in each, with flasks of gunpowder, percussion caps, bullets, &c.

Among the party there were two surgeons who had brought three cases of Instruments, wadding, lint, etc., and these gentlemen seeing how matters stood and the predicament they were in, very quietly and with great civility returned to their carriages with the seconds, I in one, Clements and Plank in the two others, and being all quietly seated, Plank took the lead bidding myself and Clements to follow. We drove rapidly to Marlborough Street office, arriving about five in the morning, having then to knock, ring and wake up the office-keeper, Bill Waistcott, who in about ten minutes opened the door and was bewildered at seeing four Carriages containing eight gentlemen and ourselves making up the number to eleven, getting out and walking into the office. The next thing to be done was to call and wake up the resident Magistrate, Mr Conant, who was very soon woke up, but he wanted to know what all this stir was about at so early an hour, and the reason of so many carriages at hand. Mr Plank having made him acquainted of the circumstances, he came downstairs into the private room, and after hearing the case the whole party, eight in number, were held to bail.

Thus ended an affair which in all probability, if I had not been interrupted, might have concluded seriously if not fatally.

No account of the above circumstances that I am aware of ever reached the press and consequently was not made known, so many years having now passed away very likely that all parties are dead.

The names of the Duellists were Capt. Burton and William Ford, Esq.

Madame Vestris

On the afternoon of the 6th July, 1830, Madame Vestris, the celebrated actress who in her day and peculiar line was not to be surpassed, left her carriage in charge of the coachman and page while she went into went into Drury Lane Theatre to attend a rehearsal. She had placed her reticule under the front cushion seat, containing her purse with four five-pound notes and some silver in it. After the rehearsal was over she returned to her carriage but found the page was not in attendance nor anywhere to be seen. After waiting a few minutes she enquired of the coachman where he was gone, who replied that he thought he was behind or beside the carriage. Madame became impatient, stepped into the carriage and told the coachman to drive home to May Fair, and while on the way she looked in her reticule for her purse and discovered it was gone. As on arriving home there was no page, she at once came to the conclusion that he must be the thief and that he had decamped with the money.

On the same evening at seven o'clock she came to Marlboro' Street police office and stated the particulars of the robbery as well as the name and description of her page. On being questioned she could not tell the numbers and dates of the notes, therefore to obtain this piece of information I accompanied her next morning to the bankers, and without any difficulty obtained the required information, and so far as Madam Vestris was concerned, left the business in my hands, to deal with it in the best way I could.

My first step was to see the coachman and ask him to try and recollect the topic of any conversation he had had with the page, George Walker. I walked with him to the public house at the corner of Down Street, Piccadilly, and treated him to a pint of ale, and after drinking a glass he said he recollected about a week ago George told him that he should like to go and live somewhere in the West of England, but he could not recollect the name of the place he mentioned, and when he did so, as he, George, had not much money, it would be in one of those broad wheel waggons drawn by eight horses.

That is all the coachman recollected. After this conversation we separated and I was put into a fix to know what to do. I enquired at the last place George was in, but could get no reliable information. I must do something, whispered I to myself, and to make a beginning it struck me all at once to go to some of the large Inn yards at the bottom of Holborn and Snowhill and also Fleet Market and make enquiries about some of these West of England broad wheeled waggons. I went to several places and found that some were gone, others would go next week and another in a fortnight, but that there was one going from Fleet Market the following morning. I went to the Inn Yard indicated and was informed that a waggon for Oxford, Cheltenham and Gloucester would leave at seven o'clock on the following morning. I'll be there, I said to myself, and being determined not to let the opportunity slip, I was at the yard soon after I heard St. Paul's Church clock strike six. There was a great bustle going on, some loading the Wagon, others roughly dressed in fustian Jackets and smock frocks going in and out of the Tap, some drinking pearl, others coffee.

The morning was very cold and dark. I walked into the Tap and ordered toast and coffee, and while I was taking my coffee a smart looking youth about 18 years of age walked in with two large bundles. He sat down and asked for a cup of tea, bread, butter and eggs; he wanted it directly, he said, because he was going off by the Wagon. They were brought and he soon put them out of sight. Then he rose from his seat and said to the Landlord who was inside the bar, he hadn't got enough coppers nor silver and he should be glad if he would give him change for a five pound bank note.

"Certainly I will," said the Landlord.

On hearing this I felt a slight throbbing in my inside, and saw that he answered the description given to me by Madam Vestris. After he had received his change he left carrying his bundles to the Wagon to take his place. I immediately referred to the memorandum in my pocket book with regard to the numbers and dates of the notes, and asked the Landlord in a low voice if he would kindly inform me the number and date of the note he had just given change for.

"Oh, yes, certainly," he said. "Is anything the matter? Here it is"holding it up in his hands—"the number is 5743."

I shewed my list and found it to be one of the same, and after telling him all about the robbery I went to the waggon and told the young man who I was, that he was to consider himself in my custody for the robbery of twenty pounds from his mistress Madam Vestris.

He came down the ladder at my bidding and I told him to

hand over to me the money. He put his hand into his inside waistcoat pocket and gave me the three other missing notes together with the change he had just received.

I dispatched one of the porters to fetch a hackney coach, and while he was gone a tall rough looking man resembling a navvy full six feet two inches high, and who witnessed these proceedings, spoke to me and asked if I be a Lunnon police officer, because if I be one, he know'd a case of £100 reward and if he know'd where to find me he would see and tell me all about it. I gave him my card, H. Goddard, Police Office Great Marlboro' Street, telling him that would find me.

At this moment the Hackney Coach came up. I gave the porter a shilling and stepped in with my prisoner, bundles and all, locked him up in safe custody at St. James's Watchhouse, discharged the Coachman and went home because it was too early to go and call upon Madame. At 10 o' clock I went to her house and told her exactly what I have already stated and she was delighted. I said it was necessary that she should attend at Marlboro' Street Office at 12 o'clock punctual. She was there and the result was the prisoner was identified committed to Newgate for trial, a true bill was found, he pleaded guilty and was sentenced to seven years' transportation.

Dick Poacher

Soon after the committal of the Page, George Walker, in the foregoing case of Madame Vestris, the rough I therein mentioned, as having given my card to, made his appearance. He asked Schofield, a brother Officer who was standing outside the door, at the same time shewing my card, if that was right, because if it was he would like to see me. Schofield came in the Clerks' office and told me there was a rough looking navigating sort of man waiting outside all of a perspiration to see me, Schofield at the same time wondering what it could be all about.

I went and said, "Hallo! you have found me out."

He laugh'd and was much pleased and said he never was in Lunnon afore, and gave his name to me as Joe Bealey, and said he knew where one of the men was to be found who had been concerned in a burglary with some others who were executed about a year ago at Lincoln Castle for a Job at Hawstead Hall in Lincolnshire.

The circumstances of this burglary were as follows.

About the hour of midnight in the early part of the month of February 1829, during the raging of a fearful storm when the wind was howling and whistling thro' the crevices of doors and windows of the old manor-house, Hawstead Hall, then in the occupation of Mr William Elsey, and situate in the parish of Stixwold, about seven miles from Horncastle in Lincolnshire, was broken into by seven ruffians (navvies) armed and disguised, some wearing masks and others with their faces blackened, one carrying a gun and the rest pistols and bludgeons.

Three of these ruffians entered the bedroom of Mr and Mrs Elsey, one presenting the gun, the second holding a lantern, while the third ordered Mrs Elsey out and go to the maid servant's room, where he locked them in saying if they made any noise he would do for them; while the other four proceeded to the men servants' room over the stables, putting them in bodily fear and threatening them in the same way. During this time the other two were threatening Mr Elsey for his life, to shew them where his plate and money was deposited, and after possessing themselves of the plunder to the value of £300 told Mr Elsey he might go back to his bed room, he at the same time with great fear and trembling beseeching them to spare their lives; they followed him upstairs and locked him in and said if he did not go to the window to give an alarm they would not hurt him, so after packing up the spoil they took it in turns to go to the larder and regale themselves over sundry jugs of beer and, after demolishing a ham, some beef and two or three cold roast fowls, quietly stole away along the garden and across the fields, leaving their footprints behind plainly visible next morning till the trace was lost by taking the turnpike road, going towards Tattershall.

Mrs Elsey and her servant, as also Mr Elsey, were kept a long time in a terrible state of suspense when at last the servant saw the gang of burglars passing along the garden from her bedroom window; at this time the wind had dropped and all was hushed in silence. The servant proposed to her mistress that she could get out of the window and drop into the garden, and by this means if the gang had left the outside door open she could enter that way and unlock her bedroom door from the outside. Mrs Elsey gave her consent and assisted the servant from the window, who lost no time in running round to the front and found the door was left open. She proceeded upstairs and released her mistress, who both immediately went to the bedroom of Mr Elsey expecting to find him murdered, but before turning the key one of them knocked, and hearing Mr Elsey reply, "Who is it?" they unlocked the door and to their joy found him alive but in a great state of nervous agitation. (My readers can imagine this scene much better than I can attempt to describe it.) He immediately rose from his bed and, while dressing, the servant went downstairs and after putting two or three bundles of dry faggots into the kitchen range there was soon a brilliant fire.

By this time the servant men had found their way into the house, Mr and Mrs Elsey had come down stairs, it was then about two o'clock in the morning when Mr Elsey requested his household to follow him into the drawing room. After reading a prayer and returning thanks to Almighty God for their deliverance from the perils and dangers they had escaped that night, in which they all joined, the men-servants then returned to the kitchen while a good fire was soon got in the drawing room, the breakfast service set. After the household had partaken of a hearty breakfast the men and Mr Elsey at this untimely hour scarcely in their state of excitement knew what to do for the best, for if they alarmed the Village they said the house would soon be surrounded and by this means the foot prints along the garden would be obliterated. Under these circumstances it was thought best not to give the alarm until day-light, when they went to the village, first calling up the constable, who on hearing of the outrage a Hue and Cry was soon raised and the news was quickly spread from village to village and from town to town till it was conveyed to Lincoln and all over the country, so much so that it was not long before one of the gang was apprehended and taken before the Magistrates at Horncastle, who committed him for trial. He was convicted at the March Assizes, 1829, held at Lincoln and executed a few days afterwards at Lincoln Castle, viz on the 27th March, 1829.

Two others of these desperate ruffians—viz Tiger alias rough Tom, Timothy Brammer, and Thomas Strong alias Tipler—was apprehended some time afterwards and committed at the March Assizes at Lincoln in the year 1830 and executed at Lincoln Castle on the 19th March within three days after their conviction. (Tiger Tom was so called in consequence of his enormous strength, that he could without difficulty take a man of ordinary size by the waistband of his trousers with his teeth and run round the room carrying the man thus, as a cat would carry a mouse.)

It was the fourth of these seven burglars, viz Dick Poacher, of whose whereabouts his pal Joe Bealey came to Great Marlboro' Street to inform me.

I and Schofield searched over the Hue and Cry and found the information to be correct, and that part of the £100 reward for the apprehension was to be paid by Mr Elsey and the other part by the association for the prosecution of felons.

We then called the attention of H.M. Dyer Esq., the sitting

Magistrate, to these particulars, who ordered the man Joe Bealey to be introduced, and upon being sworn, and in answer to questions put by the Magistrates, replied that one of the gang, Richard Poacher, was now engaged working at Newbold in Warwickshire with about a hundred other navvies in digging the Oxford Canal. The Magistrates then directed his deposition to be taken down in writing, which was afterwards read over to him and was then asked if that was true. Joe Bealey replied it was and then attached his signature, a warrant was granted and placed in our hands for Poacher's apprehension.

It was arranged the trio, viz Schofield, Joe Bealey and myself, should start off by Coach the next morning. We met according to agreement and left the Swan-with-two necks, Lad Lane, at 9 o'clock, booking for Northampton; and on our way every time the Coach changed horses Joe would slip down and run to the public house for a drink of Rum and told us that if we prevented him from having it he should leave and seek work in another part of the country. Schofield told him he could do as he liked for we should be able to get on better without him; this observation seemed to trouble him and so we travelled on in peace for the rest of the journey to the Angel Inn, Northampton, where we arrived at about 4 in the afternoon.

After Joe had thoroughly filled himself with salt beef and carrots, washing it down with three pints of beer, and as Weedon was only eight miles and no coach going that way, we undertook to walk it bag and baggage; but before we left Northampton Joe would have a quartern of Rum, and after getting over about four miles of the journey in passing a rick-yard he complain'd of being sleepy and tired, and must have a downer under the rick for half an hour. We also felt tired, and allowed him to mount over the gate and take his downer under one of the hay stacks. He soon fell into a sound sleep, snoring like a pig for an hour, when we tried to wake him but in vain, therefore we thought we would give him another hour to sober him during which old Scho and myself dozed occasionally.

It was now getting on for nine o'clock and we had some difficulty in waking him. At last he got up, gaped, shook himself and complain'd of thirst. Observing a cottage near at hand, we knocked and, being answered by an old man, asked if he would kindly give us a large jug of water for we were all so thirsty. The old cottager went to the well and soon drew up a bucket of beautiful bright water and dipped a quart jug into it which was handed to Joe, the contents of which he swallowed in two draughts, which refreshed him very much. Old Scho and I also took a draft and asked the cottager if there was anything to pay; he laughed, Scho put sixpence into his hand and wished him goodnight. He stared at us, and as we walked away he seemed to wonder what it all meant and what sort of business ours was.

The water so refreshed Joe that he took it into his head all at once to start off walking at the rate of nearly five miles an hour, so that we arrived at a road side house at Weedon before 10 o'clock. After ordering three beds we placed Joe in the tap room and asked him what he should like to have for his supper.

"Beef steak and onions," he said.

The landlord looked thunderstruck and said he had not such a thing in the house, but had plenty of cold roast beef.

Joe said, "All right, that will do with some onions." He was soon supplied with a large cut, a half quartern loaf, several large onions and a quart of beer.

While Joe was employing himself over his supper we were taking ours in the parlour when it happened two sweeps came in and, seeing Joe relishing his supper, enquired of the Landlord if he could let them have some of the same sort as they had walked all the way from Towcester (they said) and were hungry. They were answered there was no more meat left in the house and it was getting late.

"Well, let us have some bread, cheese and onions," said the master-sweep, "and some beer."

Their order was reluctantly attended to, and they contented themselves with devouring a half quartern loaf, half a pound of cheese, half a dozen large onions and half a gallon of ale. While they were eating their supper Joe was doing a Pipe with a tumblerfull of hot rum and water. The sweeps, after they had finished, fell in with Joe and called for two large glasses of hot rum and water and took to doing a pipe like Joe. They got into conversation and Joe amused them by saying he could unscrew his nose, and by placing his large brawny hand before his nasal organ and turning it round, at the same time grating his teeth, made it appear like a painted wooden one, that he could unscrew and screw it on at pleasure.

It was now getting late and the landlord told them he wanted to lock up and must put out the lights; Joe said be d…'d if he'd go to bed before he had another go of rum and water, the sweeps also join'd in saying before they went they should like to have a wind up with Joe, so the big sweep challenged him to wrestle for glasses round. The challenge was accepted and to give room the tables and seats were placed out of the way when they commenced. After the wrestling continued for some time, the assistant sweep, seeing his master getting the worst of it, pitched into Joe, and then it got to a regular fight and row making a terrible noise when the maid servant went in and saw the row, and their faces streaming with blood so frightened her that she screamed out "Murder!" The Landlord rushed in and called us for assistance.

Scho and I hurried in, when Schofield swore if they did not desist he would shoot one or the other; this so terrified the Landlord that he took us to be foot pad robbers and forthwith sent to the barracks for the soldiers, and in a few minutes we found ourselves under arrest; but on informing the officer who we were, put the matter right, so that the sweeps after a good threshing left, and went on their way home to Daventry.

We had some difficulty afterwards in getting Joe to bed, and Scho having no confidence in him, fearing he might get up in the night and make his escape, took away his boots, billy-cock hat and his trousers; having done this, we apologised to the landlord for introducing such a rough customer and he expressed himself satisfied.

Thus far, the troubles, excitement and fatigues of that day and part of the night having come to an end, we were only too glad to get to bed and think what sort of a day we should have to battle through before the sun set tomorrow.

We were up the next morning at seven o'clock and told the Ostler to clean Joe's boots and take them with the trousers and call him. Joe was soon up and down in the tap room with a plentiful supply of fried eggs and bacon for his breakfast. He preferred beer to tea and coffee so we allowed him to have it. At nine o'clock we started on foot for Daventry, when our savage began to turn awkwardly quarrelsome and sulky if we did not give him more money for Rum. He had remarkable white teeth, and to try to put him in a good temper I praised them and asked him what he cleaned them with. This brought a smile and he replied, "With beer, to be sure!" Then he wanted rum, and we let him have what we thought sufficient, and so by the time we got to Rugby, within three miles of the Oxford

Canal at Newbold where Dick Poacher was at work he refused to go any further unless we paid him the reward before he went to the works to point out his pal, Dick Poacher.

We tried to reason with him, but in vain, and found it essential to have an interview with the Rugby Constable. After telling him our business he said we were going on a very dangerous and unsafe undertaking, that it would require at least twenty soldiers for our work, but he added, "I know two very powerful fellows who are fighting men, their name is Tring and are brothers and if you walk with me I will take you to them."

We followed, and he soon introduced us to the Trings, who were blacksmiths, and most formidable looking men they were; we engaged to pay them a Guinea each besides expenses for Horse, Cart, etc. We all then went to the Magistrate to get the Trings sworn in as constables for the occasion as also to have the Warrant backed. Joe was at our heels all the time and was not ignorant as to what was going on, when Schofield went up to him and told him if he did not keep to his bargain and go with us as he had promised, he should go and call all the bankers (Navvies) together and split against him what he had been doing and leave him to his fate among his fellow mates he had been working with. These words so frightened Joe that after a little parleying he consented to go.

We then engaged a Post-chaise, the Rugby constable and the brothers Tring hired a Trap and it was arranged they were to follow a quarter of an hour behind, not to take any notice of us but to keep the New Inn in view. Joe accompanied us in the Chaise, and it was agreed on our way to set him down within half a mile of the works so as not to be seen with us. Six o'clock was the hour these Navvies left work, of whom there were about a hundred, and they all had to pass through the large battery or Tap of the New Inn (a Beer shop), many of them usually staying to have supper, some bread and cheese with onions, others cold meat, some fried eggs and bacon. It being now near the time, Schofield and I left the Chaise in charge of the driver at the lower part of the hill. Before ascending the top I was dressed as a Pedlar, wearing a check shirt and Billy-cock with fustian Jacket.

It wanted now about five minutes to six when I left Schofield sitting on a style. Joe by this time had gone into the Tap. I followed about a minute afterwards, took a seat and called for a pint of beer, a small loaf and cheese. Joe faced me on the opposite side and by this time the bell struck six and the Navvies began to come in, carrying pickaxes and shovels. Some passed through while others sat down and ordered their suppers, numbering about thirty. Now it had been previously arranged that when Dick Poacher should enter, Joe was to give a signal by calling for a pot of beer, and hand over the same to Poacher saying, "Come, Dick lad! take a drink."

The Tap room was now nearly full, scarcely room to stand, when a tall powerful man carrying a shovel on his shoulder walked in, and after ordering fried eggs and bacon he amused himself while it was being got ready by playing a tune with his knuckles on the table. A few minutes elapsed and his supper was ready, which he soon eat and paid for his score, by which time several Navvies had left. At this point Joe called out for a pot of beer and according to the prearranged signal handed it to this powerful man (Dick Poacher) and said, "Come, Dick lad! take a drink," at the same time look'd at me to see if I observed his movement. Dick took the pot from his hand and drank very heartily, Joe finished it and called for another and after paying for it told Dick to finish it. Joe then rose from his seat, shook hands with Dick, and said, "Good night, Dick," and walked away, leaving me single-handed doing my pipe among this gang of ruffians.

After Joe left he walked up to Schofield, who still sat perched upon the stile reading a Newspaper, and told him it was now all right, that he had given the signal and expected Dick would be out in two or three minutes. Schofield then slipped two sovereigns in his hand and told him to make the best of his way to London and call upon us in the course of two or three days.

About a quarter of an hour after Joe left, Dick Poacher raised himself from his sitting posture, shouldered his shovel and walked out followed by about a dozen other navvies carrying pickaxes and shovels. I followed after, and as long as Dick was walking in the direction of our post chaise I let him go unmolested, but when he turned with his mates to go in another direction, I made up to him and told him who I was and that I held a Warrant for his apprehension, that he must consider Himself in custody. He then put himself in a menacing attitude, raising his shovel over his head and saying if I did not let him go he would brain me. I kept close to him with my shoulder under his armpit. Schofield at this moment came up, producing his pistols, holding one to his head and in a determined manner told him, by God if he did not drop that shovel he would shoot him.

The brothers Tring and the Rugby constable arrived at this nick of time, one fastened to him on one side and the one on the other. Schofield disarmed him of the shovel while the Rugby constable assisted the Trings, Dick Poacher calling on his mates (the Navvies) to rescue him, hollowing out to about thirty of them, "Come on! Come on! Is there never a man among you then?"

Poacher then threw himself on the ground among the flints and stones, I on the top of him and sometimes under, till at last with the able assistance of the Trings succeeded in snapping on the handcuffs, when we all got upon our legs.

At this moment a boy-sweep mounted on a pony appeared upon the scene to whom I offered a half-crown if he would gallop his pony to the other side of the top of the hill and tell the driver to bring the post-chaise he would see standing there down immediately. The boy galloped away on his errand, while during his absence we were all engaged forcing and dragging our prisoner along the road to meet it, Schofield being engaged all this time in keeping the navvies from approaching at a short distance with a pistol in each hand. In a few seconds down came the sweep galloping, with the post-chaise following. I gave him the half crown, the chaise was turned round, the door soon opened and while we were forcing Poacher into it, a gang of these Navvies, his pals, were seen advancing armed with picks and shovels along a field close by the hedge side where there was a gap, through which they were making their way and crying out "Rescue! Rescue!" while our prisoner kept bawling out "Come on! Come on!" Schofield, seeing our danger, ran to the gap foaming at the mouth, and with pistol in each hand swore the first man who attempted to come down he would shoot him dead. We had now succeeded in forcing Dick into the chaise, and I ran, pistol in hand, to Schofield's assistance standing side by his side declaring if they advanced we would fire upon them in defence of our lives.

This threat seemed to have the desired effect for a few seconds and, retreating backwards with our faces to the enemy step by step till we reached the chaise, our prisoner being well secured by the Trings, I mounted on the splinter-bar while

Schofield with some difficulty got up and perched himself on the roof with the Rugby constable. No sooner when the word "Go on!" was given to the postillion, he spurred his horses, and the sudden start nearly pitched old Schofield and the constable head foremost, they having nothing to hold on by, but the one balanced the other and away went the post-chaise at a rattling pace followed by the gang of Navvies for about a hundred yards, pelting us pell-mell with large flint stones laying on the road, coming down on the roof like hail stones in a storm, but happily without effect as the fleetness of the horses soon outstript our pursuers. We quickly reached Rugby and settled what we had promised the Trings, as well as the constable, whose indomitable courage and tact they all displayed on the occasion was beyond all praise.

Schofield and I took the places just vacated by the Trings and away we went at a dashing pace till we reached Daventry, where we changed carriage and horses and gave our prisoner what he appeared to be much in want of after his powerful and long resistance, a pint of beer. We then drove on to Northampton and saw Mr Castles, the Mayor and proprietor of the Stag's head Inn, who, after hearing under what circumstances we wanted our prisoner secured for the night, kindly gave us an order to Mr Wootten, the Governor of the Borough gaol, to place him in one of the strong cells. By this time our prisoner became subdued and felt much exhausted, therefore the Governor allowed him to have some cold meat and a draught of beer. We paid the post boy, and when Mr Wootton had well secured our prisoner for the night he returned with us to the Stag's-head. Schofield and I ate a hearty supper of cold roast fowl and a most delicious flavoured ham, of which we stood in so much need after the fatigues of such a long and exciting day.

At eight o'clock on the following morning (Sunday) we went to look after our prisoner. The Governor conducted us to his cell and, on unlocking the door, to our surprise he was stark naked standing on the wooden seat of his cell like a Colossus. He had suffered from the disagreeable odour arising from his clothes, which he said was so unbearable during the night that he tore them into remnants, and from what we experienced from the smell when the door was opened we thought he was quite justified in doing what he did. The Governor ordered a blanket to cover him and he was then conducted by three of the wardens to a warm bath. Schofield took his measure, we informed the Mayor of the man's condition, who told us of an outfitter's establishment where we could get him rigged; the outfitter with his man followed us to the gaol, each carrying two or three suits of the largest size Fustians they had, who upon seeing the man knew exactly what he wanted and fitted him at once with a good check shirt, fustian jacket, trousers and waistcoat, a pair of woollen stockings, pocket handkerchief and one to wear round his neck; all was now complete except a cap, he having lost his billy-cock in the encounter with us. He was then placed in a light and strong room, ate a good breakfast consisting of a pint of tea, two eggs and thick slices of bread and butter which, with his bath and change of clothes, refreshed him so much that he looked quite a different and respectable man and he expressed himself in thanks to us for our kindness. As there was no conveyance from Northampton to Leicester till two o'clock we took our dinners before starting not forgetting to give Dick his. At that hour we went to the Angel Inn followed by a great crowd, and while the changing of horses took place Dick walked up the wide steps of a ladder and seated himself on the centre of the roof behind the coachman, I on one side of him and Schofield on the other, and in a few minutes the guard blew his horn and we were off, arriving at Leicester about five o'clock, and as the Governor of the gaol knew me he kindly consented to secure him in one of his strong cells for the night.

On the next day while conveying our prisoner on the coach to Horncastle he expressed himself in the most subdued and penitent manner, saying how sorry he was for the trouble and resistance he had shewn towards us and hoped that we would not inform the magistrates, for if we did he knew they would hang him as they did the others. Schofield and I sympathised with and felt for him in his dreadful forlorn position, and told him we would consider.

At length we arrived at Horncastle and left him in his fetters in charge of the lock-up keeper. Next day he was examined before the Magistrates and committed to Lincoln Castle for trial. The warrant for his commitment was handed over to us to lodge him there and on going along the entrance to the Castle, Poacher called our attention by pointing to two Busts standing in niches in the wall, one on one side being that of Tiger Timothy Tom and the other that of Bob Brammer. We then left him in the hands of the Governor to reflect on his coming fate, and as Schofield and I had no evidence to give but merely to hand him over to be dealt with according to law, we kept sacred what he told us on the road from Leicester to Horncastle, respecting his resistance. Schofield and I returned to London, saw Joe, gave him a letter to take to the secretary for the prosecution of felons, who handed over to him the reward. Dick Poacher was tried at the next Assizes and sentenced to transportation for life. Thus ended our dangerous encounter at the hazard of our lives, and we were barely paid our expenses.

A Lost Diamond Ring

About half past eleven o'clock on the night of Friday, 22nd July, 1831, when the London season was at its zenith, I was engaged with others in attendance at a brilliant ball given by the Austrian Ambassador, Prince Esterhazy.

While the carriages were driving up and setting down the elite of the Aristocracy, a foreign count, whose name I have unfortunately forgotten, came down from the ball-room and told me that he arrived here in a Cab behind the rank of Carriages about twenty minutes since, and while engaged dancing with a lady, suddenly missed a ring which he would not lose for one hundred guineas, it being a present from the Emperor of Prussia of His diamond ring. He thought he must have dropped it in the Cab while changing his gloves.

"But it is now so late," said he. "Will you please call upon me at ten o' clock tomorrow morning and I will give the description?"

I asked where he engaged the cab.

He replied, "From Duke Street, St. James's."

He gave me his card, I in return gave mine and he returned

to the drawing saloon.

About five minutes afterwards it occurred to me that after the cab had set him down the cabman would drive and put up at the nearest cab rank, which would be in Oxford Street, between Argyll Street and Oxford Circus. Elated with this idea, I started away as fast as my legs would take me, and on nearly reaching the spot I was just in time to see the foremost cab leaving, and the driver putting his whip to the horse going at a fast pace down Regent Street. I ran to the head of the horse, took hold of the bridle and holloa'd, at the same time shewing my brass staff to the driver to stop.

He immediately pulled up, and I said to him, "Not half an hour ago you set down a gentleman at Chandos house."

"Yes, I did," he replied, "and I have just taken up another."

I opened the door and told the gentleman I must search, as something had been left. He got up and I looked around the seat but saw nothing. He sat down again and I then asked him to lift up his legs, and there was the ring laying under his feet on the mat.

After this little bit of excitement I returned to my duty, told my brother Officers what I had done and waited till the ball was over at six o'clock in the morning, then went home to Robert Street, Hampstead Road, to snatch a two hours' rest. At ten o'clock I called according to appointment upon the Count in Princes Place, Duke Street, St. James's, and on seeing him produced the ring, when he said, "Dat is it, dat is my ring, oh I am so much oblige, what can I do? What an obligation I am under! But I am so poor; stay, stay," he said. "I will write."

He went to his desk, and after keeping me in a state of suspense for twenty minutes said, "Dar, dar, take dat, and put it in your pocket, it is a recommendation and a character for you to shew to any gentleman similarly situated, who may some time or another so happen to be."

This I, of course, considered an ample gratuitous return.

The Murder of Mr Richardson

Early in the morning of the 25th March, 1834, before the break of day, Mrs Richardson was awoke in a great fright by her husband starting up suddenly from his sleep and shouting out with all his might, "I have been shot! I am shot! See! See! Look!! They are murdering me."

She instantly arose from the bed and obtain'd a light when Mr Richardson, in a nervous state of mind and bathed in perspiration, said he had been dreaming that he was shot while on his way home coming from Epsom Market.

On recovering from the shock of his dream through the soothing language of his wife, he soon became reconciled and then went to sleep and did not awake again till his usual hour of rising—about 7 o'clock A.M.

About an hour after his breakfast, viz at half past 9, his chaise being in readiness, he got into it and bade his wife good morning, at the same time saying, "If nothing happens to me on returning from Market this evening I shall be home before half past 7." He then started on his way, and after driving for a few miles, arrived at Tadworth Gate Tollbar. Here while paying the toll he, by a motion of his head, called the attention of the Collector to a man he had just passed on the road and who was now leaning his back against some rails which stood about 200 yards off; he said, "See! look! there he is!" He then explained that he did not like the appearance of that man, for while the wind was blowing he saw the shape of a horse pistol under his frock. He then added, "You keep your eye on him, for I am sure he is after no good." He then related his dream, and said, "Mind, if anything happens to me on my returning home tonight that will be the man". He then left and drove on to Epsom, and after transacting his business at the market, returned to the Spread Eagle Hotel (then kept by Mr Lumley) where he had put up his horse.

While taking his tea at the same table with several farmers he related to them his dream, they listening with the greatest attention. He also told them of his coming to market that morning and of his calling the attention of the toll-man, at Tadworth toll-bar, to his dream and of his at the same time pointing out a suspicious looking man whom he had passed on the road. Then he continued, "If any thing happens to me, if I am shot on returning home to night, that man who I pointed out to the toll-collector will be the man who has done it". The farmers to a man listened with very great attention to this last statement. Then they all cheered him up saying there was nothing in dreams except they always went contrary.

It was now getting on for half past six o'clock. Mr Richardson got into his chaise and, wishing them all good night, drove out of the yard. About two hours afterwards, between eight and nine o'clock, the town of Epsom and the surrounding villages were thrown into the greatest terror and alarm by the report that Mr Richardson of Bletchingly had been found laying in the road murdered.

He was discovered at a short distance from the country seat of Lord Hardinge by West the Carrier, who was on his way from Ewell accompanied by Mr Batchelor. Upon arriving within about 200 yards of where the Ewell and Banstead roads join, they heard the report of two pistols. They stopped immediately, then they heard someone groaning. Upon this, West alighted from his Cart and left Batchelor in charge while he went towards the spot from whence the groanings proceeded. Whilst thus making his way he met two men dressed in short frocks; upon seeing him they altered their course towards Ewell. West was then only a few yards from the road, upon gaining which on his arrival he saw a tall big man lying across dead, and an empty Chaise backed against the hedge on the other side, with the two wheels in the ditch.

On seeing this, he hastened back in great alarm and told his companion, Mr Batchelor, what he had seen. He then exclaimed, "Come on! follow me! for directly I left you I met two men coming from that direction who saw me, and they have gone towards Ewell. Come on!" said West again to Batchelor, "let us follow them and raise an alarm, if we lose a moment they will escape."

Batchelor hesitated, and said, "What is to become of the horse and cart and all the parcels, some of which are no doubt valuable?"

Upon this West resumed his place in the cart and drove as fast as he could to the stables of Lord Hardinge, informing the grooms and helpers what had happened. After leaving his cart in a state of security he conducted some of the grooms and ostlers to the scene of the murder, Very soon after this all Banstead and its approaches were up in arms. Some of them mounted on their horses went as fast as they could gallop to take the news to Epsom, Ewell and Leatherhead in order that it might be spread all round that part of the country.

It happened very shortly after these outcries that four men (bell ringers) came upon the scene of the murder, who had walked across the fields from Ewell to make their way towards the belfry at Banstead. Upon hearing of the murder they said, "Why, it is not long since, as we were on our way, we met two men going in the direction of Ewell—they wore short frocks, were running fast and out of breath, in fact we separated and made room for them to pass between us—they almost ran into our arms." (According to this statement, if Batchelor had followed up the pursuit as West wished, there is no doubt these men would have been captured.)

Early on the following morning Mr Bugs, a grocer, living at Epsom, came forward and stated that the previous night about 7 o'clock, he was on horseback going to Banstead, and when within 200 yards of the "Rose Bushes" he passed Mr Richardson, saying "good night." In a minute afterwards he saw two men in light coloured Frocks. One was standing under the hedge on one side of the road and another in like manner on the opposite side, which unnerved him so much that he spurred his horse into a fast gallop. The wind was blowing very hard at the time, and after a few seconds he fancied he heard the report of pistols; but not being quite sure, he rode on.

Information of this murder was forwarded next day by the Magistrates to His Majesty's principal Secretary of State for the Home department, who at once communicated the same to the Chief Magistrate, Sir Frederick Roe, of the Public Office, Bow Street. I happening to be in attendance, Sir F. Roe immediately directed me to proceed without delay to the scene, telling me to use all energy and spare no expense to discover the murderers; and he added that as it was probable that in the course of the inquiry I would have to contend with desperate characters, I was not to forget to go armed with a brace of loaded pistols which Mr Stafford, the Chief Clerk, would provide me.

On arriving at Epsom I had an interview with the Baron de Tessier, one of the local Magistrates, who was then in consultation at the office of Messrs Everest and Harding, Solicitors, who all accompanied me to the spot of the murder and also the track across the fields (where West the Carrier first met the murderers when they evaded him by suddenly turning to their left across the country towards Ewell, where they were met by the bell ringers). We proceeded on to Leatherhead and its neighbourhood, continuing our enquiries till past one o'clock in the morning; meeting with no success I retired to my hotel, the "Spread Eagle", and the Baron with the two Solicitors retired to their homes.

For several days and nights afterwards, early and late, I was on the qui vive—at Merstrum, Bletchingly, Walton, Banstead, half-mile bush, Kingston and other places, searching the low slums, the lodging houses, the Tom and Jerry's and other places resorted to by tramps and suspicious characters. In these visits I was informed of one man of the name of Cheesely, a suspicious and desperate character, living at Merstrum, who was always wandering about all night and returning home as the labourers were setting out for their daily work early in the morning.

Under these circumstances I ventured to see him at his hut to put some questions to him as to how he spent his time, and as his answers were evasive I gave him into the custody of a constable while I searched his Hut, when I found a few Snares, a Gun and a large Hare, which he said had been killed by a Stoat, adding that as he saw it lying in a field he picked it up and brought it home. He begged me to let him go; and I thought under these circumstances as I could prove nothing against him as regarded the murder it would be better for me to give him his liberty than parade him before the Magistrates on suspicion of being concerned in the murder without a particle of evidence against him. Such a course as the latter not only tends to do much harm to the accused but also gives to the guilty parties every confidence.

Soon afterwards, another man, of the name of Sam Cotterell, living in the neighbourhood of Bethnall Green, was apprehended on suspicion; he was brought down from London by Ellis, one of the Principal officers of Bow Street, and while he was under examination before the Magistrates at Epsom, some one on the Bench suggested that a Billy-cock and short white frock should be obtained for the prisoner to put on in order that it might be seen if he at all resembled either of the men who were met on the night of the murder by the bell-ringers. This I thought very unfair, but the suggestion was acted upon, and a Billy-cock and frock were duly obtained from the shop of a Jew clothier hard by; these were put on the prisoner, first the frock and then the Billy-cock, and thus attired he was surveyed by West the carrier and the bell-ringers; and these failing to identify him, the man was discharged and paid for all expence and inconvenience he had been put to.

The inquest was held at the" Surry Yeoman", Banstead. In addition to the evidence of West and the Bell Ringers, two women came forward and stated that while they were stone picking in a field near to Ewell they found a pistol lying in the track the men had taken when they were met by the bell-ringers, which was identified as belonging to the deceased whose pockets were found to be turned inside out, and who was supposed to have been robbed of more than thirty pounds consisting of two ten-pound bank of England notes and two fives.

The result of the inquest was that the Jury returned a verdict of wilful murder against some person or persons unknown.

It may here be mentioned that Mr Richardson (the murdered man) had been instrumental not long before in the capture of two notorious characters who were tried and committed for highway robbery at a former Surry Assizes.

About ten days after the murder, the Magistrates at Epsom received an anonymous letter stating that there were two men of notoriously bad character by the name of John and Harry Childs (brothers), living up a back way in the retired village of West Bedfont; that since the commission of the murder they had retired from their usual haunts and were hardly ever to be seen, and then only by chance and late at night; and that so satisfied was the writer that these were the murderers, that he would come forward with overwhelming evidence to prove the fact, directly he heard of their being in custody.

Soon after the receipt of this letter the Magistrates held a consultation upon it, the result of which was that I was directed to proceed, prepared with assistance, to the place indicated in the letter, and apprehend these men and bring them before the Magistrates. I asked, for my own protection's sake, to be furnished with a Warrant as the charge I had to make was a serious one; but this they did not accede to but told me in a very polite manner to do the best I could. With this understanding I left, and went, furnished with assistance, in a four wheel chaise on my mission to the scene of action.

Upon arriving there the first thing I had to do was to put my horse and chaise up at the hotel and then, leaving the two constables behind so as not to excite suspicion, I went single handed to work. After making some enquiries I was informed of the residence of the Childs, gaining which and finding the door wide open, I walked in, and saw a woman at the wash-tub who seemed greatly surprised at my sudden intrusion. Without making any excuse for this intrusion, I asked if she could kindly inform me where two poor women (sisters) by the name of Smith resided. She considered for a moment, and asked me what occupation they followed; to which I replied, "All I know is I have been informed they were engaged near here gathering turnip tops".

"Oh!" she answered, "then I dare say they are helping my brothers, for they are loading a Wagon of turnip-tops for Covent Garden market to morrow morning, in the far field."

I enquired, "What may be the name of your brothers?"

"Oh! why Childs, to be sure," she replied, "John and Harry."

I thanked her and said, "All right! I am going a little way up the village first, and then I'll go and ask them."

She then bade me good afternoon, and I left her with a smile upon her countenance, and returned to the hotel where I informed the constables what I had done.

We then proceeded in company, down a by-lane leading to the turnip field, and after a little reconnoitering, saw the two men assisted by about eight or ten women, carrying baskets full of tops to the waggon.

"There they are," I said.

"Yes," said one of the constables, "that's them, safe enough, for I know the big one, Harry."

It was then arranged that I should saunter in the field and go up and speak to Harry, and while I was engaged with him my colleagues were to see that the other man did not run away.

"All right," they said, "we will manage him."

So into the field I went. The big one, Harry, saw me when I was about a hundred yards off, then as I approached him, I beckoned, and he said something to his brother and came towards me. Just at this time the two constables made their way through a gap in the hedge to another part of the field ready to lay collar on the other in the event of his trying to get away.

I said to the big one, ' 'Your name is Harry Childs, is it not?"

"Yes," he replied, "my name is Harry Childs, and that," pointing, "is my brother John."

The Constables at this time had got up to John.

I said, "You know of the murder of Mr Richardson."

"Oh, yes, I have heard of it, and what of it?" he replied.

I said, "People will talk and say all manner of things, but you know where you were on that night."

"Why, at home, or in the Village," he replied, "for I have never been any distance from it for the last three weeks or a month."

"Well, then," I said, "are you and your brother willing to come along with me now and explain that before the Magistrates?"

"Yes," he said. He then shouted out to his brother, "John." John came and the two constables also, and Harry then repeated to John what I had said. "It is Friday afternoon," said he, "and when that wagon is loaded who is to take it to night to be in time for Covent Garden Market to morrow? "Besides," he added, "who is to pay all these women for their worth? Where is the money to come from, and who is to receive the money for the sale of the tops to morrow morning?"

John paused for a minute, and said, "That is true."

By this time the women were all gathered round and had began to clamour and shew signs of discontent, using violent threats towards me and the constables, so much so that we thought it would end in a riot or something serious, and this no doubt would have been the case had it not been for the interference of the brothers, who after a little set-to subdued them. Harry and John then represented to me that under the present circumstances if they left their job it would be the ruin of them, and that if I wanted them they would be in Covent Garden on the morrow and ready to go with me to Bow Street and appear before Sir Frederick Roe. All these remarks having been made, I thought they were very reasonable. Further, I could not see why I should force these poor men away from their employment having satisfied myself that they had not, as stated in the letter, vacated their usual haunts, or the parish, or their homes.

Under these circumstances, I took their word-that if I wanted them they would come forward at any time.

Having come to this understanding, I and the two constables left them to their work in the fields and proceeded back to Epsom, where as we approached there were scores of people who had ascertained my mission, waiting for us in the road for our return and anxious to see the prisoners. The Magistrates were also anxiously expecting us. When they found I had not apprehended the men they expressed much surprise and disappointment. I stated that I had nothing to act upon, but if they would take upon themselves to give me the proper authority by granting me a Warrant, I would go and execute it immediately.

They consulted about twenty minutes, after which, as they

had not been able to come to an arrangement, I left.

Nothing more was heard of this matter till a few days afterwards the following astounding and exciting intelligence appeared in most of the daily papers, viz

Copy from the Morning Advertiser newspaper of 9th April, 1834:

MURDER OF MR RICHARDSON — RE— APPREHENSION OF SUPPOSED MURDERERS

The most unceasing exertions still continue to be made by the magistrates and officers to effect the capture of the murderers of the unfortunate Mr Richardson, and there is now the strongest reason to believe that their efforts will be crowned with success, and that the actual prepetrators of the cold blooded crime are at this moment in custody.

For about a month past the Magistrates at Epsom have received numerous anonymous letters referring to the murder, all of which pointed out in the most positive manner two men of the name of Child as the parties who committed the dreadful act. No attention was for some days paid to these communications as the writer did not choose to furnish his name; but from the pertinacity of the correspondent and the strong chain of evidence which he furnished, it was considered by the Magistrates that it was necessary to give the statements some notice, and accordingly Goddard, the new made Bow street officer, who from his activity and intelligence has been pitched upon to follow out the mysterious concealment of the murderers, was desired to make some enquiries into the statements contained in these letters.

Goddard after considerable difficulty succeeded in taking the two brothers into custody, and then proceeded to question them as to the disposal of their time on the night of the murder. The men gave such plausible replies and afforded such evidence of their innocence that the officer was induced to release them, and to report the great improbability of those men having any thing to do with the foul deed. The writer of the anonymous letter, after this proceeding, continued to assert that they were the real criminals, and added other and stronger circumstances of a circumstantial nature in proof of his accuracy. The same writer also addressed letters to the Commissioners of Metropolitan Police, recapitulating his assertions and his proofs and called upon them to have the men again apprehended, and an investigation set on foot as to the truth of the story they told when first taken into custody.

The persevering conduct of the anonymous correspondent added to the apparent earnestness of his charges induced the Epsom Magistrates again to have the two Childs apprehended in order that they themselves might examine them.

A warrant was issued for their immediate apprehension and entrusted to Grossmith and Barefoot, Inspectors of the B division for the purpose of being properly executed.

The officers went to execute their mission, but they learned on enquiry that the two brothers had not been seen recently at their usual haunts. Consequently they were unable to capture them until Sunday last, when in consequence of information furnished to them, they went, accompanied by Inspector Marchant and Sergeant Reynolds. to West Bedfont near Staines, and succeeded in taking both of the men into custody. At first the officers were informed that the brothers were not there, but on proceeding to search the house, Harry Child was found behind one of the doors and his brother John was shortly after taken at a house in the neighbourhood to which be had fled on hearing that the Police were again in quest of him. By order of

Sir John Gibbon, a Magistrate, the men were conveyed the same evening to Epsom, and on reaching that place it was considered advisable that they should be kept apart and separately confined, which plan was accordingly adopted. On Monday morning they were taken before Messrs Everest and Harding's offices before Baron Tessier and — Goss Esq. For examination.

The Police officers then stated that they went to the house of a Mrs Yates at West Bedfont, where they had received information the prisoners were to be found, and upon enquiring for them were informed that Harry Child had not been there that day and that John Child had gone out about half an hour previously. Not crediting this, they insisted upon searching the house and on moving a door about three feet from the spot where they were parleying they found Harry Child behind it. When they attempted to lay hold of him he made a violent resistance, but was soon overpowered. On continuing their search they found a smock frock in the home with the right sleeve clotted with blood.

The officers then proceeded to a house in the neighbourhood, kept by a person named Lacy, and having found John Child there they took him into custody. The latter prisoner admitted to the constables that he had hid himself in the house on hearing that the police were in the neighbourhood.

The carriers West and Batchelor, with Bugden and other witnesses who saw the men on the day of the murder both before and after the commission of the deed, attended the examination of the prisoners, and upon viewing their persons they immediately expressed their strong belief that they were the men.

Grossmith and Batchelor, who stated that on the afternoon of the 26th February, the day of the murder, as they were returning towards town from Reigate, when within a mile and half of Bletchingly they saw two men in a lane lying in a hedge who did not observe their chaise until it was close to them, when they immediately rose and came towards it. Suspecting them, the Officers, in order to take notice of their appearance, made some inquiries and received suspicious replies. The officers went on, but having on the following morning heard of the murder, and noticing the description of the murderers, they felt satisfied that the men they had seen were the criminals. When they took the prisoners into custody they immediately recognised them to be the men they had seen in the lane under such suspicious circumstances. The officers, to be still more certain that the men were the same, asked them to make the same replies as the men in the lane made to the questions put to them. The prisoners obeyed, and the manner of speaking of John Child was a confirmation of their suspicions; but Harry Child, it was evident, attempted to disguise his voice, therefore the officers could not speak with the same certainty to his voice, though they had no doubt as to his person.

When asked by the Magistrates where they were on the day of the murder they replied they were the whole of the day in the neighbourhood of Staines and Egham, and mentioned the names of several persons whom they said had seen them there. In particular they mentioned a man named Jordan, of whom they alleged they had bought some turnip-tops that day. They also denied that they had ever been to Epsom or in its neighbourhood in their lives. This latter statement was directly contradicted by Mr Everest, who said he saw Harry Child at the last Epsom cattle fair with a small black pony which he had for sale and which Mr Everest inquired the price of. After some equivocation the man admitted that he had not spoken the truth, and that he had been occasionally at Epsom, and also that the statement made by other persons that were camped on Banstead-Downs and Smithey bottom in August last were correct. Mr Goss asked them if they had been lately near Brighton. They said they had not, but their brother William had. This was considered to be an important circumstance, as the only bank note traced to the possession of the deceased had been paid into the banking house of Messrs Wigney & Co. at Brighton.

After some further examination the prisoners were remanded till the next day, and the officers were directed to enquire into the truth of their statements.

At nine o'clock yesterday morning the Magistrates again assembled, when Grossmith and Barefoot stated that they had made enquiries and had found the prisoners' statements were totally false. They had not been at the places named by them on the day of the murder, and the purchase of the turnip-tops had taken place three weeks prior to the event. Also that before that time they had been very short of money, but within the last six weeks they had been seen when tipsy to pull out a number of sovereigns and offer, to pay some trifling debts they had previously owed.

On hearing the statements of the officers together with other strong facts, which it would be imprudent at this stage of the inquiry to make public, the Magistrates determined on postponing the further examination to Saturday next and to remand the prisoners to Union Hall in the expectation that the writer of the anonymous letters would redeem his pledge and come forward with the testimony, which as stated in that letter, "could leave no doubt of these men being murderers."

The prisoners seemed to treat the charge with indifference.

Their appearance was that of most determined ruffians. Their dress was smock frocks and high-lows and their age about 30. At 12 o'clock they were conveyed to Horsemonger lane Gaol.

Upwards of thirty persons have been taken into custody and examined on suspicion of this murder, and the greatest praise is due to the Magistrates and other parties for their unceasing activity in tracing the murderers. A statement which has appeared in several of the public papers that a subscription had been entered into to defray the expences incurred in the pursuit of the delinquents is untrue. The whole of the expences incurred, which were considerable, have been liberally borne by three or four Magistrates in the neighbourhood, and the valuable professional assistance of Messrs Everest and Harding has been rendered gratuitously.

Copy from Morning Advertiser newspaper, April 14, 1834:

EXAMINATION AND DISCHARGE OF THE SUPPOSED MURDERERS OF MR RICHARDSON

At an early hour this office was crowded with persons to hear the examination of Henry and John Childs, who were charged on suspicion of having murdered Mr Richardson at Banstead near Epsom.

Mr Gosse, one of the Epsom Magistrates, took his seat at the left of Mr Murray, and there were several other gentlemen present in the commission of the Peace.

At the conclusion of the usual morning's proceedings, the Prisoners, who had been brought from Horsemonger-lane gaol, were placed at the Bar. Their presence excited considerable attention from all present, the public firmly believing from the accounts published that these men were the perpetrators of the murder. The prisoners did not appear to heed in the slightest degree the manner in which they were scrutinized by every eye.

Henry Childs is much taller than his brother but both have fair complexions, with little or no whiskers. They were attired as countrymen, Henry having on a smock frock and the other a kind of jacket-waistcoat.

Mr Murray asked the prisoners if their name was Child or Childs. The prisoner John replied that he believed it was Childs. Mr Murray then inquired if the prisoners knew the nature of the charge that was preferred against them.

They said they were told the reason of their being taken into custody when they were at Epsom on Tuesday.

Mr Grossmith, an Inspector of the B division of Police, was asked what evidence he had to bring forth in support of the charge, and he replied that he had several witnesses in attendance who saw two suspicious looking persons resembling the prisoners near Epsom on the day of the murder.

John Pattey, the toll collector at Banstead, was then called and sworn. On being desired to look at the prisoners the witness stated that he never saw them before to his knowledge.

Mr Murray: Have either of the other witnesses seen the prisoners since they were taken into custody?

Grossmith: I believe not.

Mr. Murray: Then let the door be closed and remove the prisoners, that they mix indiscriminately among the other persons in the office, so that the witnesses may not see them at the Bar.

This was complied with, and by desire of Mr Murray the prisoner Henry pulled off his smock frock and they both put on their hats.

A man who gave his name as John Walters was then called in, and on being asked if he knew any circumstances connected with the murder said that on the day previous to the commission of the act he saw two suspicious looking men going towards Bletchingly, and on the same day he observed one of the men proceeding in the direction of Reigate: he should know them again if he saw them.

Mr. Murray desired the witness to look among the persons in the Office that he might see if the men were present. The witness, having complied with the wish of the magistrate, stated that he could not see them.

Mr Pound, solicitor for the prisoners, here observed that he should have no objection for the witness to see the prisoners. Mr. Murray remarked that the witness merely said that he saw two men under suspicious circumstances but he did not then recognize them in the office. Mr. Gosse said that the prisoners must be quite aware that the account they gave of themselves was given voluntarily, and as their assertions had been proved to be false they would see the necessity for a full investigation. It now appeared there was no further evidence and they were discharged,

Mr. Murray also observed that there was good reason for their detention until that day.

The Solicitor said that in the agitation of the moment the men had given a wrong account of where they were on the day of the murder. He had seven witnesses in attendance who could satisfactorily account for their time on that day. Mr. Gosse considered that the men brought it on themselves by not stating facts. John Childs said that the police never went to the parties he referred to at all. He considered it a hard case to be thus treated. Mr. Murray observed that there was ample ground originally for suspicion. The prisoner John asked what were the grounds for suspicion. Mr. Murray said that they arose out of the circumstances that took place at the time of the prisoners' capture. Grossmith then produced the bloody smock-frock. John Childs stated that he was hit upon the head with a staff and the blood flowed profusely on to the smock-frock and other parts of his dress.

Mr. Murray enquired how the prisoners obtained their living. They replied that they bought potatoes, carrots and other vegetables at different Markets and then sold them. They added that they were gathering turnip-tops on the very day of the murder.

Mr. Murray: Don't let me be mistaken; you are discharged without suspicion of being concerned in the murder.

John Childs: I have one question to ask, and that is, where did the anonymous letters come from?

Grossmith: That is what we wish to know.

Mr. Murray: I received one this morning, and as far as it goes, it is in your favour, but I regard such letters as mere waste paper. The writer of the letter to which you allude has never had the courage or the honesty to come forward.

John Childs: We have been most harshly treated since we have been in custody and were obliged to pay for every thing we had.

Mr Gosse: It must sometimes happen that men will be put to certain inconvenience for the ends of justice. You are now discharged.

John Childs: Thank you, gentlemen; you are now satisfied that we are not the men.

The prisoners then left the Office, but in a few moments returned, when John Childs (who had been spokesman throughout the examination) told the Magistrates that they were twenty miles from home without a farthing in their pockets. Mr. Murray said he would order them half a crown out of the poor box to keep them on their way. The Clerk then handed over the money to Childs, but previous to their departure Mr. Murray gave them to understand that had their character stood in a more reputable light, suspicion would not have attached itself to them. The men assured the Magistrates that they obtained their living in an honest manner, after which they left the office and joined their friends at a public house in the vicinity.

The Great Fire

At midnight on the 21st of April, 1834, the inhabitants of this peaceable and retired village were woke up from their slumbers by the shouting out of several voices, "Fire! Fire! get up, or you will be burned in your beds," attended with hammering at their doors and window shutters besides throwing handsful of gravel at the Casements. As they woke up, and seeing such a brilliant light in the atmosphere, they became so terrified that each one thought it was their own dwelling, when it was discovered to be the Revd. W. H. Goodman's extensive farm-buildings, Cornstacks, Stables and outhouses, all in one continuous blaze; and being a windy tempestuous night it was feared that all those thatched cottages that lay in the course of the wind would become a prey to the devouring element unless precautionary measures were not at once acted upon.

There were three boys sleeping in a small room in the loft over the stables, and it was with the greatest difficulty they were made to wake up, insomuch that they had scarcely time with nothing on but their shirts to make their escape by jumping down from the loft door on to a dung-heap underneath, for immediately afterwards the blazing roof came down with a crash; as it was, all the horses and harness were burnt to a cinder as also Cows, Piggeries, Wagons, Carts and implements of husbandry.

There was but one Engine, and the fire had got such hold and beyond mastery, that the playing of this Engine had not the slightest effect, but became useful in saving some of the thatched cottages by extinguishing the flakes of fire as fast as the wind carried them on to the roofs, while several of the tenants were engaged looking out for themselves by raising ladders or anything they could get to stand upon to quench the fire by throwing buckets of water which had to be conveyed from the nearest Pond, otherwise the wind was acting like a bellows and would soon have puffed these fire flakes into a blaze and caused many a poor family to be houseless through the treachery of some vile villain. It was most distressing to see the children crying and in almost a state of nude while the fire was raging-to behold their mothers moving their beds and furniture into the open, fearing every moment their homes would become a prey to the devouring element, which was visible to many passengers travelling by the night-mails and stage-Coaches for many miles around.

Next day the Magistrates held a meeting and inquiries were instituted among the Villagers whether they had observ'd any tramps or strangers in the neighbourhood; some said they saw one or two suspicious looking men like beggars with pipes in their mouths going in the direction of Marlborough, others said they saw two suspicious looking men just at dusk offering matches for sale, loitering about, and looked as though they were going towards Pewsey, a small village about a mile distant. After 2 or 3 days had passed away in making enquiries and coming to no result, the Magistrates came to the resolution of laying the case before the Home Secretary and asking for assistance to send down one of the Bow street Officers.

In this case as in all similar ones, whichever officer was in the way and at liberty would be dispatched by order of the sitting Magistrate with a letter of introduction to the parties concerned; and as it happened that I was in the way and disengaged from my other business I received my orders and went to the scene of the fire and presented the letter to the Revd. Mr Goodman, who was discussing the matter at his own house with two of the County Magistrates. As soon as the letter had been read I accompanied them to the scene of the late fire, and after acquainting myself with the locality they separated and I was left to form my own ideas and take such measures as I thought expedient.

I first walked down the village and back and then all round it, and as I passed along and being a stranger, the women and men came out and looked after me. In some places I made a stand and looked at them when they turned their backs upon me and walked indoors out of my sight. I then made up my mind to say who I was and call at each separate place to know if they would give me any information as to who was first seen at the fire.

Some said one thing and some another, till at last I was informed by a very intelligent man named Stephen Jenkins that while he was throwing a bucket of water on his Thatch he saw, from the great light of the fire, a man in a short frock coming from the direction of Pewsey, walking very slowly. "As he came near I saw it was Charles Kimmer, who made a stop and looked at me hard in the face and then, looking in the direction of the fire, said, 'The man that set a light to that ought to be chucked into it.' He then handed me up two buckets of water and went towards the fire, which would be on the way to his home at the far end of the village, and that is all I know about it."

"After midnight, and being seen coming from the direction of Pewsey," I muttered to myself; "where could he have been at so late an hour? It looks rather suspicious. I'll go to Pewsey, it is only a mile, and see what sort of a place it is." I saw there was a Tom and Jerry beer shop, I went in and enquired if they could inform me of the names as to who was there on the night of the fire.

"Let me see," said the woman to her husband, "why, now I know," said she, "I recollect we shut up before 9 o'clock, and Kimmer, who is working on Mr Goodman's Farm, was the last man I let out, for I shut the door and bolted it after him, and we went to bed almost directly afterwards."

On receiving this information I went to Colonel Wroughton, a Magistrate at Wilcot, and repeated word for word what Jenkins told me about Kimmer, as also what had been said at the beer-shop at Pewsey, and upon that I thought there was sufficient grounds to grant me a Warrant for his arrest.

The Colonel was of my opinion, and without a moment's hesitation made out and gave me the Warrant. Being thus armed I found out the Parish Constable, who accompanied me and pointed out where Charles Kimmer lived, and we found he was at home upstairs fast asleep and in bed.

"This is Charles Kimmer," said the Constable, and we had some difficulty at waking him (it was about mid-day and he appeared to have been drinking). I told him to get up and dress, for I was an Officer, and had come about the fire; and I added, "What time did you get to bed that night and where did you go after you left work?"

"I never went anywhere. I kept at home all the evening and

went to bed at the same time as my brother did—we both sleep in the same room—and it was before nine o'clock," he replied.

"Well, how about the fire at Mr Goodman's?" I asked.

"Well," said he, "we were woke up by some dirt being thrown up the window and a cry of 'Fire!' We saw a great light, dressed ourselves and went the nearest way across the field to it."

These replies I could not reconcile with what I had previously heard of his movements. I felt I must use my authority, and I told him that he must consider himself in my Custody, at the same time producing the Warrant, so I took him for safe custody to Mr Goodman's house.

As there was no time to lose I went in search of his brother, who was ploughing in a field near at hand. In answer to my questions he flatly denied all his brother Charles had been telling me by saying that he never saw his brother on that evening before the fire at all—that he went to bed by himself at 11 o'clock and had been staying up for him and had never slept at all, fearing something had happened. As he saw a great light and heard people hollowing out 'Fire!' he dressed and went to it and never saw his brother that night till he met him at the fire at 3 in the morning.

After hearing this statement I returned to Mr Goodman's, where I found Colonel Wroughton and another Magistrate talking over the matter. After hearing my statement they said they were quite ready to hear the Case, but before producing the prisoner, the parish constable had to fetch his brother as a witness.

While his deposition was being taken, the prisoner, who was sitting by the side of me on a seat under the window in the hall, was seized for a few minutes with a fainting fit, and on recovering exclaimed, "I am the guilty man! I done it all myself."

He then went on to say he had been drinking at Pewsey and left the beer-shop at Pewsey at 9 o'clock —that it came into his head all at once to go and set fire to Mr Goodman's stables—that he hid himself under a Wheat Stack till he heard the clock strike 12 and then set a light to a heap of straw between the rick and the stables, which began to blaze into a great light. "I did not know what to do, whether to go home or hide under one of the hedges. I felt all of a fright for fear of being seen and I ran across the fields to the road leading to Pewsey, and then seeing the fire raging I turned round, and while I was walking towards it I saw Stephen Jenkins pouring water onto his cottage. He saw me and asked me to fetch some water, and I went to the pond and gave him two buckets full and after that I went to the fire."

It was stated by Mr Goodman that the property destroyed was worth between three and four thousand pounds. The witnesses were bound over to prosecute and the prisoner was fully committed to take his trial at the Summer Assizes held at Salisbury.

I received the commitment; and while conveying him in a post-chaise to Fisherton Jail, he made a further confession to me and said that he was going to set fire to Mr Edmonds the Malster's place that night.

I said, "What!"

"Yes," he said, "I was!' but the reason I did not do it was, it was so near my sister's house that I was afraid she and her child would be burnt."

The result was that Charles Kimmer was tried and convicted at the Salisbury Assizes on the 18th July, 1834, before Lord Denham, who, after putting on the black-cap and passing sentence of death upon the prisoner, said that "you, Charles Kimmer, have been convicted of one of the greatest crimes it is possible for a man to be guilty of. You have set fire to the premises of a man who was doing benefit to your family"—the prisoner's father had been in the employ of Mr Goodman from the time he was 10 years, old and is now 62 years old—without the smallest provocation. The destruction of his property is in itself a most wicked act, but this case is the more diabolical for those poor things in the stable and sties who were sure to be sacrificed to your cruelty, and besides that, there were three boys sleeping in the stables which was fired, whose lives were almost sure to be sacrificed. It is a great mercy that their lives were spared, and it must be some consolation to you, even in your present situation, and in almost the last moment of your life, that you have not added the guilt of the murder of those boys to the fact of destroying your benefactor's premises. But this is not all, because there is too much reason to believe that Jenkins and other inhabitants of the village might have had their property and lives destroyed. It is my painful duty to tell you that you have but a few days more to live, and that by a sacrifice of your life, the example may induce others to abstain from the commission of crime." The usual sentence of death was then passed upon the prisoner, who, after a few days in jail, tried all his means to get out.

I am sorry to observe that the solemn warning given by Lord Denman on passing sentence of death upon Kimmer had not as it was hoped the desired effect, for in the following month of September after Kimmer's execution, and within a short distance of Oare another act of incendiarism was committed on the premises belonging to a Mr Attwater, a Farmer in the village of Conoc, four miles from Devizes.

It fell to my lot to be sent there, and whilst instituting enquiries I was being continually followed almost step by step and sometimes within hearing distance by a lad about 17 or 18 years of age who appeared anxious to know who the people were that I saw, and all that I and they were talking about. I thought, "What does this fellow mean by always following me about? Is it his conscience that strikes him?" I thought. On the following day I had an interview with Mr Warriner, a Magistrate for the County, to whom I gave a description and the circumstance of this lad.

"That lad, George Watts," said the Magistrate, "is one of the most cruel fellows you ever heard of; he catches birds and has been seen to pull the feathers from their wings and chop off their claws so as to oblige them to hop on their stumps. What makes it so strange, there is scarcely a chapter in the Bible but what he is pretty well up in."

After hearing this statement of such wanton acts of cruelty, I thought him fully capable of committing this act of incendiarism. Without further delay I went and apprehended him and charged him before the Magistrate on suspicion of being concerned in setting fire to Mr Attwater's premises, before whom he gave a very incoherent account of himself as to how he occupied his time previous to the fire, so much so that the Magistrate committed him on remand to Devizes jail, where he was placed in a cell with a man by the name of Thomas Gregory, who had been committed to six days' imprisonment for an assault.

Three days after the committal of George Watts, Gregory was set at liberty, and no sooner was he out of prison than he informed the Governor that Watts had been telling him how he set fire to Mr Attwater's premises from some tinder he had made and put into his tobacco-box—that it was "a great flare-up," and as soon as he got out there would be "a greater flare-up than ever, but don't you inform anyone what I am telling you."

This news was soon spread through the Village, and other confirmatory evidence being collected left no doubt about his guilt. He was committed to the next Salisbury assizes for trial and was convicted on the 9th of March and executed 15 days afterwards.

General observations

I beg here to observe that so far as my own experience goes I have found that the perpetrators of incendiary fires are not only local, but infectious; for as sure that a fire took place in or near a village or some unfrequented spot, another would within a very short time follow. I have found it to be so in Kent, Sussex, Cambridgeshire, Suffolk, Norfolk. and other counties, particularly in the years 1829 and 1830.

I recollect in 1830 being dispatched to Norwich by the Home Secretary through a representation made by the Magistracy as to the alarming state of the County in firing ricks, barns, Machine breaking, etc., particularly in and about the neighbourhood of North Walsham.

On my introduction to Colonel Wodehouse, the Lord Lieutenant of the County, and to the Magistrates, I was most warmly received, and after a brief consultation I was joined by Gardner, a brother Officer, with instructions to proceed to North Walsham in the best way we could. Under these circumstances, considering the difficulties that we might subject ourselves to with regard to conveyance, we engaged, regardless of expense, a strong trap that would accommodate four persons and a powerful fast horse scarcely to be equalled in the City of Norwich, one that was capable of conveying us to any part of the County where the exercise of our calling might lead us.

It was in the afternoon we started on our journey, and we reached Sharps Hotel, North Walsham, before dusk, the distance being about fifteen miles. Our business we kept to ourselves Incognito by driving about for about a day or two in order to make ourselves acquainted with the locality.

There were several inquisitorial enquiries during our absence made about us, as to who we possibly could be.

"For they are perfect strangers," said one.

"Ah," said another, "there's seldom any good going on when you see two fellows like those driving about."

"They don't seem to have an object," said another.

Soon after these remarks a report got abroad that two well dressed men, one very tall and stout, the other middle sized, had been traveling about the County firing balls as they passed along into ricks, till it began to be hinted that they should not at all wonder but what we were those two men.

Our incog. did not last long, for in the course of our duty it was soon discovered who we were by our going into enquiries and taking into custody several persons. Some were charged with machine breaking, others on suspicion of firing cornstacks and one for attempting to pull down the boundary wall of the Bridewell at Wymondham. Most of them we had to take before Lord Suffield of Gunton Hall and Admiral Wyndham and Squire Wyndham, Magistrates of the County, who committed them to Norwich Castle for trial. Some got convicted for the Machine breaking and others were acquitted.

Joseph Randall

About 2 o'clock in the afternoon of Saturday the 10th of January, 1835, while standing on the steps outside the entrance door of Bow Street office, my attention was drawn to the sight of a Post Chaise being driven rapidly by the Post boy around the corner from Great Russell Street and pulling up suddenly in front of where I was standing. A gentleman who was inside signal'd me to open the door, and as I opened it he asked me if the Chief Magistrate was in attendance as he wished to see him on a matter of great importance. I replied in the affirmative and ushered the stranger into the presence of Sir Frederick Roe, to whom in a state of great excitement he made the following statement.

He said he had just arrived by express from Southampton for the assistance of an Officer in investigating an affair that almost ended in a fearful tragedy. At about 1 o'clock on the morning in question some Burglars had broken into the house of Mrs Maxwell, a lady of independence residing in Hamilton Place, Southampton, who was woke up from sleep in great terror by the report of fire arms, discharged as it appeared in the attempt to murder her butler, the butler having stated that whilst fast asleep in his bed he narrowly escaped death by a bullet which passed through his pillow. The gentleman further stated that the butler appeared to have displayed much courage by beating off the robbers and entirely preventing them taking away their booty, which was found packed up and ready to be carried away. This property consisted of Jewellery, silver plate and other articles together representing a considerable amount in value.

I need not inform my readers that Sir F. Roe and Mr Hall listened with great attention to the applicant's statement. After consulting it over for a few minutes, Sir Frederick turned his eyes and pointing towards me said to the applicant, "There is the Officer that I and my brother magistrate intend sending down to Southampton in so grave a matter." Accordingly I was instructed to proceed by that night's mail. I went home and prepared myself for the night journey.

On the following morning at about 4 o'clock I arrived at the Star Hotel, Southampton. There was still time for four hours' bed. At 9 o'clock I knocked at the house of Mrs Maxwell, and on being introduced I found her in a most nervous and prostrated state. After I had listened to all she had to say, she rang the Bell for Joseph Randall, her Butler, who after replying to some questions I asked him, conducted me down stairs into the Pantry and called my attention to several small Hampers containing much valuable property, just as they had been packed as was alleged by the Burglars. He then pointed out the bedstead in which he lay on the night of the attack. This bedstead represented in semblance a small shut up wardrobe, and was placed in a corner by the side of the fireplace. Nearly opposite was a window well secured by strong shutters, each having a large round hole at the top part of the Panel, about the size of a breakfast saucer, for the purpose of admitting light.

And now comes the drift of Joseph Randall's story. "You see, Sir," said he, "on the night of this attack and after all the family had retired to bed I looked all round the lower part of the house as was my usual custom, to see that all the doors and windows were made fast, and I then retired to bed, it being before 11 o'clock. I soon fell off to sleep, and at about one o'clock in the morning, as well as I can remember, I was woke up by hearing a curious noise outside the pantry windows similar to the rattling a dog chain would make by being dragged along the gravel. I lay and listened and fancied I heard footsteps about the house; at that moment I saw my door, which I never kept locked, being gradually opened. I then saw the reflection of a bull's-eye Lantern held out at arm's length, on a small picture hanging on the wall opposite, and the shadow of a man before it and a man behind the one that carried the lantern.

"I felt frightened, and pretended to be asleep whilst they held the bull's eye right before my eyes. I was trembling with a palpitation in my heart, and they thinking I was asleep softly walked backwards and gently closed the door. I listened for nearly half a minute, and just as I was turning my right hand to reach my pistol from under my pillows on the left, a Pistol was fired from the outside through one of the holes in the shutters. The bullet whizzed by my ear and passed through the pillow and the backboard of the bedstead against the wall behind and dropped on the floor, and had it not been for my turning round to reach my pistol they would have left me a corpse, for as I lay the bullet must have entered my chin and lodged in the gullet. I have really had a very narrow escape and I wonder that I was not murdered.

"I trembled very much at being taken so suddenly off my

guard, but I managed very quickly to reach my pistol and fired it through the window in the supposed direction of the robbers. I then got out of bed and cried out, 'Murder! Fire!!" as loud as I could bawl, and running into the passage I had a fearful struggle with two men disguised in masks to regain possession of the property packed ready to take away. My cries woke my mistress and the women-servants from their beds, someone sprung a rattle which altogether so alarmed the thieves that they were glad to make good their escape.

"My mistress and the two women-servants were terribly frightened, and the house was in a state of great commotion. In the mean time some watchmen arrived and examined the premises, who found that "the thieves had effected an entrance by forcing open the back door and that they then made their way up stairs and had rummaged the drawing and dining rooms, the lady's Boudoir and the plate closet, turning everything topsey turvy."

Having paid the greatest attention to the above statement, I requested him to conduct me to the door where the thieves made their entry. After I had examined it I found that some considerable force had been used, no doubt by a Jemmy; but I also found the impression on the outside did not appear to my mind to correspond with the inside. This observation I kept to myself. I then proceeded to the plate closet and saw similar impressions, which also did not tally, and I felt satisfied it was not the work of a Cracksman, I then asked him to show me his pistols and also the mould and bullets if he had any. He went to his cupboard and produced the pistols, the mould and about a dozen bullets, saying, "That is the mould I cast the bullets in."

"Have you got the bullet that was fired at you?" I asked.

He put his hand in his pocket and, pulling out a bullet, said,

"Yes, here it is, I found it on the floor at the back of the bedstead."

I examined it and found some part of it to be a little flattened. On comparing it with the other bullets I had got in my possession it appeared to correspond with them as if it had been cast in the same mould. I made no remark. I then looked into the butler's cupboard and observed three knives ground into very sharp points and looking like daggers. I enquired their use; he replied that he thought of going into the business of a pork butcher.

As it was Sunday and getting rather late in the day I thought any further enquiries on my part might interfere with the family domestic arrangements. I therefore wished the butler good morning and went up stairs and bade the same to his mistress, saying that I should return at 10 o'clock on the following morning to renew my enquiries. I left, and soon after my return to the hotel I occupied myself for some little time in looking at the discharged bullet, and on comparing it closely with the others I discovered a very small round pimple on all the bullets, including the one alleged to have been discharged. In looking into the mould there was a very little hole hardly so large as the head of a small pin, and this I found accounted for the pimples. On the following morning I thought before I returned to Mrs Maxwell's I would call upon the Gun-smith who supplied the Pistols for his opinion. After very attentive examination he said he was ready to come forward and make oath before the bench of Magistrates that all those bullets including the flattened one were cast in the mould now produced.

We were in fact both convinced that there could not be two opinions about the matter. I then wished him good morning and went on to Mrs Maxwell's, to whom I stated my suspicions that it was a breaking out and not a breaking in. Then I related the circumstance connected with the bullets, and the Gun maker's opinion. I also mention'd the finding of the dagger-knives and how the butler accounted for them. Considering all these circumstances together with his saying that whilst the bull's-eye was held out at arm's length he could see the shadow of a man before it, and not forgetting the marvellous escape from the bullet, I did not believe one word of his tale. I considered it a tissue of falsehoods from one end to the other, I therefore said that under the circumstances I should have the Butler up before the Magistrates. Mrs Maxwell was astonished at what I said and expressed a wish to see the bullets, which were immediately handed to her.

After carefully looking over them and comparing them with the mould she was entirely of the same opinion as the Gunmaker and myself. She also stated that about a week before Xmas, Randall the butler had raised a report that he heard thieves about the premises and had told her that it was not safe to pass the winter without his being furnished with a brace of pistols. She added that she yielded to what he said and made him a present of a very expensive pair.

"Well, Mr Goddard, she said, "as it has come to this, I must leave the case entirely in your hands. I think you had better take him up before the Magistrates as I shall be afraid to let him remain in the house any longer, but I hope there will not be any scene, for it is really dreadful."

I pacified her as well as I could, and finding there was no other resource left but for me to go down stairs and point out to Randall his audacity in representing such a glaring case of deception. I then told him that under the circumstances I must take him into custody.

He made no reply but took off his apron, put on his coat and hat, and then said, "I am ready to go where you please to take me."

I then took him before the Mayor, Mr Le Fevre, and a full bench of Magistrates who, after hearing my evidence and that of the Gunmaker, felt bound to remand him till the following Thursday. In the mean time the Prisoner expressed a wish to the visiting Magistrate that he wished to see me. I went to the prison and he then confessed his guilt, stating that on that night he never went to bed but waited up till his mistress and the servants had retired to rest, and that when all was silent he went outside and with a small crowbar made marks to look like breaking in. "The inner impression I made," he said, "about a week before." As the night was dark on that occasion he could not see what he was doing, so that accounted for the way I found him out. He further stated that he had since thrown the crowbar and all the things down a drain, that he did it all himself to make it appear that thieves had broken in and to cause alarm, that he stood at the foot of his bedstead and fired the first bullet into the pillows and the others through the upper panel of the window shutter.

When he made this statement I enquired his motive, and he replied, "I did it because I thought Mrs Maxwell would handsomely reward me for the supposed narrow escape I had of being shot and the brave manner I beat the robbers off to save her property."

He was brought upon his remand to Thursday, and as no property was actually stolen, he was discharged on his own recognisance to appear at the sessions to answer any indictment that might be charged against him.

When the time arrived, as there was no charge made against

him he was dismissed with a severe admonition from the Bench, and cautioned as to his conduct for the future; so thus the matter ended which had caused so much excitement in the town and all over county.

Randall Montague Lewis

This young man, through the high position and respectability of his family, obtained an introduction into the large wholesale brush manufactory establishment of the Messrs. Bliss of Barbican, who, from the high recommendation they received, took him into their employ and appointed him principal cashier, collecting clerk and general manager. To all appearance matters went on most agreeably and he gave great satisfaction while he was there for two months, until one leisure day in the month of November 1835 he asked permission for half a day's leave of absence to go to see his Uncle at Greenwich. He obtained leave, and on his way he was to call and deposit £300, to be placed to the banking account of his employers.

He left the counting-house about 2 o'clock, bidding them good day; thus so far, the day finished. On the following morning his time to be at his post was half past 9; 10 o'clock came, and 11 o'clock but no appearance: his non-attendance could not be accounted for as he was always so punctual, till it was deemed expedient to send a messenger to his address to enquire the cause. He was informed that Mr Lewis had gone away, that he left about 7 o'clock the previous evening in a clandestine manner, and they knew not where he was gone to.

This information so surprised and excited the messenger that he made all haste and in a breathless state delivered it to his employer, causing them great alarm and anxiety, so much so that Mr Bliss went at once to his bankers to make enquiries. He was informed that Mr Lewis called and presented a Check yesterday afternoon purporting to be signed by the firm for £800, which amount he received in notes and 50 Sovereigns, viz 10 fiftys, 10 twentys and 10 fives besides the gold. Mr Bliss saw at once it was a forgery and returned home with all speed to his brother, and after consulting for a few minutes it was determined that one of them should at once proceed to Bow Street for assistance.

I was seen upon the subject, and after hearing the particulars of the case I went to the fugitive's address, and in addition to what the messenger had been told I was informed that he took his baggage, which consisted of a large brown canvas bag and a long hair trunk, covered with red hair cow-skin. On this information I proceeded to the different cab-stands in the neighbourhood, as well also at Islington near the Angel, and gave full particulars with my address to the different watermen, to whom I was no stranger, and promised a sovereign to anyone of them if they could find the cab man who took the fare last night from Northampton Square 7 o'clock and who would also receive the same reward by telling me where he put down his fare.

I then proceeded to Barbican to report what I had done, when it was arranged that Mr Bliss should go next morning to obtain the numbers and dates of the notes, to give information to the Bank, while I was to go to Glindon's, the printers, in

Rupert Street to order handbills of description, offering a reward to be distributed to all the Cab ranks in London. It was now getting on towards midnight, and I went home.

On the following morning at 9 o'clock, as I was about leaving home to proceed on my mission to the printers, I had hardly closed the street door when a cabman pulled up and asked me if my name was Goddard.

"It is," I replied.

He said "I have come to tell you that the waterman from the stand by the Angel at Islington sent me to tell you that I think I can give you the information you were enquiring about last night, and if so, you would give me a sovereign."

"That is true, and so I will if you can drive me to where you set him down on that night."

"Get in," he said.

I got in, he shut the door and drove me to a low public-house at the bottom of Clements Lane near Clare Market.

The Potman was standing outside, who came to assist me from the cab, on which the Cabman got off his seat and said, "This is the man that I gave the trunk to from off the roof of the cab the night before last. and he carried it into the house and afterwards fetched the brown linen bag. Don't you recollect it was about half past 7 o'clock on Lord Mayor's day?" said the Cabman. "You took the things from me."

'Yes," replied the potman, "I recollect it very well, for the gentleman slept here, and after going out in the morning he returned about 4 o'clock in the afternoon in a go-cart and left with his luggage. The go-cart man I had seen before at our house, and I know he lives somewhere by the Elephant and Castle. On seeing the Landlord he said that he recollected the circumstance of the young man sleeping here, and he knew him by his frequenting his parlor of an evening, but nothing more."

This satisfied me I was on the right scent, and having got a description of the go-cart man in addition to his having a cast in his eye, I lost no time in proceeding to the Elephant and Castle. On enquiring of several of these go-cart drivers, who all knew me from my frequent attendance at Fairs, Race Courses and other places of public amusement where my duties took me, I was told by one from the description I gave that it must be Boss-eyed Charley and that he lived at the end of Townsend Street near the Bricklayers Arms.

On this information I immediately went to the place indicated, and was fortunate enough to catch Boss-eyed Charley at home, who, without the slightest hesitation, said, in answer to my question, that he drove the gentleman and set him down at the George Inn, Crawley, Sussex. "The gentleman came one day to the Bricklayers Arms and saw me standing opposite the Swan, and engaged me to take him to St. Clements Church in the Strand and then to a public house in Clements Lane, when he got out. After going into the public house he returned with a Cow's hide trunk and a linen bag and told me to drive over Blackfriars bridge, at where, when arrived, he said he would pay me thirty shillings to take him to Crawley, where I took him to and left him about 8 o'clock at night, having treated me to my supper and also for the baiting of my horse."

This information (good reader) was worth a sovereign to me which I handed over to him, he thanking me and I thanking him in return for his information and we bade each other good night. I then hurried away to Barbican, and after giving my report I was to lose no time, but proceed at once that night by mail to the George Inn, Crawley, where I arrived in time for my supper and engaged a bed.

I was up early to breakfast the next morning, and after relating my business to the Landlord, he said the gentleman came there in a go-cart two or three evenings ago, slept there and had his supper with a bottle of Champagne, and after breakfast the next morning he ordered a post-chaise to take him on to Brighton. "I gave him change out of a fifty pound note and he said his name was Cleveland. Our Post-boy took him to Cuckfield."

On this information I followed on the same track to Brighton, where I found he went to a Jewellers and purchased a gold watch for £36, receiving the difference out in change of another £50 note, Bank of England. He also paid his Hotel bill out of another £50 note and then posted on to the Marine Hotel, Worthing, changing another £50 note: from hence to Arundel, Chichester, Havant, the Red Lion at Fareham to the Star at Southampton, changing notes at every place and going by the name of Cleveland—finally changing nearly all his English money into French Mille Franc Notes and French Gold.

I then traced him on board a Boat where a waterman by the name of Brown received a sovereign from him to row him to the Vine Inn at Cowes. From there I kept on his track to Newport and Ryde, where I was informed he went out to sea on board a Pilot boat with Captain Johnson, whose boat had not returned but was expected back some time during the night or early the next morning. So after a good night's rest at the Hotel I was up by times in the morning and succeeded in obtaining an interview with the Captain, who informed that he left Cleveland at Wheelers Hotel, Havre de Gras.

As no time was now to be lost, I crossed over to Portsmouth and took coach to London (Sunday) and reported my doings to the house at Barbican. On the following morning (Monday) Mr Bliss and I took coach to Dover and obtained our passports. Next day we crossed to Boulogne and on by the Diligence to Abrille, next day Dieppe and the next at Havre. I arrived at Wheelers Hotel about 7 o'clock, leaving Mr Bliss at a Caffe close at hand while I was making enquiries.

Mrs Wheeler, who knowing me before and anticipating something was wrong, came and whispered, "He is alright. He is gone to the opera and will not return till 11 o'clock and will not return till 11 o'clock—he has engaged a first class berth to go to New York by the Ville de Lion, she was to have sailed two or three days ago, but she sails for certain at 12 o'clock tomorrow."

I silently thanked her and pointed out the importance to keep all this to herself, and engaged two beds, and ordered a nice light supper, for myself and friend whom I said I would go and fetch. This required caution, and as Mr Bliss always wore a Wig, at my request he took it off and put it into his pocket. I was astonished at the alteration it made in his appearance. We then accompanied each other to Wheelers hotel, and after taking our supper we went and sat in company with several others in the Bar parlor. Mr Bliss enjoyed himself over a cigar while I was in communication for information with Mrs Wheeler, who gave me the key and number of his room, to where I went.

After securing the door the first thing that attracted my attention was the old red hair'd trunk, and besides two new large French black leather Portmanteaus locked and well secured with straps and addresses attached: "G. Cleveland Esq., passenger per Ship Ville de Lion, New York." These and other circumstances satisfied me that the owner of these portmanteaus must be Randall Montague Lewis and no other.

Coming to this conclusion, I took my pocketknife and opened these portmanteaus by cutting that part of the leather round the lock, and the first thing I laid my hand on were two canvas bags full of French Gold and Mille Frank notes, with a receipt for his passage to America. Also a stock of new linen, wearing apparel and a brace of loaded pistols, etc.

Now all the time I was thus engaged, the perspiration poured down my face and made me feel so excited that I felt as though I was committing a robbery and expecting detection every moment.

However, having secured the cash I put the Franks together in the best way I could and carried away my prize. After counting and placing it under my own security I walked down to the Bar-parlor, sat myself by the side of Mr Bliss and told him how I had been engaged and of my success.

It was now about half past 10, and the time was drawing near, so from the position Mr Bliss was sitting I caused him to move to a seat on the other side of the table opposite to me to escape observation.

At last the time arrived. It was now eleven o'clock, and in walked two well dressed looking gentlemen, one much taller than the other. Mrs Wheeler look'd at me and pointed behind his back to the shorter one. I knew from her signal what she meant, and I instantly quitted my seat and made towards him, saying, "I wish, if you have a moment to spare, to speak. to you."

"Oh, certainly," he replied, and I followed him upstairs into a private room which was well lit with Gas.

On his turning round to face me, I put my hand against his waistcoat pocket and pulled his watch from it by the gold chain. saying. "Is this the watch you gave £36 for at Brighton?"

At this moment Mr Bliss, on entering the room and, placing his Wig on his head, exclaimed, "A pretty scoundrel you are!"

This so shocked Lewis's nerves that he fell back in a fainting fit on the sofa, and lay insensible till the doctor came for a quarter of an hour.

Soon after his recovery I told him to come up to his bedroom and I would shew what I had done. This seemed to surprise him, and he followed me upstairs. On seeing how his portmanteaus had been cut, he wanted to know by whose authority that was done.

I replied, "If you don't mind, you will get imprisoned for being here in a false name."

Warm words ensued, and Mr Bliss threatened to send for the Police and have him locked up. This so frightened him that he fell on his knees and prayed forgiveness, and that if he was allowed to go to America he would in a short time make amends for what he had done.

This ended the conversation, and we separated for the night. Next morning Mr Bliss and I discussed over the business. Knowing there was no extradition Treaty in existence between France and England at that time, we allowed the Fugitive without any further to do to take his flight to America, and as this was Mr Bliss's first visit to France, he embraced the opportunity and we went to Paris. After seeing nearly all that was to be seen for a week we returned to London. Mr Bliss not only expressed himself how he enjoyed the Trip but also highly complimented me with a handsome present and for the able manner the business had been carried out.

The Duke of Brunswick

In the middle of the month of May 1836 Sir F. Roe sent for me to his private room at Bow Street office, and requested me not to undertake any business that was likely to call me away either to the continent or to the country.

"In fact," he said, "you must not quit London, as you will be shortly wanted to undertake an important matter and devote your whole time and energy to it; it is by the wish of the King and you are not to be sparing of expenses. His Majesty expects in a few days the Duke of Brunswick will arrive in London: I dare say you have seen his name mentioned in the newspapers, and you must be very particular, as you will have to keep him under strict observation and note down all places he may go to, which will have to be reported to His Majesty." This ended Sir F's conversation with me.

I must here insert, for the reader's information and easier understanding of my narrative, a copy from the Weekly Dispatch of 19 September, 1830, of which the following is an extract, viz

On Tuesday morning the 7th instant the City Magistrates,

alarmed at the state of things, assembled the Citizens and sent a deputation to receive the Duke's commands, in accordance with the promises which he had made the previous evening. His Serene Highness had now, however, recovered his confidence and refused to remove the cannon.

The deputation, foreseeing the chance of a conflict in the streets between the military and the people, requested arms and promised to maintain order along with the troops. The Duke objected to this proposal, till he was told that the soldiers would not act against their fellow citizens. At last he was obliged to appeal to the Magistracy for assistance, when their aid was too late for the effective defence of the Palace. The mob collected, they disarmed the civil force and set fire to the Castle, the Duke himself only having time to escape on horseback.

The whole of the Palace has been consumed, and the Duke would most undoubtedly have been massacred, had he not been preserved by the speed of his horse. The town of Brunswick has been saved from pillage and conflagration by a Burgher Guard which was immediately organized and armed to protect public and private property.

It is generally believed in his little dominions that the reign of this imprudent youth is at an end. He has outraged the feelings of his subjects, placed at his disposal by the Vienna settlement of Europe, in almost every possible way. He has refused to sanction the constitution given to his states by his uncle and guardian, George IV; he has continued in time of peace the oppressive taxes which were imposed during a season of war; he has arrested the most noble of his people without cause, and punished them without trial; he has disregarded the judgments of the tribunals and directed their decrees to be torn in pieces and thrown in the face of the judges; he has ordered the secrecy of correspondents to be violated, and letters to be opened at the Post Office: and while he discarded from his service or banished from his dominions the most respectable servants of the state, he employed persons whose only recommendation was a blind subserviency to his caprices.

The wretch who has at length exhausted the patience of the inhabitants has been guilty of every sort of robbery and fraud. Letters were seized at the Post-office, their contents appropriated without ceremony, and he caused his effrontery so as to give to an abandoned female a valuable gold chain which he took out of a letter and which she did not scruple to wear publicly. No functionary was safe under him; for he trampled on all law, and all order, and all decency, and whoever refused to degrade himself by the vilest subserviency to his crimes and vices was treated with the utmost indignity.

Most of our readers must recollect the absurd hostility of this wretch to our late Sovereign. Every German hopes that the Court of King William the Fourth will not disgrace itself by receiving such a monster.

I must now now relieve my reader of this lengthy but necessary interruption about the antecedents of the Duke of Brunswick and proceed with my narrative.

A fortnight afterwards, on Monday the 30th, I was ordered with others, according to the usual custom, to proceed to Ascott to attend at the races. Sir Frederick Roe and Mr Burnaby, the chief clerk, also had to be there.

On the following Wednesday, the 1st June, Sir F. Roe was sent for to see Sir Herbert Taylor at Windsor Castle, and shortly afterwards a messenger was dispatched on horse-back to the racecourse in search of me. I at that time unfortunately was at Sunning Hill wells, and the messenger being informed by two of my brother officers, Ruthven and Ledbetter, that as soon as they saw me they would tell me, he then galloped away towards Windsor. In about half an hour afterwards when I arrived on the course I was informed what had happened and that I was to make all speed to the Castle Hotel as Sir Frederick Roe was waiting to see me on something of importance.

No sooner was this said than I mounted on to a go-cart and away I went as quick as possible. It was a very fast horse, and I arrived at Windsor within the half hour. Sir Frederick was standing outside the Hotel yard, and when he saw me beckon'd me. He was so excited at the length of time that elapsed, the messenger having returned without me saying that I could not be found, which put Sir Frederick into a great rage that he began to reprove me; but after hearing what I had to say, how I was detained at the Wells by a Farmer who had been giving me a description of a valuable horse he had been robbed of, he became more moderate and soon cooled down. He then told me that the Duke had arrived in London and that I must take a Post chaise at once and go and find out where he was staying, and keep to the instructions he had already given.

I returned to the go-cart to take me to my lodging at Sunning-hill to get my Portmanteau, and having obtained this, I hastened back to Windsor, engaged a Post chaise and proceeded home to my house, No. 12 Robert Street, Hampstead Road, arriving there about five in the afternoon. My wife was sitting at the parlor window and saw the chaise make a sudden stop opposite the door. When she saw me get out she could not imagine what in the world was the matter, as I had arranged with her when I left home on the Monday previous that she was to come to Ascott on the following day, Thursday, which everyone knows is the Grand day, on account of the Royal

Family honoring the course with their attendance.

After taking a refreshing cup of tea I for some time considered how I should in the best manner commence these inquiries as to the whereabouts of the Duke: should I go and make inquiries at the Principal west end Hotels,? No!, I ,thought, If I do, as this enquiry is for the King, it may excite curiosity. He most probably landed at Dover and Posted to London. And then I thought again he may have come by Steamer to London Bridge. Having seriously considered over this matter I came to the conclusion that I would go to Thames Street and make enquiries at the Custom-house. Thither I went, and in less than half an hour I ascertained that the Duke had arrived from Boulogne and had gone to the Brunswick Hotel in Jermyn Street.

On this information I lost no time in going there, and I remained in the neighbourhood keeping the Hotel in view till 10 at night, during which time I saw nothing to attract notice. Next morning, Thursday, at 9 o'clock I took up my position at the corner of Bennett Street, St. James Street, commanding a good view of the Hotel, where I waited, and at 12 o'clock, having nothing to attract my particular attention, I got fidgetty; the time rolled on till 2 with the same result. At this moment my attention was attracted to a well-dressed man coming from out of the Junior St. James's Club, advancing without his hat towards me, and politely asked me to step into the Club as a gentleman wished very much to speak to me.

I left my post and on entering the Club was met by the proprietor, Mr Bond, whom I had known for some years. He ushered me to a seat in a small antiroom, and said, "Goddard, I don't want to know your business, neither do I intend to ask, but if it will answer your purpose instead of standing out in the street, and I can find a room suitable for your purpose, I can only say that you are most welcome."

I expressed myself delighted at his kind offer.

"Will this one suit?" he asked.

"Yes," was my reply.

"There it is, at your service, and not only that, he said, but as long as your business detains you in this neighbourhood, I shall consider you as my Guest, and what refreshment you may require I will give orders to my steward to that effect; so I wish you good morning."

In less than two minutes the steward came into the room and informed me that he had received orders from Mr Bond "to supply you with luncheon, that we have now got ready: turtle soup—roast chicken—ham—and roast beef."

I replied, "Turtle soup and some of the chicken, nothing more," said I.

This was sent in a few minutes accompanied with a pint bottle of Sauterne. While I was enjoying myself over this meal, I little thought when I was leaving home before 9 o'clock this morning, the unexpected fruit this day was going to bring forth.

It was now about half past 3 in the afternoon, and from that time till 9 o'clock I saw nothing to attract my attention. I then left as wise as I was when I went there in the morning, for during these twelve hours of anxiety I saw not a movement nor a sign of any description to indicate to my mind that any Royal Personage was there at all. On my way home and for the remainder of the night I thought how strange it was, and I began to be suspicious, and asked myself whether it was not a ruse on the part of the Duke to give out that he was going there when at the same time his intention was to drive somewhere else.

Bent upon this idea, I was determined the next day to have recourse to stratagem in some shape or another, and accordingly I took up the same position as before, resolving to mark well the sort of people going in and coming out, when about 12 o'clock. I saw a Porter go in. I knew him by the name of Thomas and that he belonged to Angersteins Hotel. I knew also that he knew me. He came out in about a quarter of an hour, and I followed him into Regent Street and spoke to him; he was very pleased to see me.

(Our acquaintance was formed from the circumstance that not long since I had to take a brother of his into custody on a bench warrant. It happened on a Saturday night, and as I was about locking the brother up at the police station in Vine Street, Thomas prevailed upon me not to do so, saying that as it would be so many hours till Monday morning his brother would lose his situation; that he was a married man with four children and it would cause much distress; that if I would kindly take his word he would produce him to me at Bow Street Office at 10 o'clock on Monday morning. I thought the case a hard one and yielded to his entreaties. Monday morning came and Thomas, true to his word, produced my prisoner, who was prepared with two sureties. He was taken before G. R. Minshill Esq. the Magistrate, and was liberated on the Bail produced, having thus escaped 50 hours' incarceration. This kindness Thomas said he should never forget.)

I invited him to take a glass of ale, when he talked about his brother's prosecution saying it was a malicious one, and he again thanked me for saving his brother so many hours of incarceration.

I replied laughingly and said, "One good turn deserves another, and I think you can now serve me, and at the same time I can put a Guinea into your pocket."

He replied, "I shall be most happy, Mr Goddard, without the Guinea; what do you wish me to do?"

I said, "Well, first of all, before I tell you, you must promise to keep it to yourself."

"Oh, that I will," he said, "never fear, it will be a pleasure, for I feel that I am bound to serve you."

Then I said, "You have been to the Brunswick Hotel, and have just come out."

"Yes, I have," he replied.

Then I said, "Do you know the Porter there?"

"What, Bill, do you mean? Of course I do, I know him well."

I answered, "That will do, and now what I want you to do is to ascertain whether the Duke of Brunswick is staying there."

"Oh," he replied, "that I can easily, and without suspicion, for I am going to see Bill again in half an hour."

"Well, then," I replied, "you meet me when you come out; I will be at the other end of Jermyn Street."

"All right, I'll be there," he replied.

We separated; I returned to my old spot, and after a short time I saw Thomas enter the Hotel. In ten minutes he left and came to me and said, "Mr Goddard, it is all right, the Duke is there with some French Count and two or three gentlemen and a Valet. They came the night before last, and the Duke has not been out since as he is very ill suffering from sea sickness."

Upon the strength of this information it run to another glass of ale when Thomas left, and I remained keeping the Hotel under observation till 9 in the evening.

On the following morning, Saturday, I was again at my old post at the corner of Bennett Street by 10. I had not been there more than a quarter of an hour when I spied Thomas leaving the Hotel and advancing to me in great haste and much excited, exclaiming at the top of his voice, "The Duke and his suite left the hotel in a sudden manner at 5 this morning in three cabs to be in time for the Boulogne Steamer that left the Custom House at 6 o'clock." Acting on this information, I hurried off in a cab to the Custom House and found what Thomas had said was true.

I then hastened to inform Sir F. Roe at his house at the corner of Whitehorse Street, Piccadilly, of the news. I was told by his servant that Sir Frederick had just left and had gone to the Home Office. I immediately followed and found that Sir Frederick was engaged with the Home Secretary. I told the Office Keeper that my visit was urgent and requested him to present my card. Sir Frederick instantly saw me, and after telling him what had occurred he told me to wait, and in about half an hour he gave me a letter directed to Sir Herbert Taylor at Windsor Castle saying I must take it at once and wait as it was very likely Sir Herbert would wish to see me. I left and was just in time to catch the Old Windsor Coach, leaving Hatchetts Hotel, Piccadilly.

Upon arriving at the Castle I delivered the letter, and after waiting a few minutes I was ordered into the presence of Sir Herbert. After telling him what I had done and how I had been engaged for the last week, he replied, "I am much obliged to you for what you have done, for it will please his Majesty." After thanking me he said he should go and tell the King.

I returned to London, went home and called upon Sir Frederick Roe the following morning, Sunday, and informed him how I was received by Sir Herbert. Sir Frederick appeared well pleased and told me he thought the matter was now finished and I could now go home and get my dinner.

About eight days afterwards, on Monday the 13th, I was informed by Sir Frederick that the Duke was expected to revisit England and that I must renew enquiries and keep a sharp look out; consequently I went daily to Nicholsons Wharf and the Custom House to make enquiries, watch the arrival of the French Steamers and also to look in the Newspapers to ascertain if any report had been announced as to his landing at any of our sea ports.

I was thus kept employed until the following Monday the 20th, when my instructions were countermanded as it was supposed the Duke was not going to return; but on the following Sunday morning, the 26th, as I was going to Church with my wife and family, a cab drove up to my door and a loud rat tat followed, and who should it be but Sir Frederick Roe's Butler with a message that I was to return with him to see Sir Frederick on important business. I obeyed the summons, and on our way I asked the Butler if he knew what it was all about; he replied that he had not the slightest idea but he said, "Sir Frederick appears in a fine way, therefore it must be something particular. Perhaps it's a duel or a murder." He said this with a most serious countenance.

By this time we had arrived at Sir Frederick's, and I was soon confronted before Sir Frederick in his library. Having closed the doors, he said, "Well, Goddard, I have just heard that this d....d Duke has come back, very much to the annoyance of his Majesty. You will therefore have to abide by the instructions you have already received."

I consequently took up my position as before, and on the next day, Monday, at 11 o'clock I saw a carriage draw up to the door of the hotel, taking up two gentlemen. They drove past me at the corner of St. James Street into Piccadilly, where I mounted a cab. I followed them up Park Lane into Oxford Street, then on to the Bazaar in Baker Street and to Madame Tussauds, where they stopped for an hour. They then came out and returned to their hotel. I then followed the empty carriage to Bryants Yard in Windmill Street and afterwards went to my friend Thomas, told him what had occurred and asked if he could manage, when he had time, to go and see what he could get out of Bill, and ascertain for me as clearly as possible who it was that went in that carriage I saw drive away in the morning.

"Certainly," said Thomas, "but I shall not be able to go for two hours, as the other porter has got leave to be out, but directly he comes in, I'll go to Bill."

"Then," I said, "to give you ample time, I will be in the bar at Blockeys at 5 o'clock."

Exactly as St. James's Church clock struck the hour of five Thomas, who was dressed in a new suit of Velveteen, entered at the Bar. Then, while drinking over two glasses of Blockeys renowned Wiltshire Ale, Thomas said that he had seen Bill and got it all out of him. He said that the gentleman that sate in the carriage with his face towards the horses was the Duke of Brunswick and the one that sate opposite, with his back to the horses, was the Duke's Secretary.

"All right," I said, "I shall know them both again."

"But," said Thomas, "Bill tells me that it is not like the same Duke that was here before who was laid up ill from sea-sickness. 'But,' said Bill,' as I did not have a good look at him, I may now be mistaken, but still after all I think, in my own mind he is not the same."

These last words put me into a quandary and made me think a great deal about what Bill had said. However, I thought time and constant observation would unravel this mystery, therefore day after day I kept to my post.

I should tire the patience of my readers were I to enumerate and enter into detail that many places the Duke went to, including his nightly visits to Drury Lane, Covent Garden and other Theatres, and not forgetting a flirtation at the back of the Slips in Covent Theatre hidden from view of the audience with one of the Harridans belonging to the doubtful firm of vieux Madame Levi notoriety from the neighbourhood of Whitehart Yard and Catherine Street. On August 5th I see from my diary the Duke went to Vauxhall Gardens for the purpose of making an ascent in a Balloon, but at the last moment his heart failed, and the Balloon left the Earth without him. On the following Monday, the 22nd, he ascended in one accompanied by Mrs Graham from the Tea Gardens at Bayswater.

On the 8th of September at 10 o'clock in the morning I saw the Duke's carriage drawn by four horses with two postillions brought up in front of the hotel. Amongst the baggage were 8 large duelling pistols. His Royal Highness was immediately followed by his Secretary, and as soon as his valet got seated behind, the carriage drove off. I followed on the road in a cab to Barnet, where they changed horses, and after they had left I was informed the Duke was going to Manchester to attend the Musical Festival.

Two or three days after this an application was made to the Chief Magistrate for the services of two experienced Police Officers, stating that several robberies had taken place by some of the London thieves and that the authorities had got four suspected persons in custody and they wanted them to be identified as such. George Ruthven and I was dispatched by the night mail, and on the day after our arrival, when the prisoners were brought up before the Magistrates at the New Baily,

Ruthven immediately identified all four. I could only identify three. Their names were John Hartnell, Thomas Jones, John Waklin and John Jones, all four most notorious well known thieves.

When John Hartnell cross-examined me how it was that I knew him to be a thief my answer to his question was, "It is only about a fortnight since that I saw you in company with two well-known thieves among a great crush of people in the avenue at the Pit entrance of Covent Garden Theatre, just as the doors were being opened. I cautioned you and the others to make yourselves scarce or you would be locked up. You thanked me, and you all decamped."

Mr Thomas, the Chief Constable of Manchester, was then called up, and after being sworn said he knew them all to be swell mobsmen belonging to old Ben Lewis's gang in Wych Street. Waklin, one of the most dashing of the prisoners, enquired of Mr Thomas if he recollected speaking to a gentleman who was walking through the Church yard two or three days ago and cautioning him that there were thieves about and if he did not mind he would lose his handkerchief that was half hanging out of his pocket.

"Yes," replied Mr Thomas, "I do recollect that circumstance very well!"

"Then," said Waklin, "I was that gentleman, and how is it you now say you know me to be a thief? You did not know me then; you have invented this from what you have heard from the London Police Officers."

The matter then dropped, and the prisoners were committed for one month each as rogues and vagabonds.

Not long after this, Sir Frederick Roe stated to me that His Majesty was most anxious to know whether it was the Duke himself or someone personating him who in May last went to the Brunswick Hotel, as His Majesty had his doubts. Sir Frederick added that as His Majesty was anxious to know, I must try and find it out. At this time the connection of the Hotel was removed to Regent Street where German Reeds performances are now being held. Outside that Hotel is a very spacious balcony, and from constant observation I found that His Royal Highness was frequently in the habit of making his appearance on this balcony accompanied by his Secretary, both smoking cigars about 11 o'clock on Sunday mornings; and now the difficulty I had to contend against was to know who I could find that I could trust to distinguish the Duke from his Secretary. I considered for a long time, and at last it came to my mind that someone of the waiters engaged at the Hotel, in Water Lane, close to the Custom House, whose duty it was on the arrival of Foreign Steamers to go on board to direct and conduct such passengers who were bound to this Hotel, might be able to give me some information.

Acting upon this idea, I put on my best garments and betook myself thither at half past 6 o'clock, and ordered what I thought an expensive dinner, viz Turtle Soup, filleted Soles and a delicious cut from a haunch of venison in splendid condition, pastry and desert to follow accompanied by a pint of Claret with for a finish a pint of Moet's champagne good enough for a King. I asked what I had to pay, the Bill was quickly brought (18/-), I glanced over it and paid the waiter (whose name I ascertained to be Louis) a Guinea and told him to keep the change for his trouble; this he very soon pocketed and, giving me his very best thanks, said, "I don't often meet with such liberal gentlemen as you."

"Don't you," said I, "I am very sorry to hear it."

I then bade him good night. I went again on the following evening about the same time, and the first person I saw was Louis. He smiled, was extremely polite and conducted me to the same snug box as before: dinner was nearly the same as on the previous evening, less the champagne. While he was paying attention to me I got into conversation about Foreigners of distinction and asked if ever any of them came there after landing.

"Oh, yes," he said, "sometimes they do and take refreshment while their baggage is being overhauled at the Custom house."

"Has the King of Holland ever been here?" I asked.

"No," he replied, "but we have had the Duke of Brunswick with his Secretary; we had the conducting them from on board the Boulogne Steamer."

Then after I had asked a few more questions, he said he had had more to do with the Secretary than with the Duke himself.

I said I had heard that they resembled each other.

"Not a bit," he said, "there is a vast difference, for I know them both well."

Now this, I thought, was a most important point to know, inasmuch as the King had his own suspicions, for reasons best known to himself, that his nephew, the Duke, did not arrive in England as was reported, but was being personated by the Baron, his Secretary, who feigned illness through sea sickness and kept in his bedroom during his short stay of three days as an excuse for not receiving visitors. So far I felt satisfied that I had found out someone who could, when called upon, identify the Duke from the Baron. I asked for my Bill and gave Louis for himself the same amount as before, wishing him good night, while he bowed me out in his usual polite manner.

Now during the time I had been engaged making these

inquiries Sir F. Roe had been out of Town. He no sooner returned than he sent for me to ask what progress I had made. After putting him in possession of what I had done to effect the object I had in view, viz the identification of the parties, he said, "That is all very well what you have been telling me, but how about getting Louis to point them out to you, distinguishing one from the other?"

"Oh, that can be done easy enough. I can go to the hotel and have another dinner, and while drinking my wine I can say to Louis, 'I have got a small wager pending, I have made a bet that it was the Duke himself who first came over and was laid up sick in his bedroom during the three days he was staying at the Brunswick Hotel in Jermyn Street.' Well, then," I continued, "if I tell him that, and offer him a sovereign for his trouble to come up next Sunday morning, I have no doubt he will consent to do so."

Sir Frederick agreed to these proposals, and I after sprucing myself up proceeded after the hour of 5 o'clock to Water Lane. On entering the hotel I was met by Louis, who in his usual polite and smiling manner conducted me to the old snug box as before.

"Just in time, Sir, for a most excellent dinner, beautiful crimped salmon, a saddle of mutton in high perfection."

"All right, Louis," I said. "you seem to know my taste. I'll have what you recommend, and this time bring me one of your pint bottles of Sauterne."

The dinner was brought, and while sipping and praising my wine I broached the subject about the Duke and the Baron, mentioning that I had got a Wager upon it. I then asked him if he would meet me at the foot of the Duke of York's column a little before 11 o'clock next Sunday morning so that I may decide my wager.

"Certainly," he said. "I can get leave, and shall be only too happy to oblige."

We then made the agreement; I paid my bill, giving Louis his usual fee, and bade him good night.

So far, so good, said I to myself, but as I wanted to make matters doubly sure, and that there should be no mistake, I went the same evening to see Thomas to get him to fetch out Bill the waiter, as I wanted to see him particularly. No sooner did I inform Thomas what I wanted than he immediately put on his hat and walked as fast as he could to the Brunswick Hotel, telling me to wait a little outside and he would bring Bill. In less than five minutes Thomas came out with Bill to me. I then made arrangements for Bill to meet me at the same time and place I had arranged to meet Louis. Sunday morning arrived, and before St. Martin's clock had struck eleven, both my men were at their post, and it happened fortunately that it was a most splendid morning.

We lost no time in walking up to Howells and James, commanding a view of the hotel opposite, when before we had been standing five minutes, the Duke and the Baron came out smoking their cigars and stood for some time talking, first looking to the right and then towards the Duke of York's column to their left, giving Louis and Bill ample opportunities to satisfy themselves. This they did at a glance. Bill took me on one side away from the hearing of Louis, and pointing to the Baron, said, "That is the one I saw, I can spot him out from among a thousand, because I had so many opportunities of seeing him." Bill having settled this question to my satisfaction as far as identity went, I and Bill wished each other good morning.

Louis during our conversation kept his distance, but directly we separated he lost no time in coming towards me; then pointing out the Baron he said it was he and not the Duke who came to England at the latter end of May last.

"Have you any doubt about it?" I asked. "None whatever," he replied.

Then I said, "You have settled the question and I have lost my money."

"I hope it is not much," said he, "for if it is I am sorry for it."

I gave him what I promised, viz a sovereign. He thanked me, we bade each other good morning and he went his way. and I mine, feeling delighted with how the business had come off thus far.

I hurried to inform Sir Frederick. After reporting what had taken place he was very pleased; he then said, "You be here at 12 o'clock tomorrow. and be prepared to go to Windsor with a letter to Sir Herbert Taylor."

Next morning, Monday. as the clock was striking 12 I was admitted into the presence of Sir Frederick, who at that moment had just finished sealing a letter and blowing out the taper.

"There!" said Sir Frederick "this is the letter." Handing it to me, he continued, "After you have delivered it you had better wait, as Sir Herbert may wish to talk to you."

"Very well," I said, "Sir Frederick, I will act up to your instructions.

I then retired, and as there was nothing said about hiring a Post chaise I waited for the Windsor coach that was to leave Hatchetts a quarter before 2 o'clock. I arrived at Windsor at half past 4 in the afternoon, when I lost no time in going to the Castle, and delivering the letter into the hands of Mr Payne (a close attendant upon Sir H. Taylor), who knew me. I told him I was instructed to wait, and he requested me to be seated; then, placing the letter upon a salver, he left me alone in the Hall for about five minutes, when he returned. and looking at me, said I was to follow him as Sir Herbert wished to see me. (I am happy to say that Mr Payne is now one of the Marshalmen in attendance at Her Majesty's Palaces.)

No sooner was I ushered in to Sir Herbert's presence in the Library than he requested me to sit down while he went to speak to his Majesty, when he vanished instantly from my sight. This sudden disappearance took me so much by surprise that it was some time before I could imagine how it took place; then without taking my eyes from the spot I discovered there was a secret door so artistically fitted and arranged with shelves of books that there was only the appearance of one continuous line of a well-stocked library. Still I could not help keeping my eyes stedfastly fixed on the spot, and I continued to do so in a state of suspense for nearly twenty minutes, when I was again equally astonished at the sudden reappearance of Sir Herbert. I could hear no sound of approaching footsteps, saw no appearance of light nor heard any noise from the drawing of a bolt or the turning of a door handle; but there he stood. and he said, "Goddard, the King has read the letter you have just brought from Sir Frederick Roe, and it appears you can say much more and go into more particulars than the letter contains, therefore tell me all about the matter as nearly as you can."

I replied, "Sir Herbert, it is very fortunate I have got my diary with me, and I can go through it in a very short time."

I then read from my diary the whole of the particulars from the beginning to the present time even to where I was then standing. I began and it took me about half an hour. Sir Herbert paid close attention to every word I uttered and took notes. When I had concluded he told me to wait, and at the same time vanished from my sight as before for about 10 minutes, when he returned in the same sudden manner.

He then said, "It is a long story, therefore the King desires you to come in and tell him as you have told me. Follow me!"

I did so, and found that I had no sooner passed the secret door than it closed instantly after me, leaving Sir Herbert and myself in a dark recess for a second. Then Sir Herbert opened another door, when I found myself in the presence of the King, who first addressed me thus: "Well, Mr Goddard, you have been at some pains and trouble in this affair and Sir Frederick mentions in his letter that you can go through it in a very short time."

I paused for a moment while opening my diary, I then went through it word by word as I had done previously before Sir Herbert. When I had concluded, his Majesty laughed very heartily and Sir Herbert motioned me to withdraw with him from the King's presence back into Sir Herbert's library. He then said, "Mr Goddard, I am desired to tell you that you have given his Majesty entire satisfaction, and if you wait in the next room I will give you a letter to Sir Frederick Roe to that effect."

I thanked Sir Herbert and retired accordingly, and after waiting for about 10 minutes Sir Herbert came out and handed to me the letter.

I bade Mr Payne good night, made the best of my way to London and delivered my charge to Sir Frederick, who was very much delighted to hear that I had been introduced to the King. "But," said Sir Frederick, "you must still continue to keep the Duke under constant observation, and report to me occasionally till you receive my orders to stop. "This duty occupied nearly all my time till within six weeks of his Majesty's death.

I must now carry my readers over, after a lapse of twelve years, till October 1849, when my services were called into request by Mr Steele, solicitor to Mr J. Harmer, to keep the Duke of Brunswick, his Secretary William Oddy and Cassimir Reinhold under strict observations. Oddy, I discovered, took up his abode for a short time in Guernsey, while Reinhold, was living in the New Cut, Lambeth. Both these men, I was Informed, had been employed by the Duke to give false and perjured evidence. Reinhold stated in the court of Queen's Bench "that he recently went to the Weekly Dispatch Newspaper Office in Fleet Street and asked for the paper of the 19th September, 1830 date: that the shopman opened a drawer from under the counter and gave it him." On inquiry, this evidence was proved to be false, and it was discovered that Oddy and Reinhold found out one Mr Plummer, a dealer in old newspapers, who daily took up his stand in Catherine Street, Strand, and told him they were most anxious to purchase an old Weekly Dispatch but it must be of the 19th September, 1830, and if he could get it they would make him a present of £5— and they would call upon him in three days. In the mean time Plummer discovered in a shop window in the Commercial Road a file of the Weekly Dispatch for the year 1830, to be had within; Plummer took advantage of this opportunity and bought them for a trifling sum. Oddy and Reinhold kept to their appointment and paid over to Plummer what they promised and received the sought-for newspaper. Hence this action.

The following is an extract from the Weekly Dispatch of

November 23rd, 1851:

THE DUKE OF BRUNSWICK AND THE "DISPATCH"

In the Court of Queen's Bench last week the Grand Jury brought into Court an indictment, found by them, against the Duke of Brunswick and others for conspiring to procure by false and perjured evidence a verdict to pass in favour of the Duke in an action of libel brought by him against Mr. Harmer, one of the Proprietors of this journal, in respect of an article which appeared in the Dispatch of 19th September, 1830; and for procuring a verdict with £500 damages to pass in his (the Duke's) favour in that action by means of perjury; and for procuring a witness falsely to swear to having purchased at the Dispatch Office, a few days before the commencement of the action, a Dispatch newspaper of that date (so as to avoid the operation of the Statute of Limitations, which requires any action for libel to be brought within 6 years after the publication of the libel), the Duke knowing at the time such newspaper had not been purchased. The indictment also contained counts against the Duke of Brunswick for subornation of perjury.

In consequence of the verdict of the Jury a Judges Warrant was issued for their apprehension, but it was not executed in consequence of the Duke having taken his flight in a Balloon to the other side of the Channel.

The Duke was proclaimed an Outlaw 9th May, 1853.

Incendiary at Frant

On the evening of the 19th of October 1836, Sheffield Grace Esq. of Frant, near Tunbridge Wells, was entertaining a select and distinguished party of friends to dinner among whom was Lady Hamilton.

The footman John Christie, who had been waiting at table, and whose duties called him away for a minute, returned in a state of great excitement and halloing in a loud voice "Master! Master!! your barn is all on fire! !!" this sudden alarm caused great terror to the company, who immediately rose from their seats and ran in all directions in the greatest confusion, crying out "Fire! Fire!"

The alarm-bell was rung aloud, the village folk assembled and the brilliant light which illumined the atmosphere brought many strangers from afar, as well as the fire-engine from Tunbridge Wells, a distance of four miles; but unfortunately in consequence of the hose not being long enough by about a hundred yards to reach the Pond the Villagers, to their credit, both male and female, ran with all speed to fetch their buckets and formed themselves into two lines while John Christie was ready standing over his knees in a Pond of water to fill them and so pass them on to be handed from one to another to supply the engine as fast as the empties were returned. He continued working on in this manner without intermission till the fire was so far got under that the stables and wagon sheds containing several implements of husbandry were considered to be out of danger; and from the promptness, energy and activity displayed he not only received the thanks from his master but from everyone all around.

Enquiries were instituted on the following day by the local authorities, and for two or three days afterwards, as to the cause of the fire, when they came to the conclusion that it was the act of an Incendiary. Bills for the discovery offering £100 reward were printed and distributed far and wide and at a meeting held by the magistrates it was resolved to lay the case before the Home Secretary. for the assistance of an officer to be sent down in order to have this atrocious outrage throughly enquired into.

In consequence I was dispatched by order of T. Hall, Esq., the sitting Magistrate, to proceed by the night-mail to Tunbridge Wells, and report myself to the Magistrates at Frant next morning.

Acting according to my instructions, I was introduced to the Magistrates and, after hearing all they had to say, I took my own private view of the case and said that my enquiries must commence with John Christie, as well as all the servants employed on the establishment including hostlers, wagonmen and others.

"We wish you to carry on this business in your own way, Mr Goddard, without interference from anyone," replied the Magistrates, "and we shall only be too anxious to assist you in so grave a matter in any way you may purpose."

After making this remark we all separated, and I went on my way commencing my enquiry with John Christie the footman.

I began by telling him who I was, and the business that brought me—that it was a very serious matter—that there would be the most searching investigation made to discover the perpetrator of so fiendish a crime.

"And now may I ask you, how you passed your time during the day from breakfast to the time you gave the alarm of 'Fire!'—but before you do so I must tell you that whatever you do say I shall have to repeat it to the Magistrates."

He then went on to say how he had been employed up to the dinner time, 1 o'clock, and in the afternoon for an hour and half for recreation he walked about in the fields. On his way, he said, he met James Bolton, whom he knew to be a Poacher, and they walked together about half an hour. "I left him to attend to my duties and about half past 8 o'clock, after the desert was cleared from the table, I had to go to the dairy for some cream, and seeing the fire I ran into the room and gave the alarm to my master. I then ran out, pulling off my coat and waistcoat—the alarm bell was ringing, the people from the village came up and ran for their buckets. From the great light the flames shewed in the clouds brought many people together, and in less than half an hour when the engine arrived I went and stood in the pond above my knees and filled the buckets to supply the Engine as I received them for a full hour till the fire was got under, and that is all I can tell you."

At the conclusion of this statement I left him to his household duties and went in search of James Bolton the Poacher. Within an hour I saw a man who seemed to answer to the description given to me of Bolton, standing not far from the entrance of the Abergavenny Arms, Public-house.

I went up to him and said, "Here, Bolton, I want to speak to you! When was the last time you saw John Christie?"

He, looking amazed, replied, "Yesterday."

This answer caused me to put several other questions, and he admitted having been out with him in the fields on the same afternoon as the fire at Mr Grace's farm took place at night, and about a fortnight before that he said they were out together with his master's Dogs after the family had gone to bed.

"Anything else do you remember?" I asked.

"Well," said he, "we saw a large fire burning and I said to Christie, 'You know whose house that is! it serves him right!! for he is a bad fellow to his workpeople. 'Yes,' answered Christie, 'and so is mine, and I should not at all wonder but his place will be fired some of these dark nights.'"

(Hello! said I to myself. It's coming out.)

I then told him who I was and that he would have to go with me. He appeared half tipsy, and walked by my side till I left him in custody of the Parish constable. Then I hastened to inform Mr Grace, who was greatly astonished, and who said that during my absence Mary Maddox, his cook, could give me some important information and she wished to see me.

I accordingly went, and she stated that just before the fire she saw Christie carrying the Candle-stick with a lighted Candle in it to fetch the cream from the dairy. "When he returned I noticed that he held the cream jug in one hand and the Candle-stick, without the candle, in the other, and as he passed me he laid down the Candle-stick and said he had seen a light, and he thought Master's barn was on fire and went on hollowing out, 'Fire!' into the sitting room: that is all I know."

On this information I took Christie into custody and left him in charge of a Constable at Harry Pegg's the Sussex Hotel, Tunbridge Wells.

These arrests took place on a Saturday, and both myself and the Constables were put to the greatest inconvenience for the want of a lock-up in the locality, and fearing escape I was compelled to keep the men in Irons.

On the following morning, Sunday, Christie sent a Messenger to say that he wanted to see me very particularly. When I saw him he asked if it was true that I had got Bolton in custody and whether he had said anything.

"Yes," I said, "it is true, and he has told me a great deal."

Then Christie said that he should either laugh or cry today.

"What do you mean?" I asked.

"Well, then," said he, "I did it! It came into my head one night when I and Bolton were out poaching with my master's dogs, when we saw in the distance a large fire and I said I should not at all wonder that there will be one at Master's next." Then he added how he had done it—that he went to the dairy for cream, that he took from the Candle-stick the candle, and carried it with his hand before it to prevent the wind from blowing it out, and pulled a board of the barn on one side, put the candle in it and placed some loose straw over. "When it began to blaze, I placed the board back and ran and told my master that his barn was all on fire."

After this statement I left him in the hands of the constable, and next day we took him and Bolton before the Magistrate, Daniel Rowland Esq., before whom Christie made a full confession of his guilt which the clerk took down in writing. The Magistrate had previously cautioned him that what he might say may be used in evidence against him and then asked him if he had any objection to put his name to what he had been saying.

He answered, "No! I am Guilty," and affixed his name in the presence of four Witnesses. He was then committed to the next Lewes March Assizes for trial.

On the 22nd of March following, on being brought up to the bar of the Court before Lord Tyndall, he was asked, after the indictment had been read over to him by the Clerk of Arraigns in the usual manner, "How say you, John Christie, are you guilty of the offence with which you are charged in this indictment, or not guilty?"

"Guilty, my Lord," in a loud voice replied the prisoner.

The Court thereon consulted for a few minutes, when the Judge informed the Prisoner's Counsel he might withdraw his plea and let the trial proceed. The Prisoner, acting according to his Counsel's advice, withdrew his plea of guilty to that of Not Guilty. The trial was then gone into, which occupied a considerable time, and the result was that after the Jury had conferred together for a few minutes they returned their verdict of "Not Guilty"!!!

The Prisoner looked round the Court in a state of amazement, and said, "What, not guilty!"

"There," said the Judge to the governor of the Jail, "Take him away"

Soon afterwards I left the Court for the purpose of taking some refreshment at the Tavern close at hand, when I was followed in by John Christie, who shook me by the hand and invited me to take a glass of Sherry, saying, "What a lucky escape I have had, for the Jury wouldn't believe me." I was not sorry at the result, otherwise his life would have been forfeited, and broken his poor mother's heart, who was respectably connected.

The Gold Robbery

On the evening of the 30th of October, 1836, the Defiance coach left Dover for London, carrying, among other articles, several canvass bags of gold, which had been consigned from the continent to a firm in the city, On the following morning, upon the arrival of the coach at the Golden-cross, the waybill was looked at, and upon examining the fore boot it was discovered that one of the bags, containing a large quantity of gold, was missing.

The guard and coachman were questioned upon the subject by the coach proprietors, and said that they could not at all account for the missing bag. The former said that he saw Matthews, the porter, remove the bags from the counter of the office and deposit them in the fore boot of the coach, and that he (the guard) and the porter packed the London heavy luggage upon them for their greater security. The coachman said that he left the box but once, and the guard was equally certain that he never left the coach at all during the journey.

The guard obtained the assistance of a Bow-street officer, who returned with him to the Golden-cross, where a most rigid and searching inquiry was instituted among the persons who unloaded the coach; but they failed in obtaining any clue to the perpetrator of the robbery. The officer immediately visited all the stations between London and Dover at which the coach had changed horses, questioning "boots", ostlers, stable-keepers, passengers, and searching and overhauling stables and lofts. A similar ceremony was repeated at Dover, the office-clerk stating that he had placed the whole of the bags containing the gold on the counter, from which they were removed by the porter in the presence of the guard. The porter said that he placed the whole of the bags at the bottom of the boot. The officer examined the coachman, guard, the two ostlers who had stood at the horses' heads, and the porter, and he at once communicated to the proprietors of the hotel his suspicions that the last-named person was the thief.

The proprietors of the hotel, however, were of a different opinion, and said they thought the officer was mistaken, as the porter had been in their employment a great number of years, and they had always found him strictly and thoroughly honest. This did not get rid of the suspicions of the officer, who all along doubted whether the missing bag had been placed in the boot at all. By way of ruse, and with the consent of the coachman and guard, he searched their houses in order that the porter might not suppose that he was the party suspected. Shortly afterwards the house of the porter was inspected by the officer, and having a strong impression that the gold was buried in the garden he dug, raked, and pierced it in various places, in the expectation of finding the booty. Thus the matter remained for a time, the officer thinking it desirable to make it appear that all hope of recovering the property was gone.

About a month afterwards the house of Matthews, the

porter, was again searched, when the officer found that he had got a quantity of new furniture, bedding, etc.; and he found secreted in one of the rooms 20 sovereigns. Goddard, the officer, immediately took Matthews into custody, and, from inquiries which he made, ascertained that Matthews on the night of the robbery was seen in one of his journeys with the bags to walk behind the coach to the fore boot. Matthews was examined before the magistrate and committed for trial. The evidence, however, failed to connect him with the robbery, and he was acquitted.

About three months afterwards, while Goddard was standing on the steps leading to Bow-street Police-office, a stout, broad-shouldered man, dressed in a suit of dark velveteen, presented himself to him. He immediately recognized him, and said, "Matthews, is that you?"

"Yes," was the reply; "I want to see you very particularly to tell you something. Can you meet me this afternoon?"

"Yes," replied Goddard.

An appointment to meet was made, which Goddard was unable to keep, on account of his being despatched into the country on business connected with the Home-office. Matthews, finding that Goddard did not keep the appointment, at once proceeded to Dover, and told the inspector of police there that he was a wretched man and had never been happy since his trial. He admitted to the inspector that he stole the bag of gold, and that he had buried it in his next-door neighbour's garden; that he had made repeated attempts to possess himself of it; that his heart always failed him, and that he was afraid of being seen. The inspector forthwith proceeded to the spot indicated, and found the hidden treasure close to the border of Matthews's own garden. Matthews stated that the way in which he effected the robbery was this:—On the occasion of his walking behind the coach, as if for the purpose of proceeding to the boot, he concealed the bag of gold in a large inside breast coat pocket, and so deceived those who were in attendance on the coach. He also said that as the safe was being repaired, and was not fastened in the boot, he concluded that the way in which the robbery was committed would never be discovered.

Looking at one self in the glass

In the Month of December 1836 Mr Lauderdale Maule, Brother to the late Lord Dalhousie, applied to Sir F. Roe for a warrant against a man of the name of Charles Atkinson for conspiring and by false pretences to rob him of the sum of one thousand pounds, in the following manner, about a month since. He said:

"In answer to an advertisement I saw in the newspaper, that the advertiser was prepar'd to advance from one hundred to two Thousand Pounds for long or short periods at five per cent to officers holding appointments in the Army and Navy or to clergymen and others of good connections at a day's notice on borrower's note of hand—Address Private

To C.A.

Blue Post Tavern

Cork Street

will meet with immediate attention—

I replied and an appointment was made for a meeting at 12 on the following day. We met, and after making myself known to him I stated that I only wanted the Loan of £100 for a month.

'There is no difficulty about that,' said the advertiser, 'for you can have it tomorrow.' While this conversation was going on he took from his Pocket Book a blank bill stamp and with great plausibility of manner requested me to sign it, and after putting my name, it was arranged that either himself or his clerk would be ready to hand over the cash at 12 tomorrow. I kept to the appointment and waited for two hours with no result, and thinking there was some accident or misunderstanding I went again on the following day, but no Mr Atkinson or clerk was to be seen. By this time, and not without a reason, my suspicions became aroused. I had searched and made every enquiry after him but without success, when. to my utter astonishment, after the expiration of the month, a notice was served upon me for the payment of £1000. Under these circumstances without fear of exposure I am determined to have this scoundrel Brought to Justice, for I can be on my oath that I never signed my hand to a bill for £1000 in my life."

Sir F. Roe granted the warrant with instructions, as I knew the man, to execute it as quickly as possible. On enquiry and not without some difficulty I ascertain'd that this Atkinson occasionally visited a Lady who occupied two Parlours in German Street. After keeping this House for a short time under observation I crossed the road and looking in at the window, there being a bright light from the fire, to my surprise I distinctly saw the face of a man reflected in the large looking glass over the mantel shelf whom I discovered to be no other but the identical man wanted.

As no time was to be lost I took an envelope from my Pocket book and, after directing it, rung the bell and presented it to the servant. She said it was a mistake, "for the Gentleman in the Parlour is Mr Jones."

"Yes," I said, "Mr A. Jones, it is all right, Atkinson Jones, and I must see him."

"You cannot," she said and began to scream, on which I pushed her on one side and forced myself into his presence.

He, knowing me, made no resistance, and after telling him my business he put on his great coat and Hat and walked with me to Bow Street. Mr Maule shortly afterwards appeared, and he was committed to Newgate, tried at the Old Bailey on the, 6th of January following, found Guilty and sentenced to seven years transportation.

This Atkinson was connected with Tom Prestcott, Minter Hart and Bill Richardson, well educated and most Gentlemanly looking men, all notorious Bill stealers. They were all transported after victimising clergymen and others for several years.

Joseph Reiteroffer

About nine o'clock on Sunday night the 28th of May, 1837, I took this man into custody, without a Warrant, and I believe with the exception of George Ruthven I was the only other officer who knew that he had been indicted for keeping a Gaming-House in St. James's Square at the suit of one Thomas Bennett and others. Ruthven and I had spent a great deal of time and at considerable expense in going to Brompton and Chelsea, staying out very late at night, where our informant led us to believe that we should fall over him.

Having met with no success, we retired from the enquiry till such time as we could get more direct information, but in the meantime Mr Bennett was continually agitating Sir F. Roe that he did not think we exerted ourselves, which caused Sir Frederick to feel dissatisfied. In the midst of this agitation George Ruthven was suddenly called upon by Mr Bush, solicitor to the Society of Bankers, for him to follow up an important case that he had previously got in hand, and he was dispatched at once to the Continent. Shortly after his departure Mr Bignold, Mr Bennett's lawyer, called on me in a Cab and informed me that if I met him at eight o'clock that evening, Sunday, at the corner of the Haymarket, Piccadilly side, he could put me upon Reiteroffer, as he said "he has had already a thousand escapes, but he shall not escape this time."

I consented to meet him, and after his departure I made all haste I could to the residence of George Ruthven to enquire of his wife if he had left the Warrant in question under her care. She replied that he had not, but she would allow me to look over his papers in his desk: we searched, but all in vain, it was not to be found. I felt very annoyed as it put me in a great fix that I scarcely knew what to do. However, I had to consider and kept my appointment, and at nine o'clock Bignold took me to the corners of Jermyn Street and Regent Street to nearly opposite the Strangers Club, and in less than five minutes we saw a very tall stout well dressed fine looking gentleman descending the steps of the Strangers Club and turned to the right hand.

The lawyer immediately exclaimed as loud as he could bawl, "See, Goddard, there he goes, that is him, that's Reiteroffer, the Count, do your duty and go and take him into custody. (This bawling annoyed me very much.) I followed after him at a fast pace, and joining him in his walk by his side I told him who I was and my errand. By this time we had got to the corner of Church Court and walked on to Piccadilly opposite St. James's Church and then called a cab one of those with the seat for the driver fixed over the wheel, and on being seated I told the Cabman to drive to Bow Street Police Station. On our way Reiteroffer requested me to shew him the Warrant, so I pulled an old one out of my pocket which I was carrying about for some one else, and as he saw Her Majesty's Coat of Arms engraved upon it this satisfied him.

When we arrived at the Police Station Mr Landrock, the Superintendent, paused about receiving him in custody without a Warrant; seeing this, I at once said, "I charge him with conspiracy." With that he took the charge, I signed the book, the prisoner was locked up and I left.

Early next morning I went to the office of the Clerk of the Peace, Clerkenwell, and on stating the circumstances I obtained a certificate of the Indictment and then made all haste to Bow Street office before 11 o'clock in time to tell the Chief Magistrate, Sir F. Roe, that I had last night succeeded in apprehending Reiteroffer. But when I said that I had taken him in custody without the Warrant, as Ruthven had not left it behind, he exclaim'd, "D… n it, what have you done!" On telling him the particulars of what I had done, as already stated, and producing the certificate, he was at once pacified. He then desired me to place the prisoner before him at the Bar. This having been done he committed him to the New prison, Clerkenwell, and to give forty-eight hours' notice of bail.

He had to remain in prison for some length. of time, and when he got his liberty he told several of his associates how I had deceived him in taking him without a Warrant, and that he would never forget it, and if it ever occurred again at any future time that I should have to take him into custody, he would shoot me. This information, I need not say, was the reason why I made my Will.

Deer Stealers etc.

On the 10th July 1837, an application was made to Sir Frederick Roe by Mr Wade, the house-steward to the Ladies Fitzpatrick of Farming Woods, in the County of Northamptonshire, for the assistance of an officer under the following circumstances.

The residence of Mr Height, their Ladyship' bailiff, had been during the night of the 8th inst. burglariously entered and his bureau broken open and a large purse containing about forty sovereigns and three pounds in silver stolen. It was the wish of the ladies for an officer to go down to make inquiries.

As it happened that I was present when this application was made and heard what was said. I was directed without delay to go down by the night mail to make inquiries.

On arriving at the spot next morning I was informed that it was high time something was done, what with the Poachers, the deer stealers and sheep stealers, with other robberies in that part of the county which was growing to such an alarming extent that it was not considered safe for people to be travelling about after dark. On hearing so many complaints it took me some time to consider in what form or manner of way I was to shape my course to make a beginning.

In the first place I found that entry had been made at the back of the premises by using a crow bar and forcing open a door which led them into the parlor, where I discovered the same impression was made in breaking open the bureau as at the door outside. As I was unable to obtain any clue, I heard that Weedon fair would take place in a day or two and would bring together no end of roughs and bad characters, such as Poachers, Idlers, Thimble riggers, Skittle sharks, Horsestealers and thieves of every description.

Now before this fair took place I got acquainted with Mr Chard, a doctor of great experience, living at Brigstock, who from his profession knew almost all the bad characters for many miles round. Through him I found an acquaintance with a Baker at Oundle who knew most of these characters. Therefore as the Doctor, the Baker and I were in each other's confidence it was arranged that they should meet me at the fair, and that I should be disguised as a countryman, and as opportunities turned up they were to point out to me the worst and most desperate of these characters.

So on the morning of the Fair their Ladyships' Bailiff accompanied me to an old barn to help me on with my disguise, and on his taking charge of the clothes I had taken off wished me "good morning", and said he should go and report to the Ladies how I looked in my new attire. After this I made the best of my way with about thirty shillings and a few coppers in my pocket to Weedon Fair, arriving there about 2 p.m. in time for a hearty dinner of salt beef, potatoes and carrots. When I had finished I strolled into the Fair, first looking at the skittle-players, then to the Pea and Thimble riggers, where to my astonishment I saw the Doctor and the Baker among several others staking their money which they soon to their cost found to be a losing game. After this we associated ourselves together looking on at the skittles and four-cornered sharpers how they gulled the flats and picked up the money. While this game was going on the Baker espied two notorious characters (Brothers) by the name of Clair, rushing into one of the booths ready to challenge and toss anyone for a sovereign. At the same time one of them, taking a number of sovereigns from his pocket, exclaimed, "Look here! look here!! these are none of your counterfeits." Turning them out of one hand into the other he said, "See, I am doing this to prevent them getting mouldy."

This freak not only attracted the attention of the Baker but of others, and after a few minutes' consideration the Baker signalled the Doctor and me to follow him. Calling our attention he said, "Why, I now recollect it is only a few days since and before the robbery I saw these two Clairs with scarcely any thing on their backs and almost barefooted. I think it looks suspicious to see such a sudden change in their being fresh togged out in new clothes with their pockets full of sovereigns, and all this money and new clothes without working for."

These appearances, I thought, would justify me in going to the Rev Mr Hogg, the Magistrate at Kettering, and telling him that from information received I suspected these Clairs to be concerned in the Burglary at Farming Woods and under the circumstances to ask him to grant me a warrant for their apprehension. So next day I went, and on this representation he granted the warrants, which were executed without delay.

Samuel Clair I apprehended at Oundle, and in his possession was found a Jemmy and ten sovereigns. On comparing the jemmy it corresponded with the impression made in forcing open the outer door and the bureau before mentioned. I immediately hired a conveyance and took him before the magistrate at Kettering, who remanded him to Northampton Gaol. The other Clair I apprehended at Stamford, and on his person found, with a few sovereigns in it, Mr Height's identical "large purse" stolen from his Bureau on the night of the Burglary. Because of this and other circumstances connected with the case, both prisoners were committed for trial.

While these exciting inquiries were going on I received information that if a young man named Richard Knight was taken into custody, certain persons would come forward and prove how he was implicated with a gang of sheep stealers, deer stealers and poachers. So inquiring into the antecedents of this said Richard Knight, I found that he was of loose habits, doing no manner of work, and was seen occasionally by different gamekeepers far and wide from home prowling about all hours of the night and in the day time frequenting the beerhouses and passing away his time in tossing, playing at skittles, shove halfpenny and drinking beer from morning till night. As there had been a lamb stolen from a neighbouring Farmer by the name of Vickers, I thought by apprehending him on suspicion of being concerned in this last case it would not be very injurious to his character. Acting on this impression I took upon myself this responsibility, and while conveying him from Brigstock to Mr Hogg, the Magistrate at Kettermg, he confessed to me the names of the whole gang of sheep and deer stealers, and also that I had got the right parties for the job at Farming Woods (meaning the Clairs); but if it was known, he said, that he split upon them, they would murder him.

In consequence of this information I obtained warrants against two brothers by the name of Bird, Brown, Briggs,

Jackson and Finedon, all of whom were apprehended for sheep and deer stealing, committed for trial and convicted at the October sessions held at Northampton in 1837.

Now with regard to Richard Knight, it was considered that if he returned to Brigstock his life would be in danger. This was represented to the Ladies Fitzpatrick, who said that if he had no objection, and was willing to leave the country and go to America, they would not only pay his Passage but furnish him with liberal means on his arrival there. Knight was delighted, and I took him to London and kept him at my house and shewed him about London for nearly three weeks, when I obtained for him a comfortable berth on board one of the New York monthly liners. After paying for his passage, including all extras for eating and drinking, I gave him a sovereign to put in his pocket and twenty Pounds to the Captain to give him after his arrival at New York.

About ten weeks afterwards, when the ship returned, I saw the Captain, who gave me a receipt for £20 from Richard Knight as a warranty that he had paid it over to him according to my instructions.

The Captain, in reply to my questions, said that Knight was a well behaved lad throughout the whole passage—that he got acquainted with a passenger who was going to Canada, and it was agreed for Knight to go with him; which is now 42 years ago, but how he got on at Canada I am sorry to say I have never heard.

One word about the Ladies Fitzpatrick. Their charity was unbounded, they were universally beloved and respected by the poor—their house was open to all comers—soup was liberally given twice a week according to the number amongst the families who stood in need. They had, when they drove out in their four wheel pony chaise, a small basket fastened on he side partly filled with silver consisting of coins from sixpences to half crowns ready to give to the needy they might pass or meet in their rural drives.

The stable-yard clock was always kept one hour fast.

The Cold Shoulder

In the early part of September 1837 Mr W. Winter, an extensive outfitter, made application to G.R. Minshull Esq., the sitting Magistrate, for a Warrant under the following circumstances against a young man who wore the full dress uniform of a naval officer and who had represented himself to be second in command on board her Majesty's ship Caledonia, laying off Chatham, and who had by means of a forged signature obtained goods and money from him to the amount of Fifty Pounds. After answering several questions put by the Magistrate a Warrant was granted and placed in my hands—that I was to take such steps under the circumstances as were necessary.

It was not long before I found out, from inquiries at the Theatres and from Mr Goodried, the proprietor of the Saloon situate near to the Haymarket in Piccadilly, his real name to be Henry Brooks and that he had duped other tradesmen in a similar manner. I soon got onto his track in finding out that he had been staying with a lady by the name of Read at Waites Hotel Gravesend and from there moved to Sheerness and Folkstone. From the last place I wrote, giving a full description of him, to the constable at Dover to give a full look out and that if he saw such a person to keep his eye upon him, and that I should be there before 12 o'clock the next day.

On my arrival there I found to my astonishment that the constable had within an hour before my arrival succeeded in arresting him and that he was now, he said, safely locked up in the Town Gaol. I lost no time in going to see him. I found that he was sitting in a well furnished room quite at his ease smoking a cigar with a small decanter of sherry wine before him, which I was rather surprised at. Finding that he had not been searched, I took from him a quantity of letters and memorandums, all torn up, from out of his coat pocket tied up in a silk handkerchief.

Having possessed myself of these and other articles, I left him to make further inquiries at the Dover Castle Hotel, and on my return I found that he had been examined before the Mayor and another Magistrate who ordered him to be locked up. At this instant the Constable said I was to go before the Mayor. When I appeared he asked me by what right and by whose authority I had come and searched a prisoner confined in their Gaol. In reply I briefly explained the circumstances that led me there and the importance of searching a prisoner in custody on a charge of Forgery. He replied that if I did not give up every thing he would commit me and report me to the Secretary of State. I then yielded to his threat and left Dover to proceed to London.

On the following morning, soon after the night charges had been disposed of and just before I was going to report how I had been treated by the Mayor, the Dover Constable came to me and delivered up the prisoner as also the articles found upon him, saying, "Here is the prisoner, I am in a hurry," and instantly disappeared from my sight.

The prisoner was taken before the Magistrate and after two or three remands was committed to Newgate for trial, which came on the 30th November, 1837. Verdict, guilty: and I was complimented by the Recorder for the energy and activity displayed in the manner the case was got up.

The Murder of Elizabeth Longfoot

Early in the morning towards the latter end of March 1838 a shocking murder was discovered at Easton, near to Burleigh Hall, the seat of the Marquis of Exeter, by a laborer. On attempting to draw water from a well situate in a garden close to a cottage inhabited by an old woman named Elizabeth Longfoot, he saw at the bottom the body of a woman floating on the surface. On alarming the neighbours, they, after some difficulty, succeeded in recovering it when it was found to be Elizabeth Longfoot, greatly disfigured by severe bruises about the head and face, and a cord with a running noose tied tightly round her neck. On further search it was found that deceased's cottage had been broken into, making an entrance at the back and plundered of what little money she was supposed to possess.

The information of this outrage soon reached the town of Stamford and caused a great sensation all over the county. The Magistrates consisting of the Marquis of Exeter, the Revd. Charles Atley and Dr Hopkinson, lost no time in taking up the matter and at once dispatched a messenger with a letter to Bow

Street office to send an officer as quickly as possible to the scene of tragedy. As it happened that I was the only Officer that was in town, I was dispatched forthwith by the night mail, arriving early on the following morning.

After my introduction to the Magistrates we proceeded with Mr Reed, the Chief Constable of the Borough, to the scene of the murder. At the back of the cottage we saw the prints of three different sized footmarks, which led us to believe that three persons had been concerned in this murder. Now one of these footprints was much above the ordinary size and I may say unusually long. From enquiries made I was informed that there was a man of bad character by the name of Stancer, with large feet, supposed to be living occasionally under the same roof as his sister, in the parish of Easton, not far from the scene of the murder. It was found from enquiry that he was a lay-about skulking fellow, away from his supposed home sometimes for a week, or a fortnight, sleeping in barns and under hayricks with no visible signs of doing any work. On asking after him of his sister she informed me that she had not seen him since the night of the murder, when he said he was going to Bourne.

In consequence of this information, my enquiring with Mr Reed took us to Bourne, Gosperton, Deeping, Peterboro' and Spalding. At the latter place we found that Stancer had been two nights after the murder and had been seen there at the Cross Keys with three or four sovereigns. At last we came upon him and apprehended him at Uppingham, and found over two pounds in his possession. While conveying him to Oundle, locking up and charging him as one being concerned in the murder, he admitted that on that night he was in company with Richard Woodward and Jack Archer, but he had nothing to do with the murder; it was Archer and Woodward.

In consequence of this statement, after locking him up, we went in pursuit after these men, and our enquiries led us to Weedon, Crick, Colly, Weston, Rode, Barnack, Brigstock, and Market Deeping to Duddington and back to Easton, where we succeeded in apprehending them, conveying one to Oakham Gaol and the other to Stamford lock-up, so that there should be no communication.

These apprehensions caused the greatest sensation.

Woodward, while being conveyed from the lock-up to undergo his examination before the Magistrates, admitted that all he had to do in the business was that he only forced the back door open with a small mortar chisel. The examination of these prisoners occupied much of the Magistrate's time, who after hearing the evidence admitted Stancer as an approver and committed the others to Northampton for trial at the next Assizes.

While conveying Woodward to Gaol he asked me who was the first that told me about the murder. On his being informed that it was Stancer, he said it was all true except that he did not commit the murder and it was the first robbery he had ever been concerned in, and he should not have been in that only as he was a bricklayer he wanted the money to take him to America.

On being arraign'd at the Bar for trial of these prisoners, the trial was postponed for eight months, to the following March assizes in consequence of the absence of two material witnesses: Mr Farrer, clerk to the Magistrates who took down the deposition, and Mr Reed, Chief Constable, both through the horse falling were pitched out of the chaise and so severely injured they were obliged to be assisted into a Post chaise and taken back home to Stamford almost in an insensible state. Ultimately the time for the trial of the prisoners came on, which occupied the whole day till 8 at night, when an additional witness, who was undergoing his sentence of imprisonment, was brought forward as to a conversation he said he had heard between Woodward and Archer. They were confined in separate yards, and as his yard of confinement was close to theirs he heard them hollowing to each other about how they strangled the woman. When this statement was made without corroboration, the Judge sent for the Governor to know how it was that such irregularities were allowed to exist. The reply was that it was an utter impossibility (altho' it was found out after the Assizes were over that "it was quite possible"). What with this statement, together with the death of a witness, and after a long retirement of the Jury, they returned a verdict of acquittal, to the surprise and astonishment of the Judge and everyone in court.

This finished the Assizes.

Joseph Reiteroffer again

In the month of September 1838, Mr Handley, an eminent Solicitor residing at Penton Hill, placed a Warrant in my hands for the apprehension of this alias Count charged with a false and malicious libel against the Marquis of Downshire and members of his family of an unpleasant nature for the purpose of extortion. This man had formerly been in this noble family's service as courier for many years and had travelled all over the continent of Europe and a great part of Africa and the most implicit confidence was placed in him.

Sometime after he had left the service of the noble Marquis he was continually importuning and making demands for large sums of money to the tune of some thousands of pounds, and finding his requests not noticed, he threatened to expose them in a way that would not be very palatable to their feelings. As no attention was paid to his idle threats, this man, out of bravado, employed two scavenger looking men to carry and exhibit over their shoulders large boards with very offensive and ugly pictures painted on them and with these boards to parade up and down in front of the house of the Marquis in Hanover

Square and its neighbourhood, followed by several men and boys, to the great annoyance of the Noble family.

This nuisance however did not last long, as the men were taken before the Magistrates and on giving up their employer's name were discharged on bail. In consequence of these proceedings Reiteroffer kept himself in a manner so secluded and out of sight of everyone that knew him, not the slightest clue could be obtained of his whereabouts. I was out early and late searching in all parts of London and displaying the greatest anxiety for my own credit's sake but in vain.

Months had passed away till at last the Marquis came to the conclusion that he was hiding in Italy not far from his native home. Not long after this a very agreeable sudden change took place in this affair, which happened while I was attending at the Mansion house the examination of a prisoner who was apprehended at Liverpool and charged on suspicion with being concerned with others in the great robbery of the Aberdeen bank at Aberdeen in Scotland, from which place I had not long arrived.

At the close of the examination, as I was about to leave, a man that I was known to came up to me, and said, "If you go to the fruiterer's shop kept by Mr Irish at No. 9 Arabella Row, Pimlico, not far from the 'Bag of Nails' you will find Reiteroffer! He has a bedroom there on the first floor back; any time after eight o'clock will do, and beware of his stiletto and pocket pistol." He added that Reiteroffer had only just arrived from abroad—and "you know as well as I do the desperate man he is." On receiving this information my informant vanished, crossing the road between the cabs and omnibuses out of my sight.

I was very excited but lost no time in conveying this news to

Bow Street to get assistance; but finding all my brother Officers were engaged out of town, I obtained Tyrol, our gaoler, and after telling him the whole of the circumstances, we got into a Hackney Coach and drove to the sign of the "White Horse", situated at that time opposite the side and present entrance to Buckingham Palace, where (under the peculiar circumstances and the knowledge I previously had of Reiteroffer's desperate characteristics) I thought it prudent to make my will, which I did in the presence of Tyrol and to which he attached his name.

We left the "White Horse" about nine o'dock, and proceeded to Arabella Row, and after reconnoitering the back of No. 9 house and seeing a light in the room indicated we returned to the front. After instructing the Coachman, it occurred to me that I should gain admittance sooner by knocking a loud rat-tat-tat than by giving a sneaking single knock, so by this means the door was instantly opened by a person from the shop whom I asked no questions but bounded, in the twinkling of an eye, followed by Tyrol, upstairs to the door on my right, which was not quite closed. As I was about placing my hand upon the handle, the door was being closed by some one inside, but my foot prevented its being shut to and I pushed it open, entered the room followed by Tyrol and upstanding in front of me like a giant stood Reiteroffer in his shirt sleeves, holding in his right hand an open razor and his face covered all over with lather and a white towel fastened under his chin.

On seeing me in he stepped back and seated himself on a chair opposite his dressing glass and laid the razor on a table, and while I was engaged in calling his attention to the warrant which I held close before him, and saying how sorry I was that it had fallen to my lot to have to execute it, Tyrol, taking advantage of the moment, possessed himself of the razor, a stiletto and a double-barrel loaded pistol laying on the table, all of which he put into his pockets. Reiteroffer saw all that he was doing, made no remark, was very reserved and rose from his seat, went to the washstand and after an ablution and drying his face, put on his neck-tie, waistcoat and coat; complained of being very unwell and asked for Brandy, but as there was none in the house I told him there was a coach waiting and if he would get into it at once it would not take long to drive to the "White Horse".

He immediately left his room with us and hurried to the Coach, which took about five minutes. I ordered a shilling tumbler of cold brandy and water, which he drank off at a draught and appeared to quite revive him. I and Tyrol had the same quantity which to us had the same effect. After being thus refreshed I directed the coachman to drive to the "Grapes" public-house in Bow Street, and having arrived there we walked upstairs where there was a strongroom with barred iron windows and a very strong door which had been made many years, in Lavender's! time, for the accommodation in case of need for the old Bow street officers in similar cases to that of mine. This room was well furnished with a capital four post bed, wash stand and every convenience. Having lodged him in safety so far I told him whatever he wished to have for his comfort he had only to ask as Mr Tyrol would attend to him. I then left him under the charge of Mr Tyrol.

This being Saturday night we had to keep him there till Monday.

On the following morning (Sunday) I went and informed Lord Marcus Hill of my proceedings, who expressed himself well satisfied with what had been done and said he should post off at once and report the news to the Marquis. In the afternoon of that day I went and relieved Tyrol of his charge for about six hours, and at nine o'clock on Monday morning when I saw the prisoner I was very much alarmed by his appearance, he at the time being without his coat and waistcoat, his shirt sleeves tucked up and sitting on a chair with his elbows on the table resting his head on his hands and apparently in a state of insensibility. His arms and hands were quite blue.

On asking Tyrol if he could account for his being in this state, he replied he had been so ever since four o'clock in the morning. I bathed his temples with vinegar and gave him some brandy, afterwards a cup of strong coffee which revived him, otherwise I should have called in a doctor. With assistance we then partly carried him downstairs and lifted him into a hackney coach and drove to the Judges Chambers, Sergeants Inn, Chancery Lane, and left him in charge of Tyrol while I went to the court where Judge Baron Gurney was presiding. I called his attention to the Warrant I held in my hand and other particulars as to the state of the Prisoner's present health in an apparent condition of unconsciousness, which I believed he was assuming as he had once on a former occasion represented and made people believe to answer his own ends, as he had been shot and wounded in a duel at the Bois de Boulogne near Paris.

On my making this statement the Baron ordered that I should be sworn, and then addressed me thus: "You are now on your oath and what you have stated you believe to be true?"

"I do, my · Lord."

Then said the Baron, "Let the prisoner be brought into court:

The prisoner was then with difficulty assisted from the coach into an arm chair and carried by four men into court, still in an unconscious state of all that was going on. I was again sworn in the Prisoner's presence and repeated my former statement which was taken down in writing by the Judge's Clerk and I signed it.

The Judge then said, 'Joseph Reiteroffer, I commit you to the New Prison, Clerkenwell."

He was then lifted by the same four men back to the Hackney Coach, and on arriving at the New Prison, as the prisoner was being assisted out by two of the prison officials he coughed and expectorated, when one of the officials remarked that from its appearance he had taken opium. He was then led to his room for confinement, and shortly afterwards the Governor visited him with the Doctor. The latter, seeing the state he was in and after examining him, ordered him immediately a warm bath and drink copiously of lemonade. The Doctor enquired of me what had been given to him since he was in custody, to which Tyrol replied that he had nothing out of the way; yesterday morning he ate two eggs and some bread and butter for breakfast and dined from a roast leg of mutton, had bitter ale in the evening, tea and toast, and after that smoked two cigars and drank two glasses of cold brandy and water and had slept in a comfortable bed till a quarter to four in the morning, after which he did not appear well. Thus so far matters terminated.

Three days afterwards a messenger was sent from the Governor to me saying that Reiteroffer had died that morning and that the Governor wished to see me soon as possible.

I went accordingly and saw the Governor, who said to me in a very solemn tone that there would be a most searching enquiry made into this matter as to how the deceased had been treated and what had been given him to drink during the time he had been in my custody. I replied that I had nothing to fear and was ready to answer any question, and the more searching the enquiry the better, for I knew that the deceased had had every comfort and that he was well attended to. I then bade the Governor good-day and left the prison.

On the following morning I received a summons to appear before Mr Baker, the Coroner, and after the Jury and the Coroner had returned from viewing the body they expressed to each other, in which the Coroner joined, "how much he resembled King Henry the Eighth".

I was the first witness examined and deposed to what I have hereinbefore stated, after which the Coroner asked me if I did not think the deceased was like King Henry the Eighth, as he and the Jury all thought he resembled him very much. I considered for a moment and replied that I could not tell, for "I never saw King Henry the Eighth and therefore I cannot say."

"Oh no," said the Coroner, "I don't suppose you ever did", at which he and the jury laughed. Then said the Coroner, "I shall not add that to your evidence."

F. Tyrol and Joseph Shackle were afterwards examined. The Jury and the Coroner then commented upon the case and returned a verdict of apoplexy caused by taking opium, but not with the intention of destroying life. These particulars having been communicated to Sir F. Roe, he complimented me for the manner and means I had taken in the apprehension and the comforts I had bestowed upon the prisoner while in custody.

This business having come to a finish I was requested by the Marquis to send in my account to Mr Handley, which was a large item. It was soon settled, and the Marquis expressed himself well satisfied, and made me a present of a £50 Bank note in addition.

The Revd. R Stephens

In the early part of the month of December 1838, when Chartism, Incendiarism and Torchlight meetings were being held in the manufacturing towns of Leigh, Bury Todmorden, Ashton under Lyne and other places, to the great terror and alarm of the respectable and peaceful part of the inhabitants, I was dispatched by order of Sir Frederick Roe to visit the above towns—make enquiries—take notes—observe and obtain what information I could as to the names of the Authors and ringleaders attending these seditious and Torchlight meetings, which, with the setting fire to the Cotton Mills, were so prevalent at the time. All I had to do, Sir Frederick said, required silence, discretion and activity—to have assistance at hand but not to cause alarm by shewing it.

One of these torch-light meetings, held at Bury, was headed by Fergus O'Connor. At the conclusion of a long seditious speech in speaking of the new Poor-law Bill, and pointing with extended arm towards a flaming torch close at hand, he exclaimed aloud to his hearers, "Look!! at that!!! it speaks a language so intelligible that no one can misunderstand, and those who are not within the hearing of my voice can comprehend the meaning of that silent monitor." In another speech at Manchester he recommended that the people should rise on a certain day simultaneously throughout the country and pass a resolution withdrawing all their money from the Savings Banks and organize a Run on any Bank for gold, and neither speak to Master nor Master's man till the "man-of-their-choice" was restored to them (great shouts of cheering from all parts of the crowd).

Another agitator, the Revd. R. Stephens, in alluding to Mr John Jowette, a Magistrate and Mill owner, said he had good ground to be afraid of Torch-light meetings, for it was a question with him if that Devil Magistrate's house would not ere long be too hot for him (hurra! hurra! and great cheering!). At another Torch-light meeting this same agitator, in addressing the mob at Leigh, said that he should be sorry to see those houses on fire, (pointing) that Church in flames and the streets deluged in blood, but "Arm yourselves, carry pikes, have two, and if any poor-law Guardian asks you for one, give it him, and with the other, six inches, for to destroy a poor-law Guardian would be doing God a service." (Great cheering.)

On another occasion, in his Chapel at Ashton under-Lyne, a large building capable of holding a large body of people, he at the conclusion of his address and looking round to his hearers said, "I perceive there are spies among this assembly, but as there is to be a collection made to night I need not tell you that you will soon be able to know who those spies are because they will not contribute anything. But woe," he said, "to that man who attempts to capture me, for I am armed with my brace of loaded pistols and polished steel dagger with its silver handle." (Under this device everyone contributed rather than he should be considered a spy.)

My readers can imagine my position altho' I was incognito, to be in company at this time with these ruffians of the lowest type.

At another speech given at Leigh he tells the people to arm them and keep their pikes and guns on their Chimney pieces so as to have them ready, and he would come over and be their leader and tell them what to do, and that if he lived at Leigh, he would take off a Poor-law-Guardian's coat, waistcoat and shirt, that he would get a barrel of Tar and he would tar him right well all over and would then get a pillow of feathers and would feather him, and that done would say to him, "Go to roost, thou Devil" and added, if he had wings and were to fly they would wonder what kind of bird he was. While he was delivering the above speech there was a constant firing of pistols, and at the top of one pike was stuck a red herring, and on another a loaf of bread; and on the top of a pole in large letters was the following

For children and Wife
We'll war to the Knife
Down with the Bastiles
Stephens for ever.

On the following day 500 Special Constables were sworn in. About this time a vast mob of Rioters assembled at Todmorden and, after pillaging Mr Greenwood's house, set it on fire. These acts of violence brought out the Military, and after the riot act had been read I was instructed to go into Fieldings Factory while the Military, about 30 in number, attended by two Magistrates were standing under arms opposite to the entrance gates to arrest a man supposed to be one of the ringleaders by the name of Thomas Sutcliff, Alias one of Tom of Light's lads.

A Parish constable who knew him went in with me, and we had not been in there very long before the constable pointed him out from about 600. As I was taking him out they were beginning to hiss and groan at me, but through the prompt and kind interference of Mr Fielding this clamor was stopped, otherwise I don't know what the consequences might have been. After bringing him out he was handed over to the authorities to be dealt with according to law.

Having accomplished this duty I was informed by the Magistrate that as my face now was so well known among the operatives, it would not any longer be safe for me to stay in Todmorden. I therefore took the hint and returned to Ashton under Lyne, where a young man, a spinner, who was in my confidence, had succeeded in gaining admission to a private room in a spinner's house where they held a discussion and raffled as to whose Mill should be fired next, Mr Saxon's or Mr Lees, both Millowners. "But we must mind what we are about," one said to another, "and to be careful of a strange man who had been watched and was seen, after he left talking to Owen the constable, at Mr Saxon's. He appears to have nothing to do but always prying about."

"From their description," said my informant, "I am sure they mean you. Therefore you had better be upon your guard, or they will serve you as they did young Ashton"—whom they shot—of Apeworth."

On receiving this caution I made myself scarce and moved my quarters to Leigh, where, in consequence of these tumultuous assemblies, Sir Frederick Roe had visited. He gave me instructions to report my doings to the Magistrates at Ashton under Lyne, and in consequence, of these reports I made to them and other information they had received from other quarters, a Warrant signed by J. B. W. Sanderson and John Kenworthy, Magistrates, was placed in my care for the arrest of the Revd. R. Stephens, one of the Chartists' leaders.

A discussion took place as to the best means to be adopted how it was to be executed without the sacrifice of human life. It required great caution, as there were some thousands of spinners who would rise to a man and come forward to resist his lawful apprehension. Under the circumstances it would not be considered safe to attempt it without the aid of Military power, inasmuch as Stephens was so idolized and worship'd by all the operatives that there was not a family in all Ashton and other places but had got his Portrait manufactured on all their tea cups, basins, plates and saucers, he was held in such high estimation by them.

At this moment the Church clock tolled the quarters and the clock struck the hour of one. The several Magistrates looked at their watches and on replacing them in their pockets one of them, Mr James Jowett, said he thought they had better adjourn the court for luncheon till two o'clock and they would on their return reconsider what was best to be done. The motion was agreed to. In less than ten minutes afterwards, while Mr Owen, the Chief Constable, Shackell and myself were looking over a wall in the Churchyard towards the direction of Dunkinfield, we saw in the distance to our great surprise the Revd. R. Stephens advancing towards us, upon which we separated and hid ourselves from his view. I concealed myself in the Porch of the Church until he passed, making his way down Stamford Street in the direction towards Manchester. I followed him in the distance, Owen and Shackell by the same rule, following me for a full half mile. Stephens never looked back but crossed the road, and I could see that he was making up to a house. I hastened my pace and saw him knock at the door, and as it was opened I was close behind him and in the passage. I told him who I was and had got a Warrant for his apprehension; we walked into the parlor, and by this time Owen and Shackell arrived.

When I had explained to him my business he wished to see the Warrant, to which I gave consent. He made an observation to the effect that he ought to consider himself highly honored by Lord John Russell! in sending such a person.

"But where are you going to take me to?" he asked.

"To Worsley," I replied.

"What," said he "to Lord Francis Egerton's?

"Yes," I said, "those are my instructions.

"Then, Mr Goddard, I want to ask a favor. As you have come upon me so suddenly will you allow me to go in the Custody of Mr Owen, our Chief Constable, and see my wife before you take me to Worsley.

I replied I could not consistently do so, but that he could write a note to his wife and I would see that a messenger should take it at once. This was consented to, and while he was writing, I slipped out the back way leaving him in custody of Owen and Shackell, while I ran to the Commercial Hotel and immediately obtained a Post Chaise which got to the door just as Stephens had finished his letter. This was no sooner done when the Landlady promised its safe delivery. This done, Shackell stepped into the Post Chaise, followed by Stephens and myself, while Owen mounted on to the Splinter-bar, so away we went.

While on our way he said, "You know, Mr Goddard, we won't have the new Poor-law bill, that won't do, and am I the only incendiary Lord John Russell has picked out; is there none other but me, because I consider I am very highly honored?" He then talked on, saying that an old Dragoon Guard admired his speeches and since he had read them it had quite alter'd his opinion, and so much did he respect him that he carried his portrait under the flap of his saddle bags "that he might think of me whenever he buckled them on."

At length we arrived at Manchester and stayed a few minutes at the hotel for refreshment. As we were retiring from the refreshment room I was met by a Magistrate, who express'd himself that it was desirable the soldiers should be called out.

"It will soon get wind and the people will be all up in arms. Look!" he said, "they are beginning to assemble already, and if you don't make haste, Stephens will be rescued."

I was astonished to see so many people gathered together in so short a space of time all round the post-chaise, on the foot pavement and up the steps to the entrance of the hotel, some enquiring what was the matter and what it was all about, so that we had considerable difficulty in pushing our way through the crowd to get into the Chaise. After being seated the postillion drove away with all speed to Worsley. .

I would here say that, before I proceed further with my narrative, I would inform my reader that after our departure with the prisoner from the hotel to Worsley, the following notice appeared in the Manchester evening papers:

We stop the press to inform our friends that the bloodhounds have laid hold of Stephens. This night's post has brought a great number of letters from Ashton, of which we give the following: viz "Manchester, Dec. 27, 1838. Gentlemen, The time is come—Stephens is arrested on some charge by the authority of a warrant from the Magistrates of Leigh: he was brought from Ashton by two officers in a chaise—they stopp'd at the Royal Hotel for refreshment and afterwards went off to

Worsley—J. Richardson."

To resume my narrative—What the Magistrates said or did after their return from luncheon to the Court at 2 o'clock I am unable to say, for the Capture I had made was so unexpected and sudden that I had not the time to inform them. On our arrival at Worsley I reported myself to Lord Francis Egerton, who said he was not able to go into the case himself without forming a Bench of Magistrates and that I had better hire a post-chaise and find Mr Smith, the Magistrate's clerk, and the Magistrates who granted the warrant.

This I found to be no easy task, with the uncertainty of finding them at home. After going a distance of about thirty miles, to Leigh and other places, I succeeded in returning to Worsley about 9 o'clock at night, when I found the place where the Magistrates held their meeting to be surrounded by a body of Dragoon Guards about 40 in number, commanded I think by Colonel Weimess. The Magistrates after sitting till midnight committed the prisoner under remand, and Owen, Shackell, the prisoner and myself were escorted by the mounted Dragoons, flourishing their drawn bright sabres under a brilliant moonlight, which, together with a hoar frost that had settled on the hedges and trees, with a deep snow upon the ground with the tramping sound of horses' hoofs on the frozen icy road, produced a very novel effect.

On our arrival at the New Bailey Prison, Manchester, about 1 a.m., the Bell was loudly rung, and after waiting nearly a quarter of an hour the strong gate was opened. The Governor appeared with two of his warders, each carrying lanterns, who, on seeing a post chaise conveyed by so strong a Military guard with drawn sabres formed in a line before the prison gates and with the smoke arising from the horses, wondered what it could be all about at such a late hour in the night.

On explaining my business I delivered over to him the prisoner with the commitment to be dealt with for further examination, which occupied the two following days, viz the 27th and 28th December, 1838. Then he was again remanded till the 3rd of January, and after a lengthy examination was committed for trial or to find bail himself in £1000 and two sureties of £500 each.

Fitzherbert Batty Esq.

On Monday morning April 8th 1839 at a quarter before 11 o'clock a pair-horse post-chaise was driven up to the door opposite to where I was standing at Bow Street Office, and the first thing attracting my attention was two human naked feet and legs exposed. One foot and leg up to the calf were out of one window in the front and the fellow to it in like manner out of the other, both resting on the sash frame. Behind them in a sitting posture was a well dressed stout robust dark eyed good looking man, who on seeing me beckon'd me towards him.

As I advanced he drew in his legs, opened the door, pushed down the steps and jumped out, holding his boots and stockings in his hands, and enquired of me if I was an Officer. "Because if you are," said he, "I wish you to introduce me to the Chief Magistrate, as I have come over during the night from Jamaica in a hurricane and I must see him on a matter of great importance to the people and to the Country, for you know and you must see that I am the finest man in the world and there was no man so handsome, and he would give me ten thousand pounds, but I must see the Magistrate."

At this instant I saw Sir Frederick Roe coming, who was let in by Goodson the door-keeper into the private room, followed by me.

"What is all this about?" enquired Sir Frederick. "Who is that person in the waiting room so well dressed and without his shoes and stockings? Did the post-chaise standing outside the door bring him?"

I informed Sir Frederick of what had passed previous to his coming. "Why he must be a lunatic," said Sir Frederick, "broke out of some Asylum."

Mr Vine, one of the Office Clerks, came, and Sir Frederick ordered that I should bring him before him.

I withdrew and informed. the hurricane traveller that if he followed me I would introduce him to the chief Magistrate.

He knelt down and with clasped. hands exclaimed, "The word as it is written is coming to pass," and on rising said, "I will see him and rejoice at the sight of him."

I asked him for his name.

"O," he said, "my outside name is Fitzherbert Batty Esq,. and in that name he was so introduced. "But before going into this matter I must," he said, "have the Bible, for you must know I am Jesus Christ, and that George the 4th who had risen was to be married to his daughter."

Sir Frederick would hear no more and told me to have assistance and keep him in security and find out who his friends were.

I took him to the Garrick's Head Hotel as also his ponderous Portmanteau, which contained some valuable India Shawls, some dozens of Silk Handkerchiefs, Jewellery, Shirts, etc. I provided him with very comfortable apartments, and on enquiry found that he had just arrived in one of the monthly liners from

New York, and the weather during the voyage had been very severe.

I took him to Blacklands House and the following is from Mr Hall, Medical Superintendent, Blacklands House, abstracted from the books of that establishment, viz

Fitzherbert Batty Esq., aged 46, Barrister at Law, from Spanish Town, Jamaica, admitted as a patient to Blacklands House the 11th April 1839 upon Certificate from Doctor Munro and Doctor Warburton, discharged cured May the 9th 1839. Brought in by Henry Goddard, a Bow Street Officer, the 8th of April, 1839.

Concerning the Emperor of Russia

On his first arrival in this Country in the beginning of May 1839, when he was the Grand Duke Alexander, application was made by Baron Benkhausen, the Russian Consul, to Sir Frederick Roe for the services of two of his Principal Police Officers, as a protection from Annoyances to his Imperial Highness during his stay in England; so as to be always in close attendance and to escort him on horseback or otherwise wheresoever it was the pleasure of the Grand Duke to visit.

The application being granted, I and Ballard received instructions to proceed at once to Mivart's Hotel in Brook Street, Grosvenor Square, where we were only just in time to witness the arrival of the Grand Duke, Count Orloff, Lord Torrington and a numerous staff. (I here beg to remark, that in all my travels over the four quarters of the earth and Australia, I don't think I ever saw two finer men than the Grand Duke and Count Orloff.)

Our duties commenced on the following day by being in attendance at the Russian Chapel in Welbeck Street, the Zoological Gardens and at Prince Pozzodi Borgo's in the evening, and afterwards from day to day to the end of the month as hereinafter mentioned, chiefly on Horseback with but few exceptions, Ballard at the rear of the carriage on one side and I on the other so as to be in readiness to prevent Petitions being thrown in and other annoyances by beggars running and laying hold of the carriage door importuning for alms. Several such attempts were made but were frustrated by keeping a good look out and by the activity of our horses.

I and Ballard continued our attendance and among the places His Imperial Highness visited were Westminster Abbey, Tothill Fields Prison, Chelsea Hospital, Newgate, Christ's Hospital, St Paul's Church, Egyptian Hall, The Duke of Cambridge's Royal Stables, The Ball given by Her Majesty at Buckingham Palace, Woolwich Artillery ground, Greenwich Hospital, Italian Opera with the Grand Duke sitting in the same Box with the Queen, The Penitentiary, Millbank, Whitbread's Brewery, The House of Commons, Bridgewater House, Duchess of Gloucester, Epsom Races when Bloomsbury won the Derby during a severe snowstorm, The Royal Mint and witnessed the process of coining, The Opera, The Marquis Anglesea, The Duke of Wellington, Horticultural Fete at Chiswick, Russian Ambassador's, Star & Garter, Richmond, The Review at Wormwood Scrubs, to a dinner given at the London Tavern, by the Russian Company.

The Grand Duke then left Mivart's and proceeded to Oxford in three of the Queen's Carriages; I following in company with the Chevalier Benkhausen, leaving his Office at Argyl Street at 2 o'clock in the morning, travelling by post chaise all night, arriving at Oxford to breakfast at 9; afterwards attending at the different Colleges: same evening at 9 o' clock after seeing the Duke set into his carriage, I mounted on to the seat behind, with one of Her Majesty's servants, each carriage had four horses with two Postillions. The changes occupied but little time, all be on the alert. On arriving at Mivart's at 10 minutes before 3 o'clock in the morning, I jumped from my seat and was at the door of the Hotel before the carriage door was opened. His imperial Highness, seeing me standing at the entrance to the Hotel in passing, expressed his astonishment, and made this remark: "Why, how did you come to get here before me on the road, as I left you at Oxford! it is very odd!" —and after saying these words bade me good morning.

Next day the Grand Duke attended the Drawing-Room, after that, out on horseback—at night at the Marquis of Landsdown's, then to the Countess of Pembroke's, next evening at Labloche's concert, next day at the Hippodrome Races at which the Duke presented a Hundred Guinea Silver Cup.

Now as Ballard and I were well mounted during all these visits, altho' there was a great gathering of people, we had very little difficulty in keeping the course clear by the production of our bright brass staves and with civil requests for the people to stand back, which they in perfect good humour obeyed without a murmur.

When the Races were finished and soon after our return to Mivart's, the Grand Duke sent a Messenger to say that he wanted to see me. When I saw him he was standing in the Stableyard leading into Davies Street and he asked to look at the Staff I exhibited at the Races. On presenting and examining it for a few minutes, he said, "What an extraordinary thing that the sight of this should have such control over the people."

The same day we visited Mr Theobald's, a great breeder of horses at Stockwell; at night, Lord Londonderry's. The next day we visited the Queen at Windsor Castle, and the next were with her Majesty at Ascot Races; the following day at a Review in Windsor Park, afterwards at dinner with the Queen, when toasts were given to the Emperor of Russia, King of the Netherlands, and the Queen. The next day he returned to London and went to Marlboro' House and the Duke of Wellington's.

The next and last day, the 31st, the Duke left at one o'clock, arriving at Deptford Dock Yard at 2 o'clock, boarded the Fire Brand Steamer, receiving at the same time a hearty cheer from a large body of Marines and the Officers in Command; when the Steamer left for Rotterdam.

The Reader will be surprised to hear that after a lapse of 35 years, when the Emperor returned to this country in May 1874, he quickly recognised me while I was on duty at the House of Lords. The Emperor paid his visit there accompanied by the Duchess of Edinburgh leaning on his arm, attended by some of the Royal Family. Lord Torrington called the Emperor's attention to me, who at once exclaimed, I recollect you very well indeed, Goddard," and, after exchanging a few words about the different places I had accompanied him to in 1839, His Majesty passed on.

The Eglington Tournament

In the early part of August 1839, Mr Pratt, Camp Equipage Maker to her Majesty, made application in behalf of Lord Eglington to Sir Frederick Roe, the Chief Magistrate, for his permission to allow two of his principal Police Officers to be in attendance at Eglington Castle, during the forthcoming Tournament.

Sir Frederick, in glancing his eye round the office; and seeing that Ballard and myself were in attendance, called us forward, and enquired whether we had any engagement that was likely to call us from London, "because," said he, "this gentleman"—pointing to Mr Pratt—"is making application for the attendance of two Officers at Eglington Castle, during the Tournament, which from what I have heard will be a very grand affair; and if both of you are disengaged from any other business, you have my sanction to go."

We replied that our hands were quite untied.

"Very well," said Sir Frederick, "you had better retire to another room with Mr Pratt, and make your arrangements, and after you have one so, come to me.

We retired, and Mr P. informed us that it was Lord Eglington's wish that we were to spare no expense, but that we must take all necessary precautions—as there would be much valuable property exposed—so as to prevent the possibility of the light-fingered gentry congregating for the purpose of exercising their calling in the vicinity of the Tilting Grounds, as well as the interior of the castle, and its surroundings.

After discussing this important matter over for half an hour, we came to the determination to adopt the following scheme: first that Ballard and myself would make it our business to visit the flash houses and other haunts resorted to by thieves, denominated under the cognomen of Swell Mobsmen, in and about London, as well as at Birmingham Manchester and Liverpool, so as to apprise the ringleaders of our engagement, of what was coming to pass, and at the same time warning them that if they had any regard for themselves, and their liberty, not to venture their calling at the forthcoming Eglington Tournament, as our orders were (we would say) most rigid, that is to say to lock up all well known suspected characters, be they male or female.

Our consultation having now come to an end, there was nothing else left but to return to our Chief Magistrate and communicate to him our scheme. After having paid great attention, and considering it over, he fully concurred in our views, and wished us every success.

Having now got Sir Frederick's approval, we arranged to go on the following night and pay our first visit to the Sol's Arms in Wych Street at the end of Drury Lane, kept by old Ben Lewis, being a noted resort for swell thieves of the first class, denominated Swell Mobsmen: and on going into the back parlor, the first batch we came against was the notorious Bill

Caughty, and Elephant Smith, remarkable for his large proportions, Jack Vanderville, the notorious Burglar, who drove his own Cab, with a very fast trotting horse, deaf Brown Ned Eggerton of pick-pocket notoriety, and several others, who at the time of our entry were engaged playing at cards, while others were tossing for sovereigns. I need not say that our sudden presence put a stop to their gambling, and for a few seconds all were silent, and looking at each other's countenances, wondering among themselves who was wanted. At this moment the door from the outside was opened by Ben Lewis, who, on putting in his appearance, quietly enquired was there any thing the matter.

Ballard replied, "No, Ben, it's all right, don't be alarmed, but keep yourself easy, and we will tell you."

At this moment the company appeared in great suspense, and I then disclosed the nature of our visit. One and all their countenances brightened up, and they thanked us for the manly and straight-forward manner in which we had come forward to give them the warning. Bill Caughty called them to order and asked to be allowed to speak, not only for himself, but for all. Addressing us by our names, he said, "You may depend and make sure that none of us here will trouble you at Eglington with our presence, and that we will not only keep away ourselves, but will make it our business to go the rounds, and tell others of the same calling, to do the same and keep away."

Having executed part of our errand so far, we bade them good night, followed by the Landlord, who invited us into the bar parlor, and drew the cork from a bottle of champagne, of which we partook out of tumblers, and most delicious wine it was. I must here inform my readers, that it is policy sometimes for Police Officers to be civil and obliging to the latter, for in many instances they give behind-back information which often leads to the most beneficial results.

And as we were bidding old Ben good night, he whispered and told us what a singular circumstance it was, for it was only about half an hour before we arrived they were talking among themselves about going to Eglington, and intended to take three of their ladies.

"But this," said he, "what I have told you must be kept dark; and I think your coming here and talking to them in the way you have will stop their game, and a good many others as well. Good night!" said he.

"Good night!" we replied, and came away; and this finished that night's adventure.

After this we were occupied in following up the same system at all the Bash houses, in and about the Metropolis, as well as at Birmingham, Manchester, and Liverpool, finishing with the same result of promises as at the Sol's Arms.

This piece of performance on our part having come to an end, we proceeded on the 26th August on board the Royal George to Ardrossan, arriving at Eglingten next day, and in the afternoon went to Irving to be present at the swearing in of 200 special constables.

It is now just upon 40 years age since this Tournament was given, and it may be read with some little degree of interest to the rising generation. This Tournament excited the most extraordinary interest throughout the Kingdom.

About 15 steamers had been advertised to leave the Clyde for Irving and Ardrossan, and in addition to the steamers, one to arrive from Liverpool, Ireland, and other places, some of which were chartered for the occasion, in all there would be about twenty steamers at the Ports in the neighbourhood of

Eglington. To accommodate in addition to what the castle would hold was erected close to, a large tent about 300 feet long, part to be occupied as a dining room, and part for a ballroom, with about 20 feet in the centre for a saloon—the lists of 650 feet long, and 250 wide with a barrier in the centre for tilting 4 and a half feet high and 300 feet long, and the grand stand erected at a distance of about 60 feet back from the centre, commanding a full view, which was very conspicuous, beautifully adorned and carved in gilt Grecian style. Irving, Ardrossan. Saltcoats. Kilmarnock and Kilwinnie and all the farm houses in the neighbourhood were crowded with visitors, every bed was taken and numbers were obliged to bivouac under the trees.

Among the arrivals were Prince Napoleon, Marquiss of London-derry, Waterford, Lord Glasgow, Prince Esterhazy, and a host of others. It was calculated that some thousands would attend, and consequently numerous preparations had to be made, stately tents striped with red, black and blue, with all the appearance of grim waged war about to commence; ornaments of the time of Louis the 14th, Barons of beef, Haunches of venison, legions of all sorts of game, and wildfowl. In the scenes of the castle, there was revelling, eating, drinking, carousing and laughing, every room and gallery was filled with people buckling Harness; Knights, Squires, ladies and damsels were hurrying through the corridors, and crowding the staircases and halls of the castle, while a regiment of Cooks was preparing the viands for the banquet, and the piles of iced champagne, hock and claret, the corks of which were momentarily extracted. The company was dressed in the costume of the time of Henry the 8th and Queen Elizabeth, adorned in great display with diamonds.

In conclusion I have only to say that in consequence of the precautions that were taken in the first instance, they had the desired effect inasmuch as that there was not a complaint reported of a piece of gold or silver large or small missing, nor a diamond or pearl lost; so that previous to our departure his Lordship came forward, shook hands and congratulated us for the manner in which the duty was done, and gave each of us a handsome check, independent of our charges, and a letter to Sir F. Roe, paying us a great compliment, and expressing satisfaction at the manner in which we had done our duty.

Delicate Enquiries

On the following day, after my return from Eglington to London, I was dispatched on an important errand of a confidential nature at the instance of Lord—— to institute enquiries at Bath, in consequence of some very unpleasant reports affecting the honor of his Lordship's wife whose absence caused some very painful feelings in his mind.

These enquiries led me to Portsmouth, Bristol, Southampton, Havre de Grace, Rouen and Paris, where, after very considerable difficulty I found the object of my pursuit to have taken up her residence in one of the Entresols in Rue de Rivoli. With the assistance of Monsieur Rousell, Chief of the Paris Police, her Ladyship was kept under observation for a long period. It was seen that a gentleman, a Mr C—— who was staying very near, at Maurice's Hotel, paid frequent visits and at all hours, sometimes as late as one o'clock in the morning, besides meeting her at certain distances and making it appear as if by accident, then seating himself by her side in the carriage paying visits to different parts of Paris and its environs. All these movements and some of a suspicious nature were made known to his Lordship.

As this affair was of an entirely private nature I feel myself bound to be for ever silent, but the reason why I feel disposed in bringing the above case forward is to show the reader, by way of interlude, how it happens that sometimes when engaged in one enquiry one is led on to the foundation of another. For while so engaged I found that I myself was being continually kept under observation by a person of gentlemanly bearing and superior address and who—from his manner towards me—appeared desirous of making my acquaintance, whilst I at the same time had some difficulty, under all circumstances, to keep myself as much secluded from him as possible.

He first addressed me while I was taking refreshment at the Fountain Hotel, Portsmouth, when he said he had the pleasure of seeing me at the York House Hotel, Bath.

I replied, "Yes, I have been there"; and seeing from his manner that he wanted to be inquisitive I rose from my seat and agitated the bellrope to ask the waiter for my bill, and moved about to get out of his way and went and booked myself to go by the Rocket coach to Southampton. There my enquiries led me to the Royal George, and about 9 o'clock, while taking supper in a very quiet manner, to my astonishment this same gentleman put in his figure head, and seating himself in an opposite box to mine, ordered oysters, bread, butter and stout. On his looking round he recognized me, and with a nod exclaimed, "Why, how strange; here we are again!"

I answer'd, "Yes! and I have been supping off Oysters, and most delicious they were."

"Dear me," said he, "I have ordered the same thing."

After this short conversation our eyes continually met each other, and while waiting for his oysters he endeavoured to force his conversation to find out who I was and the business I might be on. In order to get rid of him I left my seat saying I had an appointment and bade him good night, and saw no more of him till about 3 o'clock in the afternoon of the next day when I was compelled to go on board the Caliph steamer bound for Havre de Grace. I had not been on board more than ten minutes before my eyes beheld him advancing in a great bustle, just in time with not ten seconds to spare to get on board, and before he looked round the steamer was leaving the Dock.

I kept from his view like playing at hide and seek for about two hours, when he spied me in the saloon and came up to me and with a whisper said that he was going to Havre and he presumed that I was going there too as the Ship was not bound for any other Port!

I said, "Yes!"

"What Hotel do you put up?" he asked.

I replied, "I cannot tell, as I shall have to be guided by circumstances."

"Yes," he said, "I suppose that all depends upon the nature of your business

I said "No, I have got friends to call upon."

By this time dinner was on the table, and seeing there was a vacant seat between two gentlemen, I embraced the opportunity and so got rid of him for nearly all the evening till it was time to turn into my berth. It was a long time before I could get myself off to sleep on account of the rolling of the Vessel against a strong head-wind with a heavy sea, so that very few of the passengers could get any sleep at all.

Next morning I prepared myself not to have any more of his interruptions by taking from my portmanteau a book, entitled The Wandering Jew, which I had begun to read in order to free myself from his annoyances. I had not been so occupied more than ten minutes than he was again on to me asking how I had slept and what a dreadful tempestuous night we had passed and how I felt and all manner of questions and where I was going to after I left Havre.

At last I was almost obliged to be rude, saying that as I should not have much time to read after landing at Havre I must make the best use of my time as I very much wished to finish the book. So I walked away from him and seated myself in an out-of-the-way part of the vessel. He seemed to take the hint, and we had very little to say to each other till about 10 o'clock the following morning when we entered the Port of Havre. He then wished me a very good morning, saying, "There is no doubt we shall see each other in the course of the day."

I put up at Wheelers Hotel, and just as I was sitting down to dine he came in, took off his hat and after hanging it on the hook took his seat directly opposite to me. Rubbing his hands, he looked at me hard in the face and with a smile he exclaimed, "By G— this is marvellous to think how we run against each other! How long may you be going to stay here?" he said.

I replied, "Only for the night."

"And where then?"

"Oh I" I replied, "perhaps Rouen."

The devil you are! Why, that is the very place I am going to on purpose to see the Cathedral and the statue of Joan of Arc. Pray what time do you leave? Do you sail by the Normandie or go by the Diligence?"

I said I could not tell, it might be early in the morning.

Dinner being over, I left wishing him good night saying that I was going to call upon an old acquaintance. Although I remained after for two days in Havre I saw no more of him till I went on board the Normandie, and after landing us at Rouen he bade me goodbye, and from that hour I saw no more of him. I proceeded on to Paris where the business I was upon kept me for six weeks, when I returned to London.

About five months afterwards at 10 o'clock one morning, as I was preparing to leave home and while brushing my hat in the passage of No. 12 Robert Street, Hampstead Road, I heard the hard clashing noise of horses' hoofs advancing at a fast trotting pace with the rumbling rush of carriage wheels like unto a fire-engine. They made a sudden stop in front of my house, followed by a loud rat-tat-tat such as Flunkeys usually give.

I opened the door and was asked by a tall man in livery, "Does one Mr Goddard live here?"

At the same time my eyes were directed to a gentleman who was leaning forward through the carriage window who, with a loud voice and looking towards me, said, "Do you remember me?"

"Yes!" I replied, "at Havre and Southampton in September last."

"Aha, I see you know me."

On alighting he gave me one of those hearty shakes of the hand (and although it is now near forty years ago I have never forgotten it), at the same time whispering in my ear, "I want to talk to you on an important matter! can I come in?"

I nodded, signifying "Yes! with great pleasure" (at same time wondering in my own mind what it could all be about). He turned round and told his servant to come back with the carriage in an hour, so indoors we went. Before being seated he looked round with his sharp and intelligent eye and directed the doors to be closed—(I said to myself what on earth is coming!)—when he began and stated as follows:

"One morning towards the end of last August, while I was standing outside the entrance to the York House Hotel, Bath, a gentleman called my attention and pointing towards you after you had walked past us said, 'Do you see the back of that man going along there and do you know who he is? Because if you don't I can tell you.' He then told me your name and the office you were attached to in London and remarked, 'There must be something very important in hand or he would not be walking at that pace.'

Those observations caused such an impression at the time on my mind," he said, "that I thought you were employed in making enquiries into some of my family's private affairs. For you must know that I have a son who is entitled to considerable property, but unfortunately about two years ago he formed an acquaintance with a poor girl whose mother was Post-mistress at Ealing and got married to her unknown to me or any of my family. He at the time was not of age, and when I heard of it I was almost driven mad, it made such an impression on me, so much so that I was determined to take him away thinking as he was under age his marriage was not legal. So I purchased a Commission for him and sent him out to India.

And now what I want you to do with another's assistance is to keep her under strict and careful observation, noting down all the places she goes to and who she meets, whether they be male or female, from the time she leaves home in the morning till her return at night. I know it will cost a heap of money, but cost what it might, I must," he said, "have it done."

At the same time he handed me over three ten-pound notes and said, "There, when you have expended these don't hesitate or be bashful, and I will repeat the dose."

After this I consented to undertake his wishes.

He then gave me a full description of the lady and her whereabouts and said I could see him at the Portland Hotel, Great Portland Street, any evening after eight o'clock.

This interview lasted about an hour, and as my clock was striking eleven his carriage was announced to be in readiness at the door. He gave me another hearty shake of the hand saying, "Well, goodbye till I see you again, which I hope will not be long."

On the following day I made an arrangement with Ballard, one of my brother-officers, and we very soon found out the movements of the lady. She left her mother's house from three to four days a week to be in time for the Ealing Omnibus that arrived at Hyde Park corner of Tyburn-Gate-side every day at 12 o'clock; so, after making ourselves acquainted as to her identity and to prevent suspicion, we planted ourselves every day against Tyburn Gate watching the arrival of the Omnibus, being seated in Black Jim's Cab. (This "Black Jim" was a very wide-awake man who drove a very fast horse and was well known to us all Bow Street Officers for his general intelligence and good tact; he invariably took up his stand in the Rank at Charles Street near Bow Street office, and from one and the other of us was kept very lucratively employed.)

We had not been seated long before we observed a gentleman drive to the corner of Park Lane in a dashing Tilbury, looking steadfastly towards Tyburn Gate. In a few minutes the Ealing Omnibus arrived and made a stop between Tyburn Gate and Park Lane, when we saw the lady leave the Omnibus making her way towards the Tilbury. She had a fancy-dog, leading it by a scarlet riband, and she herself enveloped in a very handsome large black silk cloak.

On her reaching Park Lane the gentleman shook hands with

and kissed her and assisted her into the Tilbury and drove off at a rapid pace, followed by us, on to the "Old Swan" in the Kent Road. After baiting the horse and taking some refreshment they pursued their way without making any further stop till we saw them at a distance drive into the yard of the Bull Inn Hotel at Dartford. After this, we told "Black Jim" to bait his horse and take his dinner at a public house which was not far off and we would come and see him in about an hour. In the mean time we went to the Bull Inn and, taking a biscuit with some soda water and brandy, ordered a roast fowl for dinner to be ready at four o'clock. We afterwards saw our driver and told him to make himself and his horse comfortable and we would see him at 7 o'clock.

At four o'clock we returned to the Bull, and our dinner was served up to us in a small private room. While indulging ourselves over a delicious bottle of Champagne we succeeded in obtaining from the waiter in a round-about way that a lady and gentleman who arrived in a Tilbury a short time back were going to stay all night. This information gave Ballard and me a holiday for the remainder of the day, and as we did not know what movements the party intended to make on the following day, we instructed "Black Jim" to remain where he was for the night. We returned to the Bull at 9 o'clock, took supper and ordered our beds.

Now, as "Black Jim" was in our secrets he initiated and got himself acquainted with the Ostler of the "Bull Yard", and from him he found out the Tilbury was ordered to be in readiness at 12 o'clock to return to London. This gave us time to have a late breakfast, so after we had finished, we invited the Landlord into our room and told him in a confidential way who we were, and our business, and called his attention as to the state of the bedroom occupied by the Tilbury party. He then rung the bell for the chambermaid, who, in answer to our questions, said that with the exception of ourselves there was only one other bed occupied, and that was by the lady and gentleman who came yesterday afternoon in the Tilbury. We then told her to make a note of the circumstances and identity, as she would on some future day be called upon to give evidence of the fact.

The Landlord and his Wife's attention were also called and to be particular in keeping this matter to themselves, which they did to the strict letter.

We then paid our Bill, and at 12 o'clock the parties stepped into the Tilbury and drove away at a swinging pace towards London, we following, keeping some distance behind till they pulled up at the "Swan" as before, to bait; and as we saw they had no suspicion of us,"Black Jim" baited his horse at the Swan also. In a quarter of an hour they stepped into the Tilbury, driving over London Bridge to a very romantic and pretty cottage situated at Hornsey Rise. After ringing the Stable yard bell the two gates were immediately opened by a groom who led the horse in and closed the gates, which hid the parties from further view. Thinking that "Black Jim" who, after having played his part so well, had had enough of it, we discharged him by paying him ten shillings more than his demand, which satisfied him, and we thanked each other and bade one another good afternoon, leaving Ballard and self to watch the day out.

After keeping the cottage under observation for several hours, as some clock in the distance was striking eight, we saw the gates opened and the same gentleman with the lady by his side drive through. With a rapid pace they were soon out of our sight, leaving us to make enquiries as to who this gentleman was. We soon ascertained it was a Mr Thorn, the proprietor of a large establishment carrying on the business of an Oil and Italian warehouseman in Holborn and this Cottage was his country residence. Having now considered we had finished the business so far, after two days' hard work and anxiety to our satisfaction, we walked away into the Holloway Road and got into a cab to go home. On our way it was arranged that I should call on Mr Morgan's Solicitor (Mr. Boyes) in Ely Place, Holborn Hill at 10 o'clock the next morning to report the result of our observations for the last two days.

Having done so, to the delight and gratification of Mr Boyes, our enquiries for the time ceased, till about a fortnight afterwards, when Mr Boyes requested my attendance at his Office for the purpose of writing down my deposition. I attended in pursuance of his request, and after being detained for half an hour he expressed himself sorry that in consequence of pressure of business he must make an appointment for some other day. This was about 12 past 11a.m. As I was leaving his Office, and closing the outer door after me, I saw Mr Thorn, the gentleman before described, pass by, and go into a lawyer's Office four doors above. I waited at the corner of Ely Place for half an hour, when I saw him leave, and I followed him at a fast walking pace to the corner of Kings Road, Grays Inn Lane, when he engaged a Cab, got in and drove away. I did not follow him but took the number of the Cab.

On that same afternoon at four o'clock, as Ballard and I had nothing to do, we took into our heads that we would pass the remainder of the day away by taking a stroll to see what we could at the Cottage in Hornsey Rise. As we were walking by the House of Correction, Coldbath Fields, opposite to, was a

Cab-stand, and at the hind end of this Cab-rank my eye caught the number of the Cab I had seen drive away from the corner Kings Road in the morning.

"Hello!" I exclaimed to Ballard, who was by my side, "why look, there's the same Cab I saw Thorn get into this morning. I know it by its number"—and on referring to my pocket book it corresponded.

"Is it possible?" said Ballard.

"Yes," I replied, "look here at my book!"

We then made no more to do but walked up to the Cab. Seeing the driver was not there, we enquired of the waterman and found he was in the public house opposite, tossing with others and going the odd man who should pay for a pot of beer. We asked if he was engaged and he replied no. We then got into his cab, and before starting told him to set us down at the Public house in Museum Street close to the British Museum.

"Do you know it?" I asked.

"Yes," he said, "quite well, for the Landlord is my Uncle."

"Drive on, then," said Ballard.

No sooner was the word given than off he went at a slashing pace, and after setting us down at his uncle's door and paying him a shilling over his fare we invited him to take a glass of ale. It was at this instant he was asked if he recollected taking up a gentleman about 12 o'clock today in his Cab from the rank at the corner of Kings Road.

"Yes, I do," he replied, "quite well. I drove him to the University Hotel, Grafton Street, Gower Street, and when the waiter came to open the cab-door the gentleman, instead of getting out, gave him a letter. I afterwards put the gentleman down at Shoolbred's in Tottenham Court Road and that finished the job."

We thanked him for the information, took his address and told him to make a note of the date as it was possible he might be wanted to make the same statement at some future day.

At seven o'clock that same evening Ballard and I went to this Hotel and ordered of the waiter Coffee with boiled eggs and Anchovie toast well buttered, and in the course of a quarter an hour it was served up to our satisfaction. Soon afterwards we got into conversation with the waiter and found from his answers that the gentleman who called this morning in a Cab with the letter was for a lady who had taken apartments three days ago, and that she was confined yesterday and had got a little boy. The doctor and nurse were with her now, but who she was he did not know.

We asked no further questions, paid our bill and departed. After we left, Ballard and I talked the matter over. We had our suspicions that it must be lady from Ealing, because we said to each other "See how she was dressed when we saw her, always enveloped in a large black silk cloak."

"The reason of that must be that she was enceinte," said Ballard, "and before we go to see Mr Morgan and the Lawyer we had better go to Ealing and find out whether she is there, and if not, how long she has been away."

Accordingly we went to Ealing to institute enquiries and was informed that she had not been seen at home for the last four days, but was seen to go away in a one-horse fly, with a large trunk.

On receiving this information we felt certain that we were right in our conjectures and our suspicions confirmed. Away we went that evening at eight o'clock to report to Mr Morgan all that had taken place since my eye had caught the number of the Cab opposite to the house of correction to the time of our now seeing him.

After telling him as before stated and looking steadfastly at us he said, "What Ferrets, what Devils you are to get at it in the way you have done; what would you like to take, or shall I order some oysters?"

"Yes," I said, "they will be a treat."

I need not say that we made a splendid supper for they were most delicious. It was then arranged for us to meet at the Lawyer's by 11 o'clock the following day.

The next day came, and we met and our statement to the Lawyer truly astonished him. He thought that the history about the Cab was marvellous.

In due course the lady at the University Hotel was identified to be the same we had been following up, and the wife of the person who brought his case for the object of obtaining a divorce into the House of Lords. After the case had been fully gone into, it was proved that at the time the Father separated the son from his wife and, dispatching him to India in so sudden a manner and leaving her without provision, or the common necessaries of life, their Lordships thought it was a hard case. Lord Brougham fully agreed with them and made the following remarks, "that as this poor woman was left without resources down to the present time for nearly two years, he would not consent to a divorce unless the husband made a settlement on her for life of £300 per annum"; which was agreed to. After all these matters were arranged and the husband having obtained his divorce, the wife got married to Mr Thorn, and with the profits from his business, together with her settlement, enabled them to live in a state of comfort.

Gold Robbery

It was about eight o'clock at night in the early part of January 1841, when I held the appointment of Chief Constable for the County of Northampton, I was visited by a messenger who stated that he had come from Mr Whitworth the Banker and was anxious to see me on an important matter and not a moment must be lost. On this reprcsentation, I accompanied the Messenger to the Bank, when I was informed by Mr Whitworth that a serious Robbery had been committed by his Confidential Clerk (Thomas Haslock). "Taking with him over one Thousand Pounds in gold he left here," he said, "soon after banking hours on Saturday night. In consequence of his non-appearance on Monday morning at the usual time I sent to enquire after him at his home and was informed that he had left there on Saturday night last, taking his carpet bag leaving a message that he was going to Birmingham on business and should not return till Monday night. This aroused my suspicions and not till then did I find out that I was robb'd. I then had enquiries made at Birmingham which has caused much delay, and as I have not heard any thing of him, I have applied for your services and advice to know how I had better act under these painful circumstances."

On my asking how the robbery was effected Mr Whitworth replied, "According to the rule of the establishment it was Haslock's duty after closing hours to deposit all the Cash in the iron Safe and bring me the key. This he gave me at six o'clock when I was at dinner. Strangely enough, however, I did not discover the Robbery until two or three hours after the safe was opened yesterday (Monday) morning."

After hearing this statement and considering the matter I gave it as my opinion that no doubt he had made for the Continent with the intention of going to Havre and embark from there to America. Mr Whitworth join'd in these views, and having supplied me with the means it was arranged that I should proceed at once by the night's Birmingham Mail Train, due at Blisworth at half Past Twelve, "so that by going," he said, "in Shaw's Fly that leaves the Angel at half past 11 you will be in good time."

Having come to these arrangements, I returned home and prepared myself for the journey, and after seating myself in the Fly and being the only Passenger I proceeded on my way. It was a Cold Freezing tempestuous and dark night, It was snowing hard at the time with a Cutting North East wind, and as the Fly was descending the steep hill of Huntsbury about a mile from the Town of Blisworth down came the horse and upsetting the vehicle left it in a snow drift about a foot in depth. The coachman was thrown from his seat, one of the shafts was broken, and both the lamps being smashed we were left in total darkness. While the Horse was kicking and plunging the Coachman with great difficulty got to his head, and I in no enviable position inside endeavoured baggage in hand to make my escape overhead out at the broken glass window frame; when I had succeeded, I forced my way through snow knee deep to assist the Coachman, and to free the Horse. We had to cut the traces and other parts of the harness, which was no idle work for we had no help at hand, and it was a dark Midnight with the wind howling through the branches of the Trees whilst the violence of the storm was momentarily increasing. At last with considerable difficulty we succeeded in freeing the Horse, and left the Fly, as it fell on its side. Then as there was no time to be lost, the Coachman mounted the Horse while I managed to get on behind, making our way as best we could to Blisworth Station. Here we found that the Train had not yet arrived although it was then one o'clock or half an hour behind time.

Neither the Coachman nor myself most fortunately felt any the worse after our Midnight disaster, and when the hand of the clock dial pointed to the stroke of two the Coachman, tired out and saying that he had quite enough of it, remounted his Horse, wished me good luck and good morning and then rode away through the storm, towards the scene of the Accident, while I on this bitter night waited till nearly six o'clock, the Train having been delayed on its way in consequence of the heavy fall of snow. It was nearly 10 o'clock before it arrived at Euston Station or five and a half hours behind the usual time, thus causing me to wait in London all day till the starting from the Golden Cross, Charing Cross, of the Defiance Night Mail for Dover, where I arrived in front of the Ship Hotel about six o' clock on the following morning.

I at once began making enquiries for a clue, and obtaining my Passport proceeded on board the Steamer to Calais. After instituting further Inquiries there I left and travelled by Diligence to St. Omer, from thence to the Hotel de l'Europe at

Lille, where I obtained some vague information that a Gentleman answering the description had been, but he had left there a few days ago, by the day Diligence to Arras. Thus informed I proceeded on by the night Diligence for that place and ascertained at the Hotel de l'Union that the person described was an Englishman, for it was particularly noticed that he could not understand French or French money. He left there, they said, some days ago by the Morning Diligence for Dieppe, from which latter place I took my departure again at night, and kept on his track to Havre, Rouen and other places and ultimately to St. Malo.

Here again from information received I went to the British Consul, and on calling his attention to the case, he remarked that about a week since the Proprietor of the Hotel de la Paix introduced a young gentleman to him saying that he could not understand what he wanted, not being able to speak the language, but he thought he had plenty of English Gold. "Upon his introduction and producing his Passport as a Mr William Jones we enter'd into conversation, when he told me that he was going to take a Continental tour for about a fortnight before he went to America and that he should like to have a companion who understood French, adding that he would make him a present and pay his expences for the time he remain'd in France. After a little further conversation it was agreed that my son should accompany him, and they left here," he said, "as I understood for Rennes and afterwards went on to Tours. If you take that Route," he said, "I dare say you will find him. In the mean time I will write to the Prefect at Tours to detain him until your arrival."

Let it be remembered that travelling was a very different kind of thing from what it is now. On this information I started by the Malleposte, arriving at Rennes on the following day, where on further enquiring I found that I was on his track again, but had to wait until night before the Diligence left for Angers. I arrived at Angers the following day, still on his track, and after again travelling all night I arrived at Tours and succeeded at 10 o'clock at night in tracing him to a respectable boarding house.

On being introduced to Mr Hooper, a wine Merchant, I was informed that a Gentleman answering to his description, of the name of Jones, was paying his addresses to his Daughter. "But I think you must be wrong in your man," said he, "for he appears to be so very respectable and is quite a Gentleman, but however as he has not gone to bed I will take you to him."

On our confronting-one another I at once saw that he was no other than the man I was in search of, the real Thomas Haslock.

As he knew me and the nature of my errand it required no explanation, for he immediately exclaimed, "I know you, Mr Goddard, and what you have come about, here it is."

He then unlocking his portmanteau without delay handed over to me the two bags of Gold.

Mr Hooper looked amazed, and, on asking him in as polite a manner as I could, to withdraw he took the hint and left the room. During his absence, after a brief conversation Haslock then confessed to me how he committed the robbery.

"Instead'" he said, "of depositing the Gold as was my usual custom in the safe I carried these two bags out of doors and at great risk placed them on the dark side of the two columns that support the balcony at the outside entrance to the Bank. Afterwards I gave the key of the safe to Mr Whitworth, who supposed it was all secure. These bags remain'd where I placed them for full 20 minutes till I left."

While this conversation was going on we were suddenly surprised by the arrival of two Gendarmes, who on entering the room and putting a few questions said that they had received instructions from the Prefect of Police to arrest Mr Jones for travelling and obtaining a Passport in a disguised name. Without consultation they took him away and lock'd him up, telling me to appear at the office of the Commissionaire of Police tomorrow. I was not at all sorry for this interruption as it gave me the opportunity of returning to the Hotel de Faisan and of obtaining a night's rest, which I stood in so much need after undergoing the fatigue of six nights' hard travelling by Diligence at this inclement season of the year.

Next day according to agreement I made my appearance at the Bureau of the Commissaire of Police, who after hearing the case refused to surrender him out of their custody on the ground that he had committed an offence against the laws of France having been guilty of obtaining a Passport and travelling under a fictitious name. Under these circumstances they should detain him in their custody and send him to Prison.

This being their decision and as there was no extradition treaty in existence at the time, I found there was no other alternative for me, and as I was in possession of the money, I determined to make the best of my way back to England, the Consul's son having left us.

After three days' travelling I arrived at Dover, and on the following day before starting for London I was informed that soon after I had left Boulogne on the previous day the French Police were in hot pursuit of me to get possession of the gold I had taken from Haslock. "You had not left Boulogne half an hour," said my Informant, before they arrived. What a lucky escape you have had; they would certainly have taken you back to Tours and kept the money."

Thus ended this curious excursion of mine. I need only add that on my arrival at Northampton I handed over to Mr Whitworth, after deducting my expenses, all the cash I had taken from the Prisoner, for which he expressed his thanks.

Sir Francis Mackenzie

In the spring of 1841, while the usual Cattle-Fair in the town of Northampton was being held on the 4th May, there came in careering on horseback a very distinguished looking personage who from his peculiar style of dress could not fail to attract the gaze and attention of every one present. For I must tell you that he was mounted in full Highland costume wearing his kilt and all the paraphernalia of a thorough warlike natural high-bred Scotchman; but the most attractive part of his dress was his shoulder-ornaments, for in place of epaulettes, he wore bunches of Cowslips. Not caring for the jeers and remarks made by the spectators he rode up and down, backwards and forwards quite unconcerned, looking stedfastly and taking stock of the cattle as if he meant to be an extensive purchaser.

After going several times round the market he made his way in the most sudden manner through a dense crowd, who followed him to the George Hotel. (I at that time held the appointment of Chief Constable for the County and was well known among the Farmers and Cattledealers, and witnessed his proceedings.) The crowd soon quitted the site of the Hotel and dispersed themselves about the Fair. No sooner were they gone when the bonnie Scotchman betook himself a la Pedestrian back to the Cattle-Fair and engaged himself in scrutinizing and offering high biddings to outbid those bidders who felt disposed to buy; amongst these biddings he bid to Mr Farr, an extensive breeder and cattle-dealer from Herefordshire, an enormous amount of money for 80 head of fine cattle, quite the pick of the Fair. I called Mr Farr's attention to the state of mind the man appeared to be in, which he could not fail in seeing, so pretended to knock the Cattle down to him.

The same thing occurred to several other dealers in Sheep and Pigs with the like result; and in order to get rid of this nuisance, for he was quite an obstruction to the Fair, I took upon myself the responsibility and after a little persuasion induced him to take luncheon with me at the George Hotel, where there happened to be a large sale in Porcelain in an extensive room away from the Hotel, over the Stables. During luncheon, from our conversation I found his name to be Mackenzie and that he was well acquainted with Sir William Wake, a County Magistrate residing at Courteen Hall, whom he said he should go and visit in the evening.

Luncheon being over, he heard of the sale and immediately proceeded to the Sale-room and made biddings in the same random way he had done at the Cattle fair.

I whispered to the Auctioneer's clerk that it was very important I should have a word in private with his governor, Mr Freeman, which message he duly delivered. The Auctioneer apologised to the Company for a few moments' absence and condescended to leave the Rostrum to join me in a private room, when with as little delay as possible I called his attention to the stranger and what I thought of him, that he was mad, and what had taken place in the fair, that I believed from his conversation he was personally known to Sir William Wake and it was his intention to visit him that evening. This hint was quite enough for Mr Freeman, who at once understood what I meant.

Mr F's absence did not occupy more than five minutes. On his return to the sale, a very handsome dinner service was exhibited to the company: a bidding of Five Pounds from Mr W. Huggins, proprietor of the hotel, was offered, and after the bids had run up to ten pounds the Stranger rushed up and to the surprise of all present bid Thirty Guineas, causing the greatest consternation, and was knocked down to him by way of joke on the part of Mr Freemen, which brought out what I wanted, viz his correct name and address.

The Auctioneer addressing him asked if he had seen the Catalogue and made choice of any other articles. Sir Francis replied that he had but was in a great hurry as he was going to Courteen Hall to see Sir William Wake before his dinner time.

"Then of course I can depend upon you, Sir Francis, calling on me tomorrow morning to hand me over a Check or Cash for the lot you have knocked down to you?"

"Oh, yes," was the reply; "I will either send or call."

Sir Francis then took hold of my arm and accompanied me to my house, a short distance of about 100 yards, when I introduced him to my eldest daughter, who was practising on the Piano. He looked to her like a Giant, and while she was practising he began to dance a scotch reel, which soon put a stop to the practising. He walked towards the window, which commands an extensive and pleasant view over the river Nene to the Village of Hardinstone, and on observing the high trees in the distance, he exclaimed what a pity it was that those beautiful trees were all planted wrong end upwards, that the top and upward part ought to be down and the roots upward.

My Wife by this time came into the room, whom I had previously apprised of his doings. I told her I was going with Sir Francis to Courteen Hall. I then left for a few moments to have a wash and brush up, and when I returned I told Sir Francis I was ready to proceed with him, where we arrived about half past 6, and on our names being duly announced we were met by Sir William in the hall who laughed, shook hands with one and then the other and invited us into a large antique furnished room. Sir Francis began and related to Sir William, in a roundabout confused manner, how he was pursued on horseback from the Eagle at Rugby to Northampton and that Lady Mackenzie was on her way from Inverness with his two sons. Sir William after paying great attention invited us to dinner, and at same time rung the bell for the servant to shew Sir Francis into the lavatory.

During his temporary absence Sir William looked at me very hard in the face and said, "Goddard, I have known the Mackenzie family for years, he must be mad." and calling my attention, said "did you notice the number of daggers he has about his person, and that one sheathed in his stocking below his knee, besides those around his waist?"

"Yes," I said, "I observed them all."

"Well, then," said Sir William, "there is no knowing what a madman may do, therefore at the dinner-table I shall instruct my butler to seat him next to you so that he will be divided from me, for I don't like his appearance, and see what a powerful man he is, it would take the power of half a dozen men to hold him down." Just as Sir William had uttered the last word ("down") in walked Sir Francis, the dinner bell rung and we were seated according to Sir William s instructions. It was a splendid dinner and the wines perfection. Coffee followed and soon afterwards the hour of the clock struck ten. This being about Sir William's bed-time I suggested to Sir Francis that we should retire. He very politely rose from his seat and bade Sir William good night.

We reached the George at half past 10, when I saw Sir Francis into his bed-room. Before separating he invited me to breakfast at 12 o'clock on the following day, and I bade him good night. Before going home I saw Mr Young, one of my Superintendants of Police, and related to him full particulars, and instructions to go by an early train next morning to the Eagle at Rugby, and obtain what information he could relating to Sir Francis Mackenzie, as it was of the greatest importance, and to get back as expeditiously as possible so that I may know the result.

To my surprise on the following morning at 11 o'clock Mr Young came into my office in company with a gentleman and another person. The former turned out to be the brother of Sir Francis and latter Sir Francis's Valet, who it appears had only arrived in pursuit from Scotland at the Eagle about 5 minutes before the arrival of Mr Young, and the meeting therefore was most remarkable. Explanation after explanation went on, and they were only too rejoiced after hearing the particulars from Mr Young to accompany him to Northampton and that he had fallen into such hands.

After parleying the matter over it was agreed that Mr Mackenzie should proceed alone to the hotel, and when he saw his brother he was to express great surprise so as to make it appear that the meeting was quite accidental. Upon this understanding we separated and he went on his mission, leaving the Valet with me, so as to keep out of sight of his master. It was now a quarter to 12 and, as the hour struck 12, I, according to appointment, walked into the room where Sir Francis and his brother had just seated themselves down to breakfast. I was met by Sir Francis in the most cordial and polite manner, who introduced me to his brother to whom we appeared to be strangers.

While at breakfast the conversation was about travelling. How very strange it was, Sir Francis remarked, that his brother who was on his way to the North that they should meet each other in such an extraordinary manner; it was marvellous. He then went on to say how he travelled from Rugby to Northampton on horseback and it was a long ride back, but the horse had had a good rest and could easily do it.

"What, to Rugby?" exclaimed Mr Mackenzie in a state of surprise. "The very place I am going to!"

"Are you?" said Sir Francis.

"Yes," was the reply; and while the conversation was hot in this matter I put in a rejoinder by saying, "Why, that is odd, for I am going to drive over in my chaise this afternoon to ascertain the particulars about a small Farm, and if it is any accommodation I shall be happy to take one of you with me."

"Oh, that is very kind of you," said Sir Francis, "my brother will be very much pleased at your kind offer."

"Well," replied Mr Mackenzie, "it is very kind indeed, but if Sir Francis has no objection I should prefer horseback to chaise."

"Oh, by all means," replied Sir Francis, and so it was arranged; in the mean time the Valet was dispatched by Rail to Rugby.

I then said to Sir Francis I would take him up at the George at 6 o'clock. So I left him and his brother at the Hotel.

As St. Giles's church clock was striking 6, I was at the Hotel door with my chaise ready to take up Sir Francis, who was there with his brother surrounded by at least 100 people. The Police were on the spot to keep the way clear, and when Sir Francis mounted himself into the chaise there was some little delay caused by him insisting on me to change my seat so that he might handle the reins. During this parley the mob kept increasing, so to end the matter I yielded to his caprice and he drove away down Gould Street amid the remarks and jeers of the mob.

The evening was very cold, and when we had cleared the town I recommended Sir Francis to tie his wrapper round his throat to prevent taking cold.

"O," he replied, "I never take cold, for I have had all the nerves of my teeth cut, and another thing, I am never troubled with corns for I have had all the nerves of my toes cut."

So he talked and went on driving along, increasing the pace of the horse from a sharp trot into a fast gallop, saying, "This is the pace I came when I left Rugby followed by a Farmer who kept riding after me, and I stopped and asked if he took me for a mountebank or wizard or a fool, for if you do I am neither."

The evening was getting dark, and as there were large quantities of fallen timber laying at uncertain distances on both sides of the road, I was fearful of an upset. However, as it was, we had the good fortune of narrowly escaping these mishaps and arrived safely at the Wheatsheaf Inn, which stands at the top of the hill as you enter the old town of Daventry. While the horse was taking his bait and ourselves refreshment, Mr Mackenzie arrived on horseback for the same purpose. After a stay of about half of an hour we started in company for a few miles, when Mr Mackenzie spurred his horse saying he should gallop on to the Eagle and order dinner to be got ready, and he soon escaped from our view.

"There!" said Sir Francis, "look at that, and see the pace he is going! that is just the style I sat that horse when I galloped to Northampton." And so he talked till we arrived at the Eagle about 10 minutes after his brother, who had already ordered dinner.

Sir Francis retired to his bed-room, and in about half an hour the waiter informed us that dinner was on the table. After Sir Francis had partaken of a glass or two of wine he began talking in a wild manner, and told his brother of the dealings he had been having at Northampton Fair and the number of cattle that had been sold to him as well as a large and handsome dinner service, talking most incoherently till the meal was finished, when I got up, and for an excuse said that I must wish them good night as I had got some important business to attend to and hoped they would excuse me.

I was followed out by Mr Mackenzie into a private room, who said he would see me to discuss what was best to be done in this matter and would return in a quarter of an hour, and in the mean time under no circumstances must I be seen.

When the time had expired, Mr Mackenzie came into the room and said some very hasty steps must be taken. "We must continue to persuade my brother to accompany you to London, so as to have him examined by two medical practitioners as to whether he is a fit subject to be at large. "It was arranged that I was to leave early the following morning in my chaise to Northampton and return to dinner in the evening.

This arrangement was carried out, and on my return the Valet was supposed to have only just arrived from Scotland. When his master saw him, in an excited manner he enquired if he was a witch! for he must be none other or how could he have found him out?

"Found you out?" said the Valet," Why, you told me, Sir Francis, when you left home that you were going to Northampton Fair to buy cattle to stock your Farm, and on your going and coming you should put up at the Eagle in Rugby."

Sir. F. made no further answer than "I am pleased to see you," and so this matter passed away without comment.

Dinner being announced and after being seated for a few minutes Sir Francis again brought up the old story about his cattle he had purchased at Northampton and that he should go there tomorrow and see the dealers to know where they were grazing. Other subjects of no interest were spoken upon; dinner finished, coffee followed and it was close upon 10 o'clock. Sir Francis retired to bed while I and Mr Mackenzie sat up till 11, and before retiring it was arranged that I was to try and persuade Sir Francis that the cattle-dealers he was going to see at Northampton were all gone to London and if he wished to see them he must go there.

This scheme being determined on, at 10 o'clock the following morning when breakfast was over we proceeded to the Railway Station and I booked for London two first class passengers. We had the compartment to ourselves till we arrived at Weedon, when a gentleman got in, and as we were going at a speed of 25 miles an hour, Sir Francis exclaimed that he was going to Northampton!

"O," said the gentleman, "you will not be able to do that by this Train, for it does not stop at Blisworth but goes on to Wolverton."

"Won't I, by God!" shouted Sir Francis. "Here is Blisworth

upon us, let me out—let me out!!" And suiting the action to the word, he unfastened the door and jumped out safely on his feet with a sharp run down the embankment. I followed him in the same manner, and we both fortunately gained the bottom safely whilst the Guard and Passengers were gazing with astonishment out of the window.

There were two or three of Shaw's Flys from the Angel waiting the arrival Train from London. Sir F. engaged one, jumped in and I followed, and he directed the driver to go on to Northampton. On entering the town at the bottom of Bridge Street he observed an orange shop, when he signalled the driver to stop. Sir F. opened, the fly-door and jump'd out into the shop, commencing in a voracious manner to devour the oranges till he went on and consume about a dozen. His peculiar style of dress as already mentioned caused a great number of people to assemble in front of the shop, and when he had finished he asked for a wash hand basin and towel. During this process the boys and women jeer'd, which seemed to displease him, and after paying for the Oranges be carried the basin and threw the contents over those outside saying, "There! you have got it, now share it amongst you."

Thus after fighting the way through the mob with my charge we got into the fly, followed by the rabble, till we arrived at the George. After staying for about an hour talking about his cattle and where be could see the salesman, and being told by Mr Higgint that the fair was over and the salesmen had all gone to London with the cattle to Smithfield Market, these words soon put the quietus upon him. We took luncheon and went off by Train to London, drove to Stevens' Hotel in Bond Street followed soon after by his brother with the Valet.

As it had been prearranged, at 8 o'clock, while taking coffee,

Mr Mackenzie introduced two Physicians under the garb of gentlemen friends, who had been informed of his brother's antecedents. I, of course, left the room. To bring this painful matter to a conclusion after having paid their usual customary visits, they pronounced him to be insane and totally unfit to govern his affairs and granted a certificate to that effect.

After these visits the Patient became very suspicious, continually asking his Valet and myself their business and who they were and what had become of his brother.

"What are they going to do with me?" he said. "I'll break and smash everything in the house if you don't allow me to see my brother. Where are my daggers?" be exclaimed in a desperate tone.

"Your brother," replied his Valet, "has gone to pay a visit to a friend of his at 2 Wellington Road, St. John's Wood'" (a private madhouse).

"Then go and tell him he must come and see me. Take a cab and be quick, for I will not leave this house till I see him."

His brother all this time was in a room above. Fearing that something desperate was likely to take place, we talked the business over and it was arranged that his brother should address his letter as from Wellington Road and write Sir Francis to the effect that he was taken suddenly and dangerously ill and that it was important for him without delay to come and see him at once as his case might be fatal.

The Valet, who was supposed to have gone to St. John's wood to deliver the messages, after the lapse of an hour ran into his master's room, feigning to be out of breath, deliver'd the letter, and after reading it Sir F excitedly asked if he had seen his brother.

"Yes," replied the Valet, "he was in bed with the blinds drawn down and a nurse and a doctor by his side."

"Then go, fetch my overcoat and order a fast Cab immediately," said Sir Francis, "and I'll go with you only."

The Cab was fetched with another behind it, and the Valet had only just time to tell me that he thought he had secured all Sir Francis's daggers in safety, "But he has got one now concealed up his sleeve."

Sir Francis got into the Cab followed by his Valet and drove away. I followed in another, keeping about 100 yards behind, and fortunately they made a mistake as to the number of the house in Wellington Road and passed it for some distance, giving me the opportunity which I embraced by discharging my Cab and of being admitted into the house before the other Cab-driver had discovered his mistake.

When I entered the house, there were two powerful-looking men (keepers) in waiting to whom I had just time to relate the circumstances of the conceal'd dagger, which put them on their guard. No sooner was the caution given than Sir Francis jump'd from out of the Cab and with a hasty walk along the front garden gave a loud rat-tat at the door, which was instantly opened by a female. Sir F, with uplifted arm and dagger clenched in his hand, with a wild mad-like expression in his countenance, rushed his way in a violent manner followed by his Valet into the front dining room, exclaiming aloud, "Where is my brother?"

I was standing behind the door with the keepers, and as he entered we seized on to him for our lives, and threw him down on the floor. I held on to the arm that held the dagger, the keepers in the most courageous manner acted their part, and the Valet, who knew of the secret spring, took the blade while Sir F held on to the handle as though it were in a vice.

It was a desperate struggle, and now feeling the danger was over we all got up. Sir Francis was in a state of exhaustion, and the keepers made no more to do and placed the strait-waistcoat on at once, which brought tears from the eyes of Sir Francis who, finding he was mastered, became quite reconciled and asked for a draught of Lemonade.

Thus, so far as my services were required, they had come to a finish. I left him in the hands of the medical attendants and returned with his brother in a Cab to Stevens's Hotel. After talking the matter over at the dinner-table he gave me a very handsome present and thanked me two or three times over for the great pains I had taken and said how fortunate it was that his brother had fallen into such hands.

A month afterwards I received information of Sir Francis's death.

Mr John Todd

In the early part of June 1853 an agent from the establishment of Mr Hoyle, an eminent solicitor at Newcastle-on-Tyne, applied to me to know whether I would go in pursuit of a Fugitive who it was found had clandestinely left his place of residence in that town with a large sum of money, amounting to over £10,000, the property of his creditors, and was supposed to have gone to America. "Can you undertake this business?" he asked.

I replied in the affirmative.

Then he said, "You must go away by tonight's mail to Mr Hoyle and be fully prepared for a voyage across the Atlantic."

We then made some preliminary arrangements and separated. I returned home, packed up my wardrobe, took leave of my wife and family, got into a cab, drove to the London & N.W. Railway station, took my place in a first class carriage, arriving at the Queens Hotel, Newcastle, at 7 o'clock following morning (Sunday), and after breakfast went to the residence of Mr Hoyle in time to discuss the business before his going to church.

On the following day I attended the meeting of creditors at

the bankruptcy court to hear the reading of the depositions. Having got over this part of the business, the next consideration was the amount of cash I should require for so long a journey to meet expenses for myself and one Henry Luke, who was to accompany me for identification. Mr Hoyle, after a consultation with the creditors, said he thought I should be furnished with £300, and if I found on my travels I wanted more I was only to write and it would be forwarded. On the next day Mr Hoyle handed over to me the Cash, in a canvas bag, and now nothing else remained but my departure with Luke for Liverpool. Mr Hoyle saw us off by Rail and wished us every success.

After arriving at Liverpool and paying our passage to New York, we went on board the Baltic, Collins line, Comstock commander, and after a splendid trip of eleven days arrived at New York on Sunday afternoon the 25th, putting up at Collins Hotel; had a refreshing warm sea-bath, afterwards an excellent dinner at their Table d'hote, and then a stroll to the Broadway to see what the place was like, enjoyed our curiosity very much, returned to our hotel about eleven and retired to our bedrooms.

In the middle of the night I was woke by hearing a terrific noise of people shouting and calling 'Fire!" and also the sound of a tolling bell, and at the same time could see flames and sparks of fire raging near to my window. I got up in great haste and felt much alarmed, thinking the hotel was on fire, and ran to the window when I saw it was on the opposite side of the way. I hastened to my companion, who was fast asleep in a room behind, and had some difficulty in waking him by calling out as loud as I could, "Fire!!" He rose from his bed in great terror at the glare of the fire, the sound of the tolling bell and the shouting of the people. I pacified him under the circumstances as well as I was able, and in a state of nude led him to my bedroom saying, "It is all right, look here, we are in no danger for the wind is blowing the flames and sparks away from this direction towards the backs of the houses opposite." We watched for about an hour, and seeing it was subdued each of us retired to our bedrooms.

On the following morning I engaged the services of Gill Hayes, the renowned American police-officer, for his assistance in going with me to make enquiries of bankers and ship owners, but from these we could not obtain any information. We then visited and made enquiries at all the hotels and boarding houses, looking over their books; not that we expected to see the name of Todd, but as it is the custom for all travellers to write their names in these books we thought it probable as we were in possession of his signature that we might trace some letters in an assumed name to correspond with some of those in his signature. These enquiries occupied nearly two days and ended as it commenced without the slightest clue.

I then took this matter into serious consideration, and from my former experience knew as a rule that the majority of fugitives made their way West. I consulted Gill Hayes, who was of the same opinion, and he advised me to take that course, and on the following day, the 5th of July, the day after the anniversary of the Americans' declaration of Independence, Luke and I packed up our things and embarked on board the Francis Kiddy, taking us up the Hudson, had a good view of the Catskill Mountains going to Albany about 150 miles distant, where we made enquiries as at New York and of Land Agents but with no satisfactory result. We then proceeded to Buffalo, where our enquiries came to nil, and being only 18 miles from Niagara Falls I embraced and took advantage of the opportunity to go and visit them and was so struck with their grandeur that we remained at the Clifton Hotel for the night.

The next morning we returned to Buffalo, and from there to Detroit, continuing our enquiries at the Bankers and Hotels and representing to a Land Agent that we were in search of land, at the same time asking if he had disposed of any lately. He replied he had not for the last three months, but that he had got some hundreds of acres now to dispose of at a bargain. Luke said he should like to see where it was. The Agent immediately ordered out his trap and drove us about four miles. After seeing the situation, which Luke much admired, he drove us back and pressed us hard to buy.

Luke said, "We are going further into these wild lands, and if we cannot get suited you will see us again."

These Land Agents know among themselves all newcomers for miles around, and I thought if Todd made his way West and had purchased land, I must sooner or later discover his track. Emboldened with this idea, I proceeded on to Chicago, 280 miles further, and put up at the Merchants Hotel. We were shewn to our bedrooms, very small ones, Nos. 17 and 18, situated up stairs in a long gallery where there were many more rooms in front, and right and left of ours. After having a refreshing wash the Gong gave us notice that dinner was ready. We afterwards partook of Coffee and retired to bed at half past ten.

On looking round the bedroom I found the door did not to my mind look at all secure. I therefore placed the head of my small French bedstead against it, and to insure safer security I looked to the window, pushed up the sash and saw there was a cistern about three feet below which anyone could easily climb upon in the middle of the night and gain access into my room and ease me of all my gold, viz £230. Before I could withdraw my head from the window it suddenly fell down upon the back of my neck, so that I had some little difficulty in extricating myself. These windows are not like ours, with weights and cords, they have a spring which I was not aware of. It was very hot weather and to admit air I put one of my boots under the sash, and to insure further safety from robbery I placed the wash hand stand under the window, and on the edge of it the water jug, and under that the wash-hand basin to catch the jug so that the noise in falling would wake me.

After this paraphernalia I retired to bed and was soon asleep; but about one o'clock in the morning was awoke by hearing the noise of one outside tampering with the lock. I listened, and then called out, "Who's that?" Not hearing anything more, I concluded it was a traveller who had made a mistake in the room. I soon after fell asleep till I heard the sound of the Gong at 6 o'clock in the morning; I immediately rose from my bed, pushed the bedstead to its place and on looking at the lock saw it was unlocked.

I then begun to fix (dress) when all of a sudden Luke came quickly into the room, exclaiming, "I've been robbed! I've been robbed! they have got all my money! I thought they had, for when the Gong woke me I saw a piece of red tape hanging out of my trowsers pocket, and it was a good job I did not bring my watch for they would have had that too."

I asked how much money he had, he said three Pounds. I then let him see what I had done and said if I had not taken those precautions they would have served me the same, for I heard someone in the middle of the night tampering with my lock; and if they had succeeded, what a precious pickle the pair of us would have been in, being so far from home and to be robbed of all our money!

We washed and after fixing we went down stairs and saw two well dressed men standing in the Hall, whose appearance I did not at all like. I called, in their presence, the attention of the Landlord to what had taken place during the night. He replied that he was very sorry, he had so many travellers going and coming that it was impossible to tell who was who. I remarked it was a good job they did not get into my room.

"Why was it a good job?" said one of these well dressed men.

I replied in a seeming determined manner, "I would have shot him!!" (I did not carry pistols, I merely said so to make them think that I did.)

After breakfast I went to see the Sheriff and repeated all that had taken place. Hearing me out, he opened his desk and produced two steel instruments similar to a pair of nippers, manufactured for the purpose of putting them into the outside of the key-hole which by a leverage bites on to the barrel end of the key and unlocks the door with perfect ease; these instruments are called outsiders. After examining them he said he would return with me and look at the locks, which were found to be of the commonest description. He told me he had heard of similar complaints and had got his suspicions and recommended me to leave and go to another Hotel. I then related to the Sheriff the object of my errand and asked if he would kindly aid me, by the service of the police, to go round to the Hotels I should take it as a great favour and should be happy to pay him for his trouble.

We visited all the Hotels and found it was labour in vain. Nothing daunted, I was determined still to go on, and after another packing up, we paid our Bill and started on board a

Steamer on Lake Michigan, and after being put on shore. we went to Canes Hotel and renewed enquiries at Milwarkie in the same manner as we had done at all the other towns we had left behind, but without effect. I then enquired how far the next Town of importance was from here, and the name of it, which I was informed was Janesville, distant 75 miles.

"Well," I said to Luke, "the distance is not great and we will venture it." No sooner said and we were off.

On arriving there we put up at the first Hotel we saw, and after a very short time we found there was only one other Hotel in the place.

I was feeling very anxious about the business and said to Luke, "Here we are at Janesville on the Rock River in North America, and after spending so much money we are no forwarder now than when we were at Newcastle. What am I to report to Mr Hoyle?"

"It is indeed very disheartening," said Luke. "that you have nothing to report."

"Well," I said, "this is a small place, there are only two Hotels and one Banker, it will not take long. You stay here while I cross over to the other Hotel and see if there is any good to be got there."

I walked away very slowly to the Bar and called for a drink. at the, same time observing a book lying on the bar side. As it was with easy reach I took it up, and after turning over a few pages to my great astonishment I saw the names of John Todd, George Todd, William Todd and Frederick Todd. These signatures were all in the same handwriting. I compared them with the one that I had got and there was no mistake about it, for they were all in John Todd the fugitive's handwriting and no-other.

The reader can imagine the satisfaction and relief this discovery was to me after having journeyed over four thousand miles and then to tumble over him in such an extraordinary manner. My only fear now was that Luke might be seen in this out-of-the-way place by someone of the Todd family, as they all knew him well, and to prevent this he disguised himself and had to keep himself from observation as best he could. I went to the Bank, the only one in the place, it was named "the Old Badger State Bank", a small house built of wood, part of it supported by two strong uprights fixed in the bed of the Rock River, the inside was usefully ornamented in this bye part of the State of Wisconcin with a great number of Guns and Pistols ready for use in case of emergency. I saw the Manager, and it was a cautious piece of business I had to perform; I commenced by saying that I was a stranger, that I had come from London and brought another person with me at a great expence, that my business was of the utmost importance to the mercantile world, that I would be candid and that at the same time what I was about to tell him must be confidential, otherwise all the pains, expence and trouble that had been taken would be lost.

On hearing what I had said he invited me into his small private room, when I observed the emblem of Freemasonry engraved on his gold studs in the front of his shirt. I remarked, "You are a Mason. He then gave me the sign, which I acknowledged and said, I am another, and can with confidence relate to you of my errand."

He listened with great attention, and after I had finished with the finding out of the fugitives with their names written in the Hotel book, he shook hands and said, "I can give you some important information, and if you had come here the day before yesterday I could not have furnished you with any, because the person you mention was not known to me, for it was only yesterday he came with his sons and deposited a tolerable amount of cash, which I have sent away to the Bank at Chicago. The name of his solicitor is Niel, and I know he has been purchasing rather largely some land, not a great distance from here."

I remarked, "How strange, for on my way I loitered two days in staying at Niagara Falls, and if I had not done so I should have been here two days earlier, and you would not have been able to give me any information."

The banker remarked that it was to be, but "you can learn more particulars from my friend Mr Niel, and if you will wait here-his office is not far away, I will send my clerk for him."

I waited and in less than ten minutes the clerk and Mr Niel arrived, the Banker giving him an outline of the case in which I occasionally joined, and ended by my saying, "If you will kindly take the matter up in your own way without prejudice to either party it will be very much to your advantage."

He replied, "It is a business of some importance and requires consideration: I will consider the subject and see you again in about an hour."

He was about to leave when the Banker rose from his chair and said, "Before you depart, Mr Niel, I shall be happy to have the pleasure of your company with Mr Goddard to dine at my house after the Bank is closed so that we can talk the matter over."

The invitation was accepted, the hour of 7 o'dock arrived, and as I was making my way to the Bankers I met Mr Niel at the door and we entered the house together. After an excellent dinner it took some time discuss over the business, Mr Niel observing that as I had no authority, he doubted under the circumstances whether the English law could touch Todd at all. "I think the best thing we can do is to go and see him and try to get all the money out of him we can, for I am afraid the Bankruptcy law will not affect him here in any way."

I entirely agreed with these observations, and it was arranged that I should engage a pair-horse carriage and start away the following morning at 10 to Todd's residence at Rock on the Rock River, about seven miles distant. The following morning at 10 the carriage was ready, and Luke, Mr Niel and I started; and on the way, Mr Niel informed me that Todd had placed his three daughters in a convent at Chicago (they were Catholics). I told him I had heard that he had three daughters but we thought they were in a convent somewhere in France and enquiries were being made there. I lost no time in communicating the intelligence to Mr Hoyle.

It took about an hour in consequence of the roughness of the road we had to travel over to get within a quarter of a mile of Todd's Hut. We halted under the brow of a small hill, leaving Luke with the driver while Niel and I had some difficulty in climbing over several zigzag wooden fences before reaching the Hut, situated in a most lonely spot bordering on to a dark forest; not a Hut or a homested or human being to be seen the whole distance we had come.

Mr Niel knocked at the door with his foot and was answered by a hard-featured working-looking woman; at this moment one of young Todds made his appearance from the back and recognised Mr Niel and seemed to wonder what he wanted.

Mr Niel enquired for his Father and pointing to me said. "This gentleman wishes to see him."

He replied, "Very well, my Father is not here but I will go

and fetch him."

He put on a pair of boots that reached to his thighs saying he wore them to save his legs from the bites of rattlesnakes, and immediately started away at a running pace across the small coppice leading to the forest.

I remarked to Niel, "I think we had better follow, for if he tells his father you are with a stranger, he will have his suspicions roused and perhaps keep out of the way."

"Right," said Niel, "we had better follow"; and away we went. I first. He had taken a winding sort of track and I could not see him but heard now and then the snapping of small underwood.

We followed up the direction of the sound, running as fast as we could for about half a mile, when all on a sudden we cleared the Forest just in time to see him on the top of a hill, some three or four hundred yards distant, beckoning to someone. Then we saw two men making their appearance and approaching towards him, and after stopping they held a parley for two or three minutes when young Todd turned round and pointed at us, as much as to say after he delivered Niel's message, "Why, there they are."

They then picked up their coats, slung them over their shoulders and walked towards us; the elder Todd first, followed by his three sons.

As soon as the Father got within hearing distance he declaimed at the top of his voice and foaming with rage from the mouth, "I am in a free country! I am in a free country! I'll throw myself on the American Laws, what do you want with me?" and behaved in the most violent and mad-like manner.

Niel tried to pacify him by saying, "When you have cooled down, Mr Todd, you shall hear the object of our visit"; and as we all walked together returning back through the forest, if anyone had met us they would have thought we were like a set of wild men all talking at the same time.

When we were half way through I saw two of the sons speaking in a low tone to each other and start running on before us, and by the time we had got clear of this forest we met them returning from their Hut, advancing towards us each armed with a Gun. I enquired what they were going to do with those Guns.

"To shoot racoons," one of them said.

I had my suspicions, and as we were nearing the Hut I spoke as loud as I could, addressing myself to old Todd so that they should hear me and said, "I think it quite possible you can easily get out of this bother by consulting with Mr Niel your solicitor, whose advice I am sure will be most valuable and you cannot be in better hands, therefore I don't think there is any necessity for your being so angry."

At this instant Luke, whom Todd and his sons well knew, came upon the scene in such a sudden manner that he surprised them all. Luke made no to do but at once advanced and shook hands first with one then the others and congratulating how pleased he was to see them, and so far from home: they returning the compliment.

This sudden interview seemed to alter the state of affairs altogether.

The sons took their guns back into the Hut and came out directly. The ill-temper of the Father had subdued which made him look more like a rational being, and addressing himself to me said, "Well, now, as you have come all this way what are you going to do with me?"

"Do with you?" I replied. "Why, nothing! You and your solicitor can manage this, and you will have to settle it between yourselves. At the same time you must bear in mind that you have three daughters at Chicago, and here you have three sons; and as this business will very likely reach all over the state you would not like for them to lose caste. Therefore it is better that you should consider and talk the matter over with Mr Niel and make as fair a composition with your creditors as your circumstances can afford."

He then turned round and entered into private conversation with his Solicitor, and there was nothing more to do but bid each other good day and retire to our Carriage and return to Janesville, pay Mr Niel for his trouble with the understanding that I was going to Milwarkie and await instructions from Newcastle and in the meantime for him to put himself in communication with Mr Hoyle at Newcastle.

The next day Luke, who had so well played his part, and I left, and returned to Canes Hotel at Milwarkie. After staying for some days, Mr Page the Police officer called my attention to an advertisement in a New York Newspaper stating that letters and documents of importance were laying at the Post Office there directed to me.

On hearing this, I and Luke left Milwarkie and went to Chicago, where I left him to await my return with the letters from New York. I went by way of Pittsburgh over the Alligany mountains and Philadelphia, and obtained at the New York Post Office several papers and a letter from Mr Hoyle saying that documents of importance were laying for me at the French embassy. I possessed myself of these papers, which were very voluminous, with a Warrant for the apprehension of Todd, charging him with Felony.

I lost no time in returning to Milwarkie, after this trip of above 2000 miles, to lay the papers and warrant before Mr

Miller and Federal Judge, who received me in the most courteous and obliging manner. I gave him an outline of the case and he said he should be glad to assist me. At the same time, taking a slight glance over the papers, he said, "There is a good deal of it and it will take me two or three days to peruse them, therefore if you call at the end of three days I shall be able to give an answer."

I called at the expiration of three days and he said, "Well, Mr Goddard, I have devoted much time in reading over these briefs, containing several affidavits and the Warrant; there is a great deal of other information in the use and they are beautifully got up and well written, which is all done in your country to create fees; it is a pity that such enormous expences has been incurred. I am sorry I have no power. Our laws will not assist me; the Warrant and Affidavits with the rest of the papers are all founded on Bankruptcy. We have no bankruptcy laws here and therefore cannot recognise them, but that is not your fault. You have displayed most extraordinary vigilance and untiring energy in the discovery you have made: I can only compare it to placing a small needle point upwards in the middle of a forest and that you should go and find it! If you call tomorrow I will give you a letter to Mr Hoyle with full particulars of your doings in this part of the world."

I was pleased to hear these remarks from the Judge as they were a great relief to my mind. I wrote to Mr Niel informing him what I had done and that I should not return, but that he was to communicate future proceedings to Mr Hoyle. After this, Luke and I lost no time in making our way back to New York, when I found out that old Todd, on his first arrival, had been to a Lawyer to ask his opinion in a case of a man, a friend of his, who had absconded from England before he was made

Bankrupt and had gone a long way west of Wisconsin (he was representing his own Case). The Lawyer told him his friend was quite safe, he was beyond interference and if anyone dare to presume and lay hands upon him to force him away, he would be justified in making use of his fire arms. This accounted why the young Todds made their appearance as they did with their guns.

It is now the early part of December 1875 I am engaged writing this book, and before finishing my narrative I wrote to Mr Niel, the attorney I employed when at Janesville nearly 23 years ago, to know if he could give me any information respecting the Todd family, at the same time calling his attention to the circumstance of the two Todds returning from their Hut each armed with a gun. I received his reply on the 24th of January 1875, dated 7th January 1875, from 308 Chestnut Street, Saint Louis:

My dear Goddard,

Upon my return from Court I found a letter in my office which was re-addressed to me at this point. I left Wisconsin in 1866 shortly after the death of my wife. I do remember you, my dear Sir, have often recalled our visit to the Todds and of the belligerence of the sons. The old Gentleman is dead, and when in Wisconsin two years ago, the only son, John G., was living. The rest have scattered, the daughters married, etc. The family never showed any means beyond what was visible when we visited them. You did not refer to our trip to Milwaukee. When I left Wisconsin all that volume of huge papers left with me (after obtaining Judgment upon the claims) I destroyed…

I merely introduce this first part of Mr Niel's letter to corroborate my statement as to the narrow escape I had from their firearms which they intended to make use of against me!

Here I will also introduce the copy of a letter I have from Mr Hoyle:

Dear Sir,

I have the pleasure to send you Banker's bill value £158 .19 .1, the Balance of your acct., and in doing so I have to express the high sense the Creditors as well as myself entertain of the masterly way in which you have conducted the pursuit and discovery of Todd, and the acuteness and sagacity you have displayed in the business.

Yrs. faithfully

(signed) John J. Hoyle.

P.S. Please acknowledge rect. and send me the agreement and indemnity, as I shall want them.

For further particulars as to the ending of this case I have given as follows a copy of the report published in the Newcastle Guardian of November 26th 1853.

NEWCASTLE BANKRUPTCY COURT (Before Mr Commissioner Ellison)

Re JOHN TODD.—This was a special sitting appointed by the Commissioner to audit the accounts, and to consider an application for allowance out of the estate, of the costs of endeavouring to apprehend the bankrupt in America. The bankruptcy excited considerable interest at the time, and his Honour had directed Mr Hoyle, the solicitor to the assignees, to prepare and file with the proceedings a statement of all the circumstances, and of the steps taken on the part of the creditors; and before deciding as to the allowance of costs, his Honour proceeded to read the statement, which was to the following effect.

For many years preceding and up to the 16th of May, 1853, John Todd, the bankrupt, carried on the business of a whisky distiller in the Custom House Entry on the Quay, at Newcastle-upon-Tyne, and he resided for some time in a house which was his own property, called Belle Vue, about two miles from Gateshead. Todd had formerly been in the employ of Messrs Campbell & Co., who preceded him in the distillery. Up to the period of his flight Todd was in good credit and was reputed to have carried on a lucrative business, hence the report of his having absconded from his creditors was not for some time believed to be true (but, as was afterwards ascertained, he left his house at Belle Vue between nine and ten o'clock on the night of Monday, the 16th of May, and went to Liverpool, and there on the 18th embarked in the steam-ship Arctic, bound for New York), yet the fact was not known to the creditors till the morning of Saturday, the 21st.

In the forenoon of this day, some of the principal creditors, who are chiefly engaged in the corn trade at Newcastle, in consequence of their suspicions being excited, met together, and having satisfied themselves that Todd had actually fled, determined, under the advice of Mr Hoyle, the solicitor, to file a petition of bankruptcy, which was immediately done, and an official assignee being appointed, before any extent was taken out, the right of the crown for the large arrears of duty to seize any goods, except those on the distillery, was defeated. This, as it turned out, was a most important case in point for the benefit of the creditors, as wheat and barley, which had been improperly parted with by the bankrupt, to the value of above £1000, was recovered for the estate, and debts and other property, to the extent of £500 more, has since been collected by the assignees.

Todd had evidently contemplated this step for a considerable time. Some days elapsed before it could be ascertained in which direction he had fled—he had himself taken a passport for France, and his son, John George Todd, one for Belgium, but neither of these countries were ever believed to have been his destination, and it is remarkable that even if his flight had been sooner known, he could not have been arrested by any legal process, as he had not then committed any criminal offence, and none of his acceptances were at that time due, nor was there any debt payable for which he could have been taken as an absconding debtor.

Every means were taken to ascertain where Todd had gone to, and after some days' time his track was discovered, in consequence of a bank-post bill, granted to the bankrupt by the branch Bank of England at Newcastle-upon-Tyne, having been cashed at Liverpool. That bill was traced to have been paid by one of the bankrupt's sons (William Todd, who described himself as of Furnause Abbey, in Hertfordshire) to Brown, Shipley, and Co., of Liverpool, for the passage of himself and a person answering the description of the bankrupt, by the steam-ship Arctic, which sailed on the 18th day of May, from Liverpool to New York, in the United States; and that the balance of the bank-post bill was paid to the younger Todd, by a bill, drawn by Brown, Shipley, and Co., on the firm of Brown, Brothers, in New York.

On ascertaining these facts, application was made to Colonel Aspinal, the American minister in this country, who stated that, if found in the state of New York, the bankrupt would be given up to parties armed with the necessary authority from the legislature of Great Britain, and not by virtue of any of the treaties between Great Britain and the States, but under their own law; but it was doubtful whether he would be given up if discovered in the remote territories.

The creditors having determined to send after Todd, they engaged Henry Goddard., formerly one of the principal officers of Bow-street. and who had on other, occasions exhibited great sagacity, to proceed to New York, accompanied by Henry Luke, of Newcastle (who was acquainted with Todd's person), for the purpose of identifying him. An agreement was then entered into between Goddard and the principal creditors. undertaking to pay Mr Goddard his expences for going to America, and indemnifying him from any action or proceedings that might be brought against him for what he might do in the business.

On the 8th day of June, 1853, Goddard, armed with a Warrant from a magistrate at Newcastle to apprehend the bankrupt under the English Bankrupt Law, on the charge of destroying his books of account; and Luke, holding a power of attorney from the creditors, as recommended by the American Minister, sailed in the steam-ship Baltic, and though with no further trace of the bankrupt than that he landed from the steamer on the quay at New York, he immediately succeeded in finding him, not as hoped in the State of New York, but in the country amidst the Rocky Mountains, seven miles from a place named Janesville, in the territory of Wisconsin, and about two thousand miles from the town of New York. The bankrupt was found by Goddard and Luke with his trousers tucked up mowing wet grass in a prairie, and on inquiry they found a tract of land consisting of four hundred acres, with a homestead upon it, had been purchased in the name of the bankrupt's eldest son John George Todd, who with his two brothers lived there with the bankrupt; that the daughters. Marie Louisa Todd and Emily Todd, were residing in a Roman Catholic Convent at Chicago in the United States.

The discovery of the bankrupt's retreat was made before the

bankrupt had committed a felony by not surrendering to the petition on bankruptcy. and as the bankrupt denied having any money or property of his own, and as Goddard had ascertained from the Judge of Wisconsin that he (Goddard) could not lawfully in that country apprehend the bankrupt for the minor offence of a demeanour but stated that if he had a warrant for felony he would do all he could to assist him, Goddard and Luke then withdrew from the neighbourhood for a few days until the warrant from England to apprehend him for the felony of not surrendering to his bankruptcy should arrive. As soon as he had received this he again applied to the judge of the district, who resided in a town named Maddison, but after deliberation that functionary decided that neither the policy or the law of Wisconsin justified him in endorsing the warrant, or in doing any act to authorise Goddard to apprehend the bankrupt on a felony arising from mere indebtedness; and it is alleged (though the Judge of Maddison did not admit the fact) that Wisconsin is not exactly a "state" but a "territory", and one which the United States wish peopled, and have therefore recognised in it more "liberal" laws that those of the States proper—in fact have made it a refuge for knaves and vagabonds of all descriptions.

The fact that the bankrupt was not in New York or any of the Federal States, and that Goddard and his ally Luke were unable either lawfully or unlawfully (for these parties were invested with plenary powers from the creditors) to effect his transit from America to this country, or to incarcerate him there, was duly communicated to the creditors, and Goddard returned home, having done all he undertook to do, which was to "find out Todd if he was on the face of the globe". Indeed, the assignees consider Goddard exhibited remarkable acuteness and capacity in tracing and discovering the bankrupt.

It was ascertained that money had been lodged to a considerable amount in the Badger Bank at Maddison, in the name of the bankrupt's son, John George Todd.

Proceedings may be taken against the bankrupt in the courts in Wisconsin, upon the documents sent from England at the instance of the creditors, under which the bankrupt would be divested of his property; and these have been left in the hands of Mr James Niel, solicitor in Janesville, who entertains the opinion that the bankrupt has from £10,000 to £15,000 in his possession and that of his sons. This has in some measure come out by the sums the bankrupt stood indebted to various creditors here, for goods which he purchased shortly before he absconded.

His Honor the Commissioner, at the conclusion of the statement, said he had no difficulty whatever in allowing these expenses out of the estate of the bankrupt. In the first instance, they had been advanced by one of the creditors personally, and he must express his entire approval of all that had been done by the creditors, by the assignees, and by their solicitor, who had acted with promptness and decision under the novel circumstances. He only regretted that the bankrupt had been found in a land which would not, according to the present laws and treaties, give him up to be dealt with here. The conduct of Todd had been as fraudulent as ever disgraced the jurisprudence of any country, and he was sorry the bankrupt was not at the moment where he ought to be, namely, in the gaol of Newcastle.

The assignee having entered the court, the Commissioner, addressing Mr Charlton personally, repeated his approval of his proceedings and that of the creditors, whom his Honor said had acted in the course they had taken with a most praiseworthy disregard of their own interest, and were willing to sacrifice their prospect of dividend in the hope of punishing this fraudulent bankrupt, for the good of the mercantile community. The proceedings had been taken with great judgment, and had his (the Commissioner's) entire approbation.

The Great Robbery

Towards the end of the month of August 1856, soon after the treaty of Paris, it was discovered in going into some of the accounts of the Company that property in Bonds and Railway Coupons to the amount in value of about half a Million sterling had been abstracted from an iron Closet which was well secured by three different strong patent locks and placed in the Secretary's department. On enquiries being made by order of the Directors it was found that three of the confidential Clerks, named Charles Carpentier, the principal Cashier, Louis Grelet and Eugine Grelet, also Cashiers, in conjunction with one Augustus Parrot alias Dubud, a Horsedealer, had left their respective homes in a clandestine manner without leaving the slightest clue to their whereabouts. These circumstances caused the greatest commotion not only to the Directors but all over Paris and other continental cities as well as in London.

The most decisive steps were at once taken for the purpose of tracing the absentees, and as soon as information of the above gigantic robbery had reached the Mansion House, I was engaged as an agent with Mr John Forrester, an officer of

Mansion House notoriety, by the Messrs Rothschild to try and find out regardless of expence the whereabouts of the principal Cashier, Charles Carpentier. Our enquiries led us to Argyle square, in the neighbourhood of Battle Bridge; now called Kings Cross; and judging by information got, the description of his person and what he had said, it was supposed he had left London and gone to France.

On hearing this it struck me most forcibly that he made use of that expression as a ruse whilst he intended to make for America either by way of Liverpool or Southampton. We found that the Steam Ship Asia, Cunard's line, was going to sail at noon next day, and as there was not a moment to be lost I was dispatched with Monsieur de Ronsaray, a gentleman holding a high position in the service of the Company, to go by mail train to Liverpool so as to be in time to take our berths in the above steamer (Captain Lot, commander).

We arrived in Liverpool in due time and sailed accordingly, and after a tolerably fair passage reached New York on the evening of the 18th. On the following day we reported our errand to the house of Belmont, the eminent Bankers and Agents to Messrs Rothschild. We were informed that Mr Belmont had gone to Europe, leaving his partner Mr Christmass to the management. On discussing the serious business of our errand he sent for Mr De Voe, a Police Officer, who accompanied us to make enquiries on board the Fultham, a Steamer that had arrived from Southampton to New York a few days before us. We ascertained from the description and beyond all doubt that we were on the right track, and that Charles Carpentier had sailed in her as a first class passenger from Southampton.

After obtaining this information we pursued our enquiries to

New Jersey and other places till a late hour of the night without success.

For the two or three following days we were occupied on the same errand in going to Brooklyn, Staunton Island and Philadelphia with no better result.

After our return to New York, on the following day as we were strolling down Beekman Street, Monsieur de Ronsaray, who had disguised himself in green spectacles, accidentally caught sight of Louis Grelet. Pointing him out to me, he said, "There goes Louis Grelet." No sooner was this word uttered than we both saw him go into a Restaurant, No. 21, kept by A. Matarans.

In order to keep this house under observation and to prevent ourselves from being seen we obtained the sanction of the proprietor of a large dry-goods warehouse directly opposite, to go in and screen us from view. As we were about entering, Captain Leonard, a the Governor of the Prison, who saw me—in fact we recognized each other at the same moment—exclaim'd, "Why, what on earth are you doing here?"

I may here state that our acquaintance was formed from his calling at the Mansion House to see the Forrester Brothers at the time of the exhibition in the year 1851, about which time we dined together.

After having explain'd to him. my errand we all three retired to the far end of the Warehouse, commanding a full view of the Restaurant, and he said, "If I can be of any service to you, I shall be glad to give you all the assistance that is in my power." These words were no sooner uttered when Monsieur de Ronsaray exclaimed, "Look! there is Louis Grelet and his brother coming out."

We immediately followed them for a short distance, and with

the assistance of Captain Leonard succeeded in capturing them, and to the credit of Captain Leonard we conveyed them to the Gaol over which he had control.

I searched them and took away from Louis Grelet 20,000 Franks as well as a large number of Coupons; the prisoners thus in security, we immediately went to their lodgings and took possession of more Coupons and sundry important letters and memoranda.

Of course all this took up some considerable time, and from the excitement we had been laboring under we needed some refreshment, so we then went to M. Dalmonichi's well known Restaurant. After refreshing ourselves we extended our enquiries after Carpentier, but could not obtain any clue about him. I then turned my thoughts towards Augustus Parrot, another of the Fugitives, and on the following day about the same hour, 2 p.m., we took our station as before in the dry-goods Warehouse.

We had not been there more than a quarter of an hour when de Ronsaray saw Parrot go into Matarans Restaurant opposite, wearing a white hat very large in the brim. After continuing to watch for nearly an hour, as he did not shew a head in coming out, it was agreed that I and the Captain should enter the Hotel and proceed up stairs to the Table D'hote. As we were going we met Parrot on the landing coming down; he then wore a black hat and was evidently to my mind suspicious and on the Qui vive. We allowed him to pass us and pursue his way into the street, when to his astonishment and unpleasant surprise he came in contact face to face with Monsieur de Ronsaray, who at once pointed him out to us as Augustus Parrot. Unfortunately at this moment Monsieur de Ronsaray complained. of being very unwell, and was obliged to retire to his hotel.

In the mean time Captain Leonard and myself took Parrot in charge, and we convey'd him, after overcoming considerable resistance, to the same prison where we had taken his confederates. On searching him I found his address and some keys. I then left him in charge of the Captain and then without a minute's delay I engaged a carriage and drove to his lodgings. On raising the lid of the first trunk I had unlocked I found a double brace of Colt's two barrelled revolvers, loaded: most formidable looking weapons and quite ready for action. On searching further I found a large canvas bag full of gold twenty dollar pieces of the value of four pounds each, and a number of Chemin de fer du Nord Coupons (The Great Northern Railway of France) of very considerable value besides Jewellery.

This and other trunks contain'd several dozen fancy shirts, socks, drawers, handkerchiefs and washing waistcoats, enough to last for six months, and from a memorandum that came under my observation I felt satisfied that if we had been two days later he and his accomplices would have been on their way to California.

While I was thus busily engaged, a well dressed man made his appearance who turned out to be Mr Galbraith, Augustus Parrot's Lawyer, and who, in the most blackguard bullying manner, asked by whose and by what authority I dare come there, at the same time stamping his foot on the floor and demanding of me to shew my authority. I, knowing that I was standing on tender ground, answer'd that if he would go with me to the Gaol I would shew him. To serve my own purpose I was very Civil and Kept myself firm without shewing temper, while at the same time I was fearful every moment there would be an interruption of some kind.

While I was being insulted and talked at by this Gentleman

of the Honorable profession, I kept filling up a leather bag with some small account books and memorandums that were laying about, not forgetting the pistols. I closed the bag and on lifting it up he could hear the jingling of the coin. Fearing every moment from his threats and menacing attitude it would come to a fight for the mastery of this bag with its contents, I slowly walked towards the door, which I opened carrying my treasure in front and walked down stairs into the street, he following close upon me. At this moment the coachman opened the carriage door. I stepped in with my treasure, telling the coachman in a whisper to drive me as rapidly as he could to Belmonts, leaving my antagonist standing with a countenance full of surprise and dismay at the disappointment he was laboring under because he was not before me in obtaining possession of so large an amount of money and other valuables, which if he had succeeded in obtaining I may presume to say it would have been a secret between him and his client which in probability would never have come to light.

I will here give an instance of his capabilities, which is a copy from the Times dated July 2nd, 1857:

Liverpool, July 1st.

The United States Mail Steamship Atlanta, Captain Eldridge, has arrived with advices from New York to the 10th ult. and $1,128,581 specie on freight, and among the news it states:

Augustus Parrot, one of the prisoners in the "French extradition case" has escaped through the assistance of his Counsel, Townsend and Galbraith, who seized the officer in charge as he was taking his prisoner through the streets, and held him until Parrot made good his escape.

I may here remark that through the time that had elapsed before I and Monsieur de Ronsaray arrived in New York, we did not expect to find these absconding financiers there. As we came upon them in so sudden a manner we had no time for thought; and as I had learned from former experience that delay in this kind of undertaking is likely to be dangerous. I embraced the opportunity and, acting on the impulse of the moment, ran the risk of arresting them without Warrant or authority. Had it not been for the able assistance of Captain Leonard just at the nick of time, I should have found myself placed in great difficulties.

A few days after I had made these captures, Monsieur Emanuel Tissandier, an Inspector of the Chemin de fer du Nord, arrived with an Agent from Paris, for the purpose of finding out these delinquents, when to their agreeable surprise they found three of them already in custody. They visited the prison to satisfy themselves as to their identity, and when these prisoners were brought into court, Emanuel Tissandier made the following deposition on oath:

That he was Inspector of the Great Northern Railway Company in France, was acquainted with Louis Grelet, Eugene Grelet and Augustus Parrot, all of Paris in France. That he believed that in the month of August last they feloniously carried away a large quantity of the Shares of Stock with the Coupons attached thereto, belonging to the said Company, and had brought the said shares or the proceeds to the City of New York. That the said shares with the Coupons attached were worth the sum of and over One Million Dollars. That the said Grelets with one Carpentier, principal Cashier, secretly departed from France carrying with them and bringing to the state of New York said shares or the proceeds thereof.

Sworn before me 29th Sept. 1856

(signed) B. Osborne, Police Magistrate

Another affidavit which he made goes on to say that the said shares stolen were worth from 800 to 1100 Franks each.

The following is an extract from The Times of Oct. 1.—The opinion of Attorney-General Cushing has been asked as to whether the alleged French defaulters, recently arrested in New York, can be reclaimed under the extradition treaty with France? The opinion had not been given at the despatch of the message.

Unfortunately while these examinations and remands were going on I was suddenly called away to return to Europe on business of an important and private nature which I had previously undertaken for a Noble Duke, leaving the case in the hands of the French Police Agents to follow up the pursuit of Carpentier, whose capture was ultimately effected.

I left New York on the 1st of October on board the Asia and landed at Liverpool on the 13th. On the following morning before leaving home I saw to my surprise the following announcements in the Morning Advertiser newspaper of October 14, 1856, viz

ARRIVAL OF THE STEAM-SHIP ASIA

(LIVERPOOL, Monday.

The Cunard royal mail-ship Asia, Captain E. G. Lott, arrived in the Mersey at an early hour this morning, from New York after a voyage, rather protracted by heavy contrary winds. In addition to the usual mails, the Asia brought 106 passengers and 950,695 dols., and 240l. staling in specie.

Among the passengers on board of the Asia were the Right Hon. Robert Lowe, M.P., Vice-President of the Board of Trade; and Mr. Goddard (late one of the principal officers of the Bow-street police-office), who has been sent to America by the Messrs. Rothschild, and who had succeeded in capturing Louis Grelet, Eugene Grelet, and Auguste Parrot (who had changed his name to Dubud), charged. with others, with being concerned in the great robbery of the Northern Railway of France. A considerable sum of money was found in their possession, and on Parrot several of the railway company's private papers.

Upon their being arrested at New York, Grelet admitted his guilt, and said he disposed of the stock embezzled to Parrot. About 1,000,000 dols. worth of shares were disposed of by these financiers. There is but little prospect of recovering much of the embezzled funds, as Carpentier and Grelet squandered it away in the most foolish manner.

Grelet is reported to have said, "If we are compelled to go back to France. I will disclose several matters that will compromise the very men who now persecute me, and even great financiers, who now hold their heads so high on the Bourse."

In the year 1846, when the railway company was first chartered, Messrs. Grelet and Carpentier were employed as cashiers in the concern.

"My first speculations," says Grelet, "were always entered into with cash; it was not until 1852 that I borrowed the shares of the company. I hoped to be able to replace them by lucky ventures, but being without any ready cash,

Carpentier and myself were always unfortunate in our speculations.

"Mr. Rothschild, who was president of the company, had every confidence in our integrity, and in 1848 he entrusted to our care sixty thousand shares of the railway company, valued at fifty million francs, with orders if the insurrection in Paris was not quelled, to proceed to England with the valuable package. We proceeded as far as Amiens, and intended to cross the

Channel when we received orders to remain in France. These shares were the private property of Mr Rothschild, and they remained in our possession until 1851, when Mr Rothschild claimed them. They were delivered up to him, and all was found to be correct. The property was retained in Mr Rothschild's possession for six months after that, when it was again placed in our hands.

"At that time Mr Robert was cashier and right-hand man of Mr Rothschild. When he died, in the month of May last, Mr Carpentier was appointed to fill the vacancy. Two months ago we were entrusted with 70,000 francs, and proceeded to Belgium for the purpose of depositing the amount with Mr Lambert (Rothschild's agent in Brussels). If we were disposed to be dishonest at that time, we could have left the country with the large amount, and not come here, as we did, without any money, except a small sum given us by our friends. We never took any case [cash?] from the establishment (none has been missed), but merely borrowed shares of the company, with the hope of being able to replace them."

After reading the above announcements I went into the City and had an audience with the Messrs Rothschilds, stating to them the particulars of the arrests that I had made and the amount of value in Bonds and Coupons recovered. They gave me great praise for my exertions and the manner the thing was done, and directed me at once to proceed to Paris with Mr Thomas Cullen, an old and invaluable servant who has been in their confidence for a great number of years.

Having reached Paris and after an introduction to the firm, we were directed to proceed to the Chateau of Baron Rothschild at Ferier, before whom and several ladies I had again to recapitulate what I have here before stated, and which was listened to by the Baron and the Ladies with great attention. After this the Baron most kindly and pressingly invited me and Mr Cullen to join him at dinner. The ladies being present, we accepted his kind offer but begged as we were in our travelling costume and being so dusty to be allowed if agreeable to dine in a room by ourselves. He made a very graceful bow and directed his steward to provide us with dinner.

The steward conducted us to the lavatory, and after a good brush up and a wash which occupied some twenty minutes a tall handsome well grown pleasant looking man-servant in livery came to announce that dinner was ready. He conducted us into a most magnificent richly furnished saloon surrounded with mirrors and brilliantly illuminated fit for a Prince, and had we been two Noblemen we could not have been better entertain'd. The wines were of the finest brand. It was half past 9 o'clock when we got up from dinner. We again saw the Baron, who complimented me in the highest terms for the manner and the risk I had run in making the capture as I had done in a foreign Country and without warrants. He then gave directions for his carriage to be brought to the door, when one of the Junior Rothschilds stepped in, followed by myself and Mr Cullen. We were driven at a rapid rate to the Railway station in time for the Paris Train, and after remaining in Paris two days we returned to London.

This case was under litigation in New York for ten months, terminating in July 1857.

The following is an abridged account from the New York Herald:

GREAT EXCITEMENT IN FRANCE ANOTHER INTERVIEW BY OUR REPORTER INTERESTING STATEMENTS

Parrot and his companion protest against their illegal incarceration. Parrot admits that he had speculated on the Exchange. Grelet said when he left his native land that his hopes were crushed and that he was led to the verge of despair and that his resources were tendered to him by his intimate friends. If, he argued, he had those large amounts in his possession which he is charged with having, undoubtedly they would have been found here, nor can it be said with justice that the money found upon him was stolen: other frauds have been committed by several parties which are now imputed to him. The prisoners are in good spirits and express confidence in the American laws, which punish only the guilty.

The Paris correspondence from the Independence Belge says:

It is rumoured that the Northern Railway Company has asked for satisfaction of the Minister of Foreign Affairs in order to obtain the extradition of the audacious scamps who have stolen 5547 Shares from the Company. The Minister gives little hopes of assistance, for American diplomatists are not willing to renew the extradition treaty which has already expired.

In another number it says:

About fifteen or 20 days ago the Cashier, Carpentier, asked leave of absence for eight days on the pretext that he was going to be married and requested it should be kept secret. A few days after another cashier, Grilet, feigned not to be able to go on with the business alone and insinuated that Carpentier had not to discharge such a pleasant duty. This gave time for Louis Grilet to join Carpentier at Southampton where the latter was waiting for him with a Stable Keeper (Parrot) who had a commission to sell part of the stolen shares, the amount belonging to the Treasury.

I am sorry to take up so much of my reader's valuable time before bringing this case to a conclusion, but I am of opinion that the following remarks copied from the American Newspapers may not prove uninteresting.

From the New York Herald, September 29, 1856:

THE ASTOUNDING RAILWAY FRAUDS IN FRANCE. —We gave yesterday, and continue to-day, a history of the remarkable railway frauds which have recently come to light in France, and the capture here of the parties said to have been concerned therein. By a series of bold operations the Northern Railway Company has been defrauded to the extent of five millions of francs by its own officers, who, having escaped to the United States, have been captured in this city and now await examination.

In some respects these French transactions are similar to those which lately transpired in this country. There is, however, this difference: the French government pursues and arrests the runaways on our soil, while our police allow persons engaged in similar transactions to escape and live in Europe unmolested, enjoying the fruits of their dishonesty—as in the case of Schuyler. Of late years several immense frauds have been discovered here; but we are persuaded that those which have already been brought to light are nothing to those the particulars of which have not transpired. These immense corporations, with their thirty or fifty millions of capital, are full of corruption and roguery of all kinds. We expect soon to hear of some grand railway explosions which will astonish the community.

From the New York Herald, October I, 1856:

THE ALLEGED IMMENSE FRAUDS IN FRANCE— THE ACCUSED PARTIES HELD TO BAIL IN THE SUM

OF $500,000 EACH

Supreme Court

Before Hon. Judge Davies.

Sept. 30.-The Northern Railway of France vs. Charles Carpentier, Louis Grelet, Auguste Parot and -- Guerin.

Mr Morrough made application to the Court for an order for the arrest of the defendants, who are charged with fraudulently taking property belonging to the plaintiffs, as already elaborately reported in our police news. The Judge granted the order, holding each of the defendants to bail in the sum of $500,000; and officer De Angelis, who was deputized by the Sheriff, took the accused from the custody of the Second ward police, and lodged them in Eldridge street jail, to await the further action of the Court.

From the same issue of the New York Herald:

Elsewhere will be found a full account of a gigantic fraud lately practised upon the stockholders of the Northern Railway of France, by their cashiers, Charles Carpentier and Louis Grelet, and the arrest of the latter in this city by the detective police. The accused parties fled to this country, but were closely followed both by the London and Paris police. The prisoner admitted his guilt, and said he disposed of the stock embezzled to a broker, named August Parot, who was also arrested and locked up with Grelet. Carpentier has not yet been arrested, but the police are on his track. About $1,000,000 worth of shares were disposed of by these financiers. There is but little prospect of recovering much of the embezzled funds, as Carpentier and Grelet squandered it away in the most foolish manner.

In bringing this case to a conclusion I must state that remand after remand continued for two months.

On the 26th February, 1857, and on the 27th the following

account appeared in the New York Herald:

ALLEGED FRENCH RAILROAD FRAUDS UNITED STATES COMMISSIONER'S COURT

Before Geo. F. Betts, Esq.

AN EXCITING SCENE IN COURT—MR BUSTEED GETS POSSESSION OF A PAPER AND REFUSES TO GIVE IT UP—THE PROCEEDINGS SUDDENLY ADJOURNED

Feb. 26.—In the matter of Carpentier, Grelet and others, whose extradition is claimed under the treaty with France. The District Attorney and his assistant appeared for the United States, and Messrs Tillou and Morrough for the French government, and Messrs Busteed, Galbraith, Townsend and Fogarty, for the accused.

M. de Montholon, Consul General of France, was again called to the stand, and produced his commission under the great seal of France, signed by the Emperor Napoleon and also his exequator by President Pierce.

Mr Busteed commented on M. de Montholon's appointment as Consul, and objected to it as not sufficiently proved.

The Commissioner held that the commission of the witness was sufficiently proved.

Mr Busteed excepted to the decision of the Court.

Thus matters went on till June, when the following appeared in The Times Newspaper of June 12, 1857:

AMERICA

(A summary of the following, received by electric telegraph, appeared in our second edition of yesterday.)

SOUTHAMPTON, Thursday, June 11

The United States mail steamship Arago, Captain Lines, with the mails of the 30th ult. from New York, arrived off Cowes this morning about 3 o'clock, after a passage of 11 days six hours.

Mr De Voe (Deputy United States Marshal and Sergeant from the office of the Chief of Police at New York) is also on board the Arago, having in his charge Louis Grelet, one of the persons implicated in the frauds on the Great Northern Railway Company of France. A letter from a passenger by the Arago says:

"Grelet came on board with the officer in the Bay of New York, the order, under the extradition treaty between France and the United States, having arrived from Washington only two hours before the steamer sailed. The brother of Grelet died in confinement at New York. There remain only two more—Parrot and David, who may probably escape, the evidence not being strong against them. Grelet speaks in the highest terms of his treatment by his superiors, and has had the fullest liberty on board and conducted himself in every way with propriety. Both had first-class berths. After Mr De Voe shall have delivered his charge to the French authorities he will probably visit London on his return, to inspect the police system, and place himself more intimately in correspondence with the detectives of London."

Carpentier and Augustus Parrot were conveyed in another steamer to Havre by Lorenzo De Angelis, who held the same position as Mr De Voe, and the case ended in the following manner:

THE JUDGMENT

By the decree of 25th July 1857 The Court of Assize of the Seine has acquitted Augustus Parrot of the accusation brought against him, and under the articles of the Penal code, has condemned Jean-Baptiste Charles Carpentier, clerk, to five years' imprisonment, and Louis Grelet, under-clerk, to eight years' banishment.

Julius Tode

The New York papers announce that a Russian named Julius Tode, who absconded from St Petersburg in 1859, with about £10,000, belonging to Messrs Earle and Co., shipowners of Hull, has at length been taken into custody; and this enables us to give a few particulars of the proceedings adopted under the advice of Mr Henry Goddard, formerly one of the principal officers of Marlborough-street Police-court, whose acquaintance our readers have already made; and they now have a further opportunity of admiring the perseverance and address that accomplished officer displays in those cases where his professional experience is engaged.

This Julius Tode was brother to Rudolph Tode, who was agent to Messrs Earle and Co., and being without employment, his brother, who had implicit faith in his honesty, employed him during an indisposition, which ended fatally, to discharge the business of the firm. This enabled Julius Tode to get possession of the proceeds of the sale of a ship belonging to Messrs Earle and Co., amounting to upwards of £7,000, and with this sum and other moneys he had collected, he absconded. The flight of the defaulter was not discovered for about a month afterwards. One of the firm proceeded to St Petersburg, but failed to trace the fugitive.

Mr Goddard, whose private inquiry office is at 7, Harrington-square, was applied to, and he went to the Continent to continue the investigation. Finding that the brother Rudolph was at 'Wiesbaden, ill, the first step was to set a watch on his movements, as it was conjectured that the fugitive would, as soon as he thought pursuit had cooled, pay him a visit. The next step was to communicate with the consuls and the officials at the different ports in Europe, Asia, Africa, and America, to trace out the fugitive's antecedents, which was done in the following effective manner:— Ostend, in 1856; Paris, 1857; Montpellier, 1857 and 1858; Weldbad Gastern, 1858, and again from May to July, 1859; Algiers and Constantine, 1859; Tyrol, Geneva, Bordeaux, Marseilles, Lyons, etc.

The opinion of Goddard, from the first, was that Tode had gone to America, and it will be seen that subsequent events proved his opinion was right. To give some idea of the completeness of the chain of information which was drawn round the delinquent, Goddard sent photograph likenesses of Tode, and particulars of his offences, to Amsterdam, Algiers, Bordeaux, Berlin, Bremen, Constantinople, Constantine, Dunkirk, Frankfort, Geneva, Genoa, Havre, Hamburgh, Malta, Menan, Montpellier, Messina, Madeira, Marseilles, Milan, Nice, Odessa, Paris, Rome, Rostock, Vienna, Venice, Wilbad Gastern, New Orleans, New York, and twelve ports in South America.

It was no doubt owing to the complete publicity given to the case, to the full description of the culprit's person, and his photographic likeness sent to these and other places, with the large reward offered for his apprehension (£500) that ultimately his capture was effected. Indeed, had the gentleman from the firm of Earle and Co., who went over to look after Tode, taken Goddard with him, there is good reason to suppose that Tode would have been captured before he got out of the Baltic.

It was subsequently ascertained that Tode, after visiting several places, probably to elude detection, and put pursuers off the scent, found his way to St Petersburg, and was rowed to the Peperell, American barque, then lying about two miles from Cronstadt. Having ascertained from the captain that the Custom House officers had already paid their visit, he urged the immediate departure of the vessel. The vessel got as far as Elsinore, and was detained by adverse winds for about seven days, during which period Tode feigned sickness, and persuaded his fellow passenger to go ashore and purchase a few requisites for a transatlantic voyage. The Cronstadt pilot, some time afterwards, when the robbery was made known, gave information of the passenger who had so mysteriously come on board the Peperell, and there would have been plenty of time to have gone after Tode and taken him at Elsinore had the particulars been brought out in time, which they certainly would have been had such an experienced officer as Goddard been engaged at the outset.

The fugitive got away and arrived in America. He travelled about from place to place—South America among other localities; but here he found he was on dangerous ground, and made his way back to New York, and from the New York Herald we make the following extract:

Every effort was made to find some clue as to the whereabouts of Tode in this country. Some time in September Detective Elder learned through a Wall-street broker that there was a Russian nobleman in town who corresponded in appearance with the fugitive. The officer, seized with the idea that the Russian nobleman and the man he was so long in search of were one and the same, went to work and searched for him accordingly. After several days and nights of hard toil, he succeeded on the 3rd inst. in meeting the object of his search in Broadway. He immediately accosted him and, informing him of the nature of his business, conveyed him to the police head-quarters. Subsequently Tode accompanied the officer to his hotel, where, on searching a trunk, the latter found 50,000 dols. in paper roubles.

The prisoner took the matter very coolly indeed, and told the officer that he would have all his trouble for nothing, as there was no treaty in existence whereby he could be sent back to Russia. In answer to some questions put to him by the officer, he stated that he had been travelling all over the United States, and, after visiting all the watering-places, came to New York, for the purpose of spending the winter here.

He talks English quite fluently, although he has been in this country but a short time, and is very gentlemanly in his appearance and manners. Whether the police will succeed in sending the accused to Europe is a matter of extreme doubt. There will be an effort made to make Tode disgorge his wealth, for the benefit of his mends in England, but with what success it will be attended it is hard to say.

Edward James Farrer Esq.

The following announcement appeared among the notices of Deaths in The Times newspaper of the 21st September, 1864, viz

On Saturday, the 17th Inst., from Dysentry, Edward James Farrer Esq. of 37 Old Jewry, London, for many years Actuary and Secretary of the Gresham Life Assurance Society. Friends will please accept this intimation.

The above advertisement having attracted the attention of the Directors, and being coupled with the circumstance of his nonattendance in his official capacity for the last four or five weeks, caused them to have their misgivings, and they held a meeting thereon. After a long consultation it was deemed expedient to send for their Solicitor, Mr Devonshire, who advised that inquiries should at once be instituted and that his Wife and relations should be seen.

His Wife was residing in a cottage at Belvidere, called the Retreat.

She said that for some time past Mr Farrer had been complaining of indisposition, and he thought a trip to the

Continent for a short time would do him good.

"I went with him," she said, "a week ago to Folkstone, and before he boarded the steamer for Boulogne he said to me that after he shall have crossed the Channel he would write. After the boat had left we signall'd each other until it was lost to view. Two days afterwards I received a letter from him bearing the Folkstone post-mark, complaining of the very stormy rough and disagreeable passage he had had in crossing which had made him very sick and ill, so much so, that he had been confined to his bed ever since, but that I was not to despair as he hoped to be better in a day or two, and I should hear from him soon. On the following morning to my great alarm I received a letter edged with black, bearing the same post-mark, but written in another hand saying that the writer was grieved and much pained to have to inform me that his old friend Mr Farrer after a short and painful illness died in his arms. There was no signature nor any address, nor mention made when and where his death took place, and I was going to town to shew it to the Directors."

Inquiries were afterwards made of his two Nephews, who were living at Chelsea, when it was ascertained that they had just received two large Trunks from their Uncle, Edward J. Farrer, containing nearly one thousand pounds in French gold pieces, besides his wearing apparel and linen. There was no letter, they said, to say where these Trunks came from; they thought they had been sent from France but were unable to say for certain. This and other circumstances led to the supposition that there was a mystery attending the affair, Mr Farrer's family believing he was dead.

The Directors after holding several meetings were not of this opinion, and not feeling satisfied, were determined to institute the most searching enquiries, and that without delay. They employed an enquiry-agent to go with one of their clerks to Boulogne and to continue their enquiries at every town between there and Paris, or wherever it was needed.

While these enquiries were going on in France I was employed to do the same thing in London. I was informed by the Solicitor that a Shoemaker of the name of Walsh, living near the Hospital at Chelsea, made his boots, and requested me to go there as Farrer had a deformed foot and walked lame, and Walsh being an anatomical bootmaker, would give me a proper description. I went as directed and Mr Walsh told me he had supplied Mr Farrer with boots for many years, he was one of his best customers, and had fitted him out with six pairs about two months ago. He then went on and gave me his general description, viz that he was "a tall stout gentleman about 60 years of age, walked with a stick, rather lame on the left leg," and he had promised him £50 if he could make a boot that would fit him so that he could walk without the appearance of being lame and so to look like other men and thus to hide his deformity.

"I will describe it as well as I can," said Walsh. "His heel was a little more than three inches above its natural position, and to remedy this I cut and fitted a large piece of cork to fill up the cavity of the deformed part, so as to make the heel level with the ball of the foot. To keep this in its place I made a thin slipper-boot to fit over it, and over this, another boot of the same size to correspond with the other, the right one. A short piece of steel was passed through the boot and cork below the ankle to the other side, and to this was attached two lengths iron with rivets, one on the outside under the trousers to the thigh and the other to come a little above the knee inside. By bracing these with straps made for the purpose the leg was kept apparently straight and thus hid the deformity." (The reader will find the importance of this description.)

Having obtained this information I returned to the Solicitor, when it occurred to me that if I could be in possession of the trunks, they might probably be of great assistance to obtain a clue upon which to work. He thought that if he gave me a letter to the Nephews they would let me have them. I delivered the letter, and without the slightest hesitation they gave them to me. I thanked them and brought the trunks away in a cab in the same state, with the directions fastened on, as they were when delivered, barring their contents.

Having got possession of these trunks, I had to consider what I was to do with them. My first thought, which I acted upon, was to take them for the inspection of Mr Day, the Trunk Makers in the Strand, to know whether they were French or English make. On surveying them he expressed his opinion that they were of foreign manufacture. I took them home and again considered what I should do with them.

I thought about the vague report of his death, that it was a fabrication. If so, and his intention was to leave France and return to London, he would not come by way of London Bridge, for fear (as he was so well known in the City) of being seen, but would make for his point, Charing Cross, and then retire to some hotel near at hand. Having in my former experience got acquainted with Mr Louis Watson, a bookkeeper in the service of Chaplin and Horne at the office under Gardners Hotel at Charing Cross, I asked him if he would allow me to leave a couple of Trunks in his care, also if he would kindly ask the hotel porters and waiters if they could identify them as having belonged to anyone that had lately been staying with them, for they would sooner tell him than me.

Mr Watson said, "I have known you for a great number of years, Mr Goddard, and I shall only be too happy to do what you ask."

We afterwards had some brandy and water, and it was agreed that I was to let him have them under his care for two or three days. I accordingly left them.

Three days afterwards I went to him again, and directly he saw me he came hobbling over from the other side of the booking-office, and in a whispering voice said, "I think it is all right, for I have seen Gregory Stiff the Porter and he seems to think that he knows something about them, and also the gentleman. But sit down and stay here," and with a nodding knowing sort of wink he said, "I will bring him to you."

After waiting a short time he returned with Gregory Stiff, who gave me a full description of the gentleman which exactly answered in every way to that given to me by Walsh and Mr Devonshire the solicitor.

Believing I was now on the right track I questioned him very minutely and in reply he said, "I recollect a gentleman arrived here some time ago from France with those very trunks, and a few days after he had been staying here he ordered me to send them as directed to Mr Farrer, Whiteheads Grove, Chelsea, by the Parcels-delivery."

I asked him if he was sure they were the same.

"I can swear to them," was his reply, "for the gentleman gave me these very directions that are on now. He told me to be careful and stick them on tight, and I was careful for I glued them on, and they are in the same state as they were then. His name was Williams, he occupied a bed and sitting room and I recollect he ordered me to go and buy at Allen's, the

Trunkmaker in the Strand, a gentleman's Portmanteau, to be three feet long, and just high enough to fit under the seat of a Railway Carriage and also to find a shop and purchase a hairbrush with a looking-glass at the back. He frequently sent me with Telegraph messages but I have forgotten to whom they were addressed."

After giving me this information he had no time to give me more as his duties called him away. After he left, Louis Watson introduced Isaac Collins, one of the waiters, who told me that Mr Williams had been staying at the hotel for four or five days. "He seldom went out, and one day I picked up a paper that had fallen from the table and upon it was written, '£144 Passage money paid by Joseph Williams' and the name of a Ship which I cannot remember. He was occupied all one Sunday I recollect in sorting and burning papers, and had a profusion of money on his table, consisting of Bank notes and French gold coin. He gave me a book called Les Misirables and left behind him a quantity of waste paper and a Bradshaw." (This the waiter gave to me.)

After receiving this information I wished him and old Watson good night, saying I would call again. I then made my way home and felt satisfied with my day's work. Before I went to bed I took up the Bradshaw from the table where I had laid it and in examining it I saw that the only part that appeared to have been among the pages much used was Liverpool; in fact every time I laid it down and took it up it opened at Liverpool. The next morning I again examined it with the same result.

I communicated to the solicitor the information I had obtained and called his attention to the page in Bradshaw notifying the departure from London and arrival at Liverpool, and how much it appeared the Bradshaw had been used, which gave us the idea that enquiries should be made at Liverpool. These circumstances was reported to the Director, who at once agreed that I should proceed to Liverpool. I then received a Cheque and lost no time in setting out on my journey to Liverpool.

On my arrival there I went to the Queen's Hotel, and made a few preliminary inquiries of the lady attending at the bar as to whether she had any recollection of an elderly gentleman named J. Williams, who walked a little lame, within the last two or three months having stopped there. She replied that she had a vivid recollection of such a person and said she would look over her books. She rang for the waiter, and having to my astonishment found the name and relating the matter to him, he observed, "Oh, yes, Miss, I recollect the gentleman very well, he left a small packet of cards with his name 'Mr J. Williams.' He told me he came from the Wolds in Gloucestershire, and I recollect he was continually going to McTaggots the outfitters, that he never walked out but always had a close carriage and he was fond of playing upon the flute."

I thanked the lady for her trouble and went off at once to McTaggots the outfitters and enquired the price of outfits, representing that I was about going to Australia," and that a friend of mine, Mr Williams, who had been staying at the Queens Hotel, recommended me.

"Oh, yes," said the shopman, "I recollect him very well. He bought a very expensive outfit. It cost £150, and McTaggot changed for him a £1000 Bank of England note. Amongst his things he had two black bags like these and a portmanteau and a silk skull cap like this, besides shirts, velvets, furs, etc."

After the shopman had showed me all these things I made a few purchases and said that I was going to leave Liverpool for a short time and would call again.

I then left to renew enquiries at the Queens and was informed by the waiter that Mr Williams arrived there on the 12th of the previous month (September) and remained until the Saturday following, when he left by the 11.30 a.m. Train saying that he was bound for Bristol. (This no doubt was a ruse.) "And after he had left I found in his room," continued the Waiter, "these cards, being his name, a receipt for a gold watch, some music and a flute; previous to which he gave me a walking stick."

All these things I asked the waiter to produce in order to put my private mark upon them, telling him it was very probable either sooner or later he would have to produce them to give evidence in a Court of Justice and on no account to let them go out of his possession.

Having now considered my commission over as far as Liverpool was concerned, I returned to London and made my report to the Directors, who were highly satisfied with these enquiries and came to the conclusion that I was on the right track. On the same afternoon I told the solicitor that if he sent a clerk to the "Beaureau de Change" in the Haymarket, from information I had received, he would learn that a Thousand-pound Bank of England note had been changed. The clerk made the enquiry and found that a gentleman answering the description of J. Williams did get change for a Thousand-pound note and it was all in French gold. This no doubt was the same that he had sent with other things in the Portmanteau to his nephews at Whiteheads Grove.

I then took my way to the Peninsular and Oriental Steam Navigation Company's Office,. Leadenhall Street, to ascertain whether they could furnish me with information by turning to their books of last September as to a gentleman passenger booked to Melbourne or any other part of Australia by the name of J. Williams. They very readily looked over their books and informed me there was no passenger of that name.

I felt disappointed and advised with the Solicitor that I should proceed to Southampton, whither I went and commenced enquiries at Randalls Hotel. On seeing the lady manager I apologised for intruding and said that my errand was most important as I was anxious to learn if in September last a gentleman by the name of J. Williams had been staying there. To give her time to refer to the books I retired to the Coffee room for some refreshment, and in about twenty minutes the lady sent for me and in the most polite manner said that she now well recollected the name, for the gentleman had given them a great deal of trouble. He had telegraphed from Liverpool to engage a bed and sitting room, with fires in each got ready, and then he again telegraphed that if any black bags came directed in his name, not to fail to take them in for they were important. They did arrive and were taken in. On the next morning another telegram arrived saying that he should be there at 12 o'clock, and at the time appointed a carriage brought him to the door, but he did not get out, he beckoned for the waiter who was standing at the door and inquired for the black bags and his bill, which were no sooner given to him than he paid and drove away to Hills the Shipping Agents.

From this information I went to Hills and was informed that he went from there on board the Poonah (a Peninsular and Oriental Company's Steamer), which sailed at 1 o'clock p.m. immediately after he got on board.

Having obtained this information I returned to London and made my report, and afterwards went again to the P. and O.

Company and explained the information I had obtained at Southampton. They then referred back to their books again, and said there had been some mistake as to dates in consequence of another name appearing in the place of J. Williams, but it was now quite certain that J. Williams sailed from Southampton on board the Poonah for Alexandria at 1 p.m. on the 29th September last, that she had since returned, and was now in Dock at Marseilles and would sail again for Alexandria on Wednesday next the 19th inst. As no time was now to be lost, Mr Hill, a gentleman of the establishment, gave me a letter of introduction to his brother, who was the Purser.

This was Monday the 17th, and I left by the Mail that evening to proceed to Marseilles. I arrived at Paris by 7 the following morning and went to my oId friend Outhwaite, the proprietor of Byron's tavern, Rue Fanart, had a refreshing wash and an excellent breakfast afterwards, took a "Remise" and drove to the Chemin-de-fer de Lyon and proceeded on to Lyons, where I was detained from midnight till nearly five in the morning. I arrived at the Hotel de Empereur, Marseilles, at 7 o'clock the next morning, Wednesday, all in good time to get on board the Poonah, which was for sailing at 12. I had a hasty breakfast and engaged a waterman to row me to the ship, and on boarding her I was immediately in the presence of Mr Hill.

I gave him his brother's letter, and after he read it he said, "Oh, yes, I recollect Mr Williams very well, he was a little lame and was fond of playing on the flute. After arriving at Alexandria he disembarked and went on with the other passengers by Rail to Cairo. He told me that his wife and children were all dead and his lameness was caused by an accident on the Railway. He praised the good qualities of the ship and said he would purchase shares—he appeared to be a perfect gentleman—he left a packet of cards under his pillow with his name engraved.

My interview with Mr Hill having come to an end I returned to London and made my report. Thus matters remained quiet till the 10th of November, when I received instructions to obtain my outfit and prepare to be in readiness to proceed to Australia by the overland route. On the 6th of the following month, December, I left Charing Cross Station and travelled on to Paris, Lyons and Marseilles, embarking on board the P.O. Company's Steamer Syria, commander Captain Christie, who was very amusing to the Passengers by his anecdotes.

We passed the Islands of Corsica—Sardinia—Bonne de Facie in the distance. The Captain made for the Strait but the weather coming on foggy, he would not risk it, saying that 1100 French soldiers had been cast upon the Rocks at the time of the Crimean war. On the following day we passed along the Coast of Sicily and the Island of Maritimo, arriving at Malta in the afternoon of the 15th, giving myself and fellow-passengers the opportunity of visiting the Church of St. John's, the Palace and other places of note. We returned on board at 8, bound for Alexandria, where we arrived at half past 9 on the morning of the 19th, casting anchor within half a mile of shore.

At this time a large Egyptian barge was brought alongside to receive the passengers' luggage, some of the trunks being large and very weighty, and instead of being lowered by a sling, were thrown down from a considerable height, helter skelter one upon the other, breaking and doing considerable damage. This barge contained from thirty to forty wild looking native Arabs dressed in all sorts of colored costume, all hollowing and shouting at the top of their voices in the most confused and unintelligible manner possible, enough to break the air.

The passengers were conveyed to shore by boats, and after I landed I was obliged to be as expeditious as possible to make my enquiries of the different bankers and money changers as to whether they had had any dealings within the last three months with a gentleman from England by the name of J. Williams and who it was supposed was on his way either to India or Australia. I found the most ready and cheapest way to do this was to engage a donkey-boy, telling him in the first instance what I wanted. I then mounted his donkey and in the course of an hour he took me to the places I had told him, from where I gained no information. Had I engaged a Dragoman he would have charged me at least a guinea and taken at least three times as long to do it; as it was I paid the boy half a crown which made him quite satisfied.

I had but little time to spare before the train started at half past 1 for Cairo, arriving there at 9 p.m. The night was dark and I had to scramble for my valise and get into a large carriage holding about twenty four gentlemen, driving us to Shepherds hotel. On enquiry I found all the beds engaged but one, which was at the very top of the building and that would not be vacant before 11 as the party occupying it was resting till the midnight train from Suez arrived. I felt fatigued, and under the circumstances was glad to accept it. In the meantime a fellow-passenger invited me to a bottle of soda water with a small glass of brandy; we had one each, for which we had to pay four shillings, and it was anything but refreshing for it was hot and had a nasty taste it being of their own manufacture.

The time had now arrived to retire to my bedroom. A Mahomedan walked before me with a lighted candle and led me up two or three flights of stairs and very long passages to the bedroom, which to my surprise had not been put in order since the last occupant left. The chamber towel was wet and crumpled, the wash-hand basin full of dirty water and other utensils in a most disgusting state, the bed, bolster and sheets disarranged, in fact they had never been touched, and to crown all, the bed was quite warm so that the last occupier could only have just left.

All this was very discomforting; so after complaining about it I had to retire down stairs for half an hour before it was at all in a fit state for occupation.

When I got into the room, voices could be heard right and left, and on casting my eyes aloft I found the ceiling to be nearly 12 feet in height with a wooden partition on each side of the room about 8 feet high, so that if inclined you had only to stand upon a table and see into your neighbour's room, and as long as they wished to talk and keep their lights burning after your own was extinguished you had to put up with the glare over your eyes.

What with these disagreeables and the annoyance from the buzzing and bites of Mosquitoes I had a sorry time of it and very little sleep. I was down early to breakfast on the following morning and had time to ask at the bar if they would kindly refer to their books for two or three mails back to see if they had got entered a gentleman named J. Williams, and on searching they found his name as being there on the 3rd and 4th October last, telling them he was going on board the Simla as he was proceeding to Calcutta.

Now mark; this information was given to me on the 20th of December, therefore he had seventy days' start of me. As I had been informed that the Simla had returned from Calcutta and was laying off in the Gulf of Suez, I made the best of my way with the passengers to Suez, arriving there at half past 4 p.m.

While the passengers in the large courtyard covered with canvas from the glare of the sun were being entertained to a sumptuous dinner accompanied with superior music and singing, I engaged a boat rowed by four Arabs to the Simla, laying at anchor about six miles down the gulf:

I was fortunate in having an immediate interview with Mr Standerwick the Purser, and asked him if he had any recollection of Mr Williams, a lame gentleman, who was a passenger on his last voyage to Galle.

After considering a short time, "Oh, yes," he replied, "he wrote to me from Cairo to engage, at any cost, one of the best berths in the ship, but unfortunately I have destroyed the letter. I remember while sailing down the Red Sea through the straits of Babelmamdeb he told the Captain and myself that he was one of our Directors. We believed it and paid him every attention. I remember my wife, who happened to be with me on that voyage, called my attention to him, saying, "Don't you know that gentleman? If I am not mistaken he lives at Belvidere, not far from our house at a place called the Retreat.' After she mentioned this it brought to my recollection that I knew him by sight quite well. He left our ship at Galle and went on board the Northern for Australia, he said."

At this time, the passengers from Suez came rushing on board which ended our conversation, he being obliged to leave me and attend to them. We bade each other farewell, and I descended to the small steamer that had brought the passengers, the Arabs fasten'd their boat astern and we steamed back to Suez, where I had to wait for the next Australian Mail in expectation of receiving letters from England.

After remaining two or three days I made a temporary acquaintance with three gentlemen, one was a son of Mr Kilpin the member for Northampton, and we arranged to engage a sailing boat of a very tall arab named Absolem with his three Arab men to take us to the Fountain of Moses. which I think took about three hours. As there was no landing stage they let go the anchor, jump'd overboard up to their waists and carried us on their backs to the dry sand for about 200 yards. We then had to walk about three miles, but we could see the spot, it being surrounded with palm trees which appeared then to be very small and not more than 12 to 14 feet high, but when we arrived they were tall, stately and majestic trees. Our attention was first drawn to what we considered a very novel sight, viz to see so many camels, about fifty in number, lying down resting, with their burden on their backs, accompanied with attendants who were sitting around bivouacing before several fires. It was a noble and most picturesque sight. We were informed that when they arrived at this spot after crossing the desert, they consider themselves free from the attacks of antagonistic tribes being then under the Mountains of Deliverance.

We then turned ourselves round and walked to the Fountain, the water of which bubbles up in large quantities from the centre of an apparently deep pond of not very large dimensions and the water having a brackish taste, we partook of some coffee made from this water and found it to be very good. We then returned to our boat, being carried to it in the same manner on the backs of the Arabs. We arrived at Suez in time for the table d'hote.

On the following morning we agreed to take Rail and recross the Desert to Cairo for the purpose of visiting the Pyramids, and having arrived safely at Shepherds hotel had a refreshing wash and then took our places at the Table d'Hote. Afterwards we partook of Coffee and about 11 o'clock each retired to his bedroom. I had not been in bed more than half an hour and was beginning to dose when I began to be tormented with the perpetual hum of the musquetoes and not-to-be-mentioned innumerable insects, crawling from out of the crevices all over one's arms, face and body.

This was not to be endured. I therefore got up and lit the candle, when never had I beheld such a scene before in the whole course of my life. It was terrific, the numbers were countless, crawling all over the counterpane, pillow, bolster, bed posts, mosqueto curtains and even over one's wearing apparel. I opened my bedroom door and woke up the male attendant, a Mahomedan, who was sleeping on the floor at the end of a very long passage. On making known my troubles, he immediately came to my assistance by lifting up the tester and carrying it away with the curtains, counterpane and all, afterwards returning with another counterpane and some disinfecting powder, sprinkling it about the mattress and pillows. He then left me to do the best I could.

I left the candle burning and laid me down to sleep, but the mosquitoes were too much for me. I got up, dressed and went down stairs, laid myself down on a large sofa in the Coffee Room and slept for the remainder of the night till six in the morning, when I was awoke by the waiters coming to dust and sweep the room. I wished them any where else. I retired to my bedroom and soon afterwards took a warm bath, which refreshed me so much that I felt no ill effects from the previous night's encounter. The gong now gave notice for breakfast, and I related these troubles to my friends who said theirs had been bad enough but not so bad as mine. I afterwards told the proprietor, who promised us it should not occur again.

We now decided to visit the Pyramids, and after providing

ourselves with candles and refreshment for the occasion engaged our Dragoman and carriage. We started on to old Cairo on the banks of the Nile, where our Dragoman engaged four very fine Donkeys. We were not a little surprised to see their activity in jumping over the sides into the boat, and on arriving at Ghiseh, the other side, they displayed their activity in jumping out. We mounted these donkeys and it was a delightful ride, bordering on Cotton and Sugar plantations, passing through an Arab village where there is an open space in the centre heaped up with large quantities of thrashed wheat, entirely exposed to the elements, rain being seldom seen.

From thence we made our way along the Lybian Desert, all eyes looking intent towards this wonder of wonders the Great Pyramid, rising in broad expanse and standing against the clear blue horizon with the bright and dazzling sun, shining forth upon it in all its mighty glory. It is in itself so impressive a sight that it is not easily to be forgotten. Arriving at the base of the Pyramid we were very much beset and annoyed by a gang of uncultivated begging Arabs, one of whom was blind and guided by two others who placed themselves before us importuning for Baksheeh and were not easily to be got rid of.

The first object that attracted my attention was a party of ladies and gentlemen on the top of the Pyramid nearly 600 feet high who appeared the size of children's dolls, and another party-at the same time ascending, whose figures gradually become less, while those who were descending increased. At this moment a very smart active young Arab, dressed in white with a red silk scarf round his waist, undertook for a small sum of money to ascend the top of Cheops and descend to the base and then run for a quarter of a mile and climb to the top of Cephrenes, the other Pyramid, and returning to where he first started, and I think he did it in twelve minutes. It was an interesting sight to see how he bounded from stone to stone, and came running in with his red scarf fluttering in the wind, looking, as the saying is, more like a fairy; the effect altogether was very imposing.

After witnessing this feat we made our way into the interior, first by ascending an incline of about seven yards and then in a stooping position had to pass through an opening about four feet square into a long dark slanting tunnel very much on the descent for about sixty yards, and very slippery. I went toes first, sliding down backwards, resting on my hands and knees, in a most painful position. On reaching the bottom I could just see, with the light of three or four candles, our guides, who are ever ready to support and guide your feet from one stone to another, which enables you to climb up into the dark recesses of this great and wonderful tomb of the Pharoahs, which has been so ably described by travellers that my description would be of little interest. I was very glad to get out of it and see daylight, which I managed to do at my age, 66, after a large amount of exertion, wet to the skin with perspiration, caused by so frequently slipping backwards for want of foot-hold.

I was soon afterwards joined by my friends, and we walked all round this Pyramid till we came to the Sphynx, which is of colossal magnitude, the face from the forehead to the chin measuring over nine yards and is in my opinion as great a wonder to behold as the Pyramids.

We mounted our donkeys and returned to Cairo in the evening.

Our Dragoman afterwards took us to see the sights in this ancient city of Cairo. Next day we visited the citadel, which stands upon a lofty eminence commanding an extensive view of the city, the windings of the Nile and the Pyramids. On entering the Citadel we were requested to put over our boots very large felt-carpet shoes so as not to disfigure the highly polished marble pavement of the Colonnade. We were then taken to a spacious saloon and saw the massive brass gates leading to the tomb of Mohamet Ali. We were allowed only to approach the outside, but while waiting a few seconds, two ladies, deeply veiled attended by an Eunuch, arrived and were instantly admitted. I understood they were ladies from the Harem of the Palace of Shubra.

We were afterwards shewn into the large Court yard, the place where Mehemet Ali invited the Mamelukes to a feast and while getting ready to enter the Banquet Hall they were all murdered excepting one, who spurred his horse on and leaped over the Terrace wall 4 to 5 feet high to a fall of about 40 feet on the other side, on to a quantity of rubbish. The horse was killed but the Rider, who took courage, escaped. I was told the rubbish had never been removed, and immediately after these Mamelukes had trotted their horses inside, the ponderous gates were closed upon them, there being no chance of escape and the work of death commenced.

We left there and went to the Palace at Shubra, saw part of the interior and was allowed to explore the beautiful gardens, the trees abounding with Lemons, Oranges, Apricots, Citrons, and other fruits, all in the greatest perfection. We saw two ladies of the Harem arrive attended by Eunuchs; one of these Eunuchs gave us a few Oranges just gathered.

We returned to Cairo and I bade farewell to my friends and recrossed the Desert to Suez, and after staying a few days until the English Mail for Australia arrived, and finding there were no letter for me, I took passage on board the Nemesis, Captain

Castles, commander; this was on the 5th January. On the 7th we passed two rocks named "the brothers". 8th, The Rev. Mr Davis read Prayers, strong head winds, Port-Holes being closed; it was very hot, so much so that myself and nearly all the passengers were glad to sleep on deck. 10th, passed through the straits of Babelmandeb. 11th, arrived at Aden. 12th, nearly all the passengers went on shore and had time to walk through the Pass, and visit the Tanks, which are a great curiosity. 14th, passed the Island of Socotro, about 80 miles in length, which is famous for Aloes, and was informed it has no inhabitants. 21st, Landed at Point de Galle, where all the Australian passengers dined at Messes Bogaars, proprietors of the old Mansion-house Hotel; afterwards visited the Cinnamon gardens, passing on our way numerous and very large cocoanut trees, loaded with this fruit to a Hotel called Cinnamon Station on the Gindural River, abounding with Alligators.

Renewing my enquiries, I found that after J. Williams left the Simla he boarded the Northern, which same Steamer had now returned from Sydney ready to take us on, which left the Port on the 23rd, On the 26th January the passengers were much amused at an entertainment given by the Christie Minstrels, who had been to China and Java and were then on their way to Melbourne. 30th, saw the faint glimpse of a comet in the Southern Hemisphere very low in the Horizon.

February 5. Arrived at King George's Sound, 1 a.m. an immense shark passed alongside of the Ship, a boat rowed by four convicts with an attendant to bring and take away the Mail bags, the convicts wearing red jackets. Nearly all the passengers landed and took dinner on shore. It was here we saw several Aborigines, old and young in their native state, with a Kangaroo skin slung over their shoulders. They had returned from a burial and with their faces painted white, which with their long black coarse hair and ugly features gave them a hideous appearance.

From this time during the passage several large Albatross flew round the ship, ever ready to fly down and devour the remains of food thrown over board. Mr Bayliss the Purser told me that during the passage from Galle to Melbourne he had frequent conversations with Mr Williams, who informed him that his family had all been smashed up and killed in that dreadful railway accident on the Great Western—that he was proceeding to Victoria to arrange some important business and intended returning to England in a month. At another time he said he had an idea of going to California.

"On this passage the passengers expressed to me their dissatisfaction at the bad quality of the food, wines, etc. and they determined on laying their complaint before the Company. Each of them agreed to sign the paper, and when J.W. was asked he refused, saying that he was a Director and it would not look well, but that he would take care and represent it to the Company; and as this appeared to satisfy them, so the matter ended." There was a very poor Soldier with his wife on board and they wanted to land at King George's Sound, but the Captain being informed of their circumstances took compassion and landed them at Melbourne without further cost, and J.W. hearing of their condition gave the Purser five pounds, which was given to them.

We entered Hobson Bay on the morning of the 11th February, waiting for a short time for the mail bags to be landed at Geelong, and arrived at Melbourne at 2 p.m. I took up my quarters at Port Philip Club Hotel, which I found to be very comfortable. The next day, Sunday morning, I went to the Bar of Scotts Hotel and asked for Soda and Brandy and almost in the same breath to allow me to look at the arrival passengers book, which was at once handed, and on searching back I discovered the name of J. Williams. I was timid in asking any questions, fearing it would get to his knowledge and thus frustrate all I had done. I knew it required the greatest caution as I had no power to act and he could have laughed at and defied me.

As it would be a month before the next Australian Mail from England was due, I filled up my time in the best way I could in looking about and occasionally keeping Scotts Hotel under observation. As I was told he was fond of playing on the flute I employed myself walking round the retired outskirts to try and hear the sound of one. Sometimes I went to Collingwood, Richmond and St. Kilda, and once by Rail to Geelong for a day or two and return to Melbourne, and then to the Theatres.

On the evening of the 11th of March I went to the Opera, and at about 10 I saw a gentleman in the Saloon taking Coffee and reading over a book. I looked carefully down him and came to the conclusion from the description I had got that he must be the fugitive I was in pursuit of. I kept him under observation until 11, when he arose from his chair, and as he walked I discovered his apparent lameness and the bright steel rivet over the hind part of the heel of his boot, which convinced me that he was no other person but J. Farrer alias J. Willams.

I followed him downstairs and saw him get into a Cab and heard him say to the Cabman, "Scotts." I followed in another Cab and was in time to see him get out and walk into Scotts Hotel.

I felt a new man being relieved from so much anxiety and excitement I had already undergone, but still I had to think about what I should have to do in the future; so the next day I went and took luncheon at Scotts, and passed some of my time in the reading-room, thinking to have a chance of seeing him; not succeeding. I entered my assumed name (Hammond) for the Table d'hote thinking there would be a chance turn-up.

The hour for dinner arrived and the company including myself numbered thirty. I sat near the Landlord, Mr Scott, and during the time of dinner called for a bottle of Champagne and invited Mr Scott to take a glass of two. This I did in order to form his acquaintance, when I discovered he was a brother-mason.

As my friend J.W. did not put in his appearance, I repeated my civilities the next day, with no better result. I returned to my hotel and thought what I should do for the time, when I came to the conclusion that I would see Mr Scott next day privately and make him my confidant, telling him the cause of my errand, the distance I had come in pursuit, and at the same time let him see the Times newspaper of the 21st September, 1864, containing the advertisement relating to the death of the gentleman who was now in fact living in his hotel by the name of Williams. Accordingly at one o'clock I went and took luncheon, accompanied with a pint of Champagne, and requested to see Mr Scott, who came. After a short conversation he invited me into his private parlor, when I made myself known that I was a "Brother Mason" and I could see that he also was one. I then related to him all the circumstances of my case, how I had followed his track from the beginning to the end. He shook me by the hand and fraternised with me in the most brotherly and friendly manner, giving me information from his first coming to the present.

On this day J.W. happened to be out, and Mr Scott took me up stairs into his bedroom, where I saw several pairs of boots, supplied by Walsh, the Astronomical [sic] boot-maker of Chelsea, as mentioned heretofore. We compared these boots with one I had brought from Walsh, which exactly corresponded, shewing the holes in the sides where the rivets fitted in; in fact, they were one and the same boot pattern. Also, there I saw the hairbrush with the looking-glass at the back of it, as described by the Porter of the Charring Cross hotel. We also saw some waste-paper that was written on, and on comparing, was the same handwriting as that which was given to me when in London.

Blending all these visible facts together, I felt satisfied I was on the right scent and confident he was the man I had been so long in pursuit of. From this time my task became easy thanks to Mr Scott, who was ever ready to make me acquainted with J.W's movements. He also informed me that J.W. also dined privately, and alone in his own room, which accounted for my not seeing him him the Table d'hote.

Mr Scott being now in my confidence, I took matters more easy, and settled down quietly, awaiting the arrival of the Australian Mail till the 15th, when the Steamer Bombay carrying the mails signal'd. I boarded her while laying out at St. Kilda to disembark passengers. By her I received my letters with one from the Solicitor, stating that he was pleased to hear what I had done—that I was to act cautiously and return to England with as little delay as possible.

I should have informed my reader in an earlier part of this narrative that as I obtained information at Cairo, Suez, Aden, Point de Galle and King George's Sound, so on I sent my report to the Directors, posting the same by the return Mails from these places, thus losing no time for them to be in possession of my movements. Matters now, as far as I was concerned, came to an end and without having to make any communication to the individual I went in pursuit of.

I bade Mr Scort farewell, also a very old friend of mine a Mr William Barren, the proprietor of an excellent dining establishment in Elizabeth Street, being known to each other from our early boyhood.

Now: As everything must come to an end, I left to go on board the same steamer which brought me, viz the Northern, on Sunday morning the 26th of March, 1865. I have nothing more worth noting till my arrival homewards at Point de Galle on the 15th of April, where we were kept on shore till the 19th, most of us staying at the Mansion House Hotel, Messn H. and C. Bogaars, proprietors, when I again paid a visit to the Cinnamon Gardens and also to Walla Walla, six miles distant: the river here abounds with Alligators and the weather here exceeding hot. After seeing this place we returned to Point de Galle on board we Golconda, arriving at Aden on the 28th, staying only for a few hours: passing Laffaranna Lighthouse on the 4th of May, arriving at Suez on the same evening, when all was helter skelter, giving us hardly time to see to our baggage and obtain possession of our seats before the Train started.

We found it very cold during the night in crossing the Desert to Cairo, arriving there at 6 a.m., giving us scarcely time to take a cup of Coffee, and then away to Alexandria, arriving there at 2 p.m., staying for two days, giving ample time to visit Cleopatra's Needle. Pompeys Pillar, the Egyptian Burial-ground and other places of note; but as these places have been so often described it would be superfluous in me to give a description.

I have nothing more to add, only that I had a very delightful return passage on the Mediterranean, passing through the straits of Bonefacio, with a full view of Garibaldi's house at Capraro and from hence returned home by way of Marseilles, Lyons and Paris, reaching London on the 15th of May. I reported myself in person the next morning to Mr Devonshire, the Solicitor, who was very pleased to see me, and expressed himself highly satisfied with what I had done. A few days afterwards I was instructed to send in my account, which amounted to a goodly sum. It was soon paid, and most liberally.

I believe committees were held on this business at Cairo and other places, but the result of those meetings I was never put in possession of.

There are two or three circumstances that I had almost forgotten to mention. While I was far away on my travels following the track and in pursuit of the fugitive, it was discovered, after scrutinising those letters announcing the illness and death of Mr Farrer, that they were written by the Culprit himself in a disguised hand; also in another letter that was sent to his agent, Mr Jones at St. Mary Axe, wherein it runs nearly as follows: viz

Sir, After the death of my friend Mr Edward James Farrer I found in looking over his papers a small account due to you, and as I want to have his death announced in the Times Newspaper I enclose a five Pound note which I think will recoup you for your trouble and the expence of the advertisement as well as the small account due.

2 OTHER BOOKS FEATURING
BOW STREET RUNNERS
BOTH PUBLISHED BY QUAYSTONE BOOKS
THE ENGLISH DETECTIVE
AND
RICHMOND: SCENES IN THE LIFE
OF A BOW STREET RUNNER
VISIT
QUAYSTONEBOOKS.COM

Printed in Dunstable, United Kingdom